Dancing Naked in the Rain

Theresa Cavender

iUniverse, Inc.
New York Bloomington

Dancing Naked in the Rain

iUniverse books may be ordered through booksellers or by contacting:

iUniverse
1663 Liberty Drive
Bloomington, IN 47403
www.iuniverse.com
1-800-Authors (1-800-288-4677)

Because of the dynamic nature of the Internet, any Web addresses or links contained in this book may have changed since publication and may no longer be valid. The views expressed in this work are solely those of the author and do not necessarily reflect the views of the publisher, and the publisher hereby disclaims any responsibility for them.

ISBN: 978-1-4401-7790-3 (sc)
ISBN: 978-1-4401-7893-1 (dj)
ISBN: 978-1-4401-7791-0 (ebk)

Library of Congress Control Number: 2009937238

Printed in the United States of America

iUniverse rev. date: 10/23/2009

To my husband

I strongly wish for what I faintly hope:
Like the day-dreams of melancholy men,
I think and think on things impossible,
Yet love to wander in that golden maze.
—John Dryden *Rival Ladies*, III.i.

Acknowledgments

I am grateful to my children, Andrea Rosch, Meredythe Sweet, and Scott Cavender, and to Rayna Cameron for their incisive and helpful comments, and above all, to my husband, R. Scott Cavender, for his patience and encouragement.

Part I

Chapter 1

As we drove through a grove of trees, the road abandoned its serpentine path and made a beeline for an old, but solid-looking, farmhouse. A barn and pens rambled haphazardly a stone's throw across the drive. Beyond the weathered homestead, a hill rose sharply, but only after a narrow, rut-filled road squeezed along the border of its ascent.

We drove up to the south end, where a driveway pocked with chuckholes led to a side entrance. Fergus honked the horn, got out, and opened our door. Shannon and I scrambled out onto the soft earth.

"Okay, ladies, we've arrived at last. Set your dainty feet on sheep country. It's a sensation you will feel only in Scotland. And you'll feel it from your toes to the end of your nose before the day is done."

Our laughter subsided as we walked through an entranceway leading into a cluttered patio. An assortment of clay pots lay overturned and broken with telltale hints of better days as soil and faded blossoms spilled out onto the ground. An old wooden stool, crippled from time, a tire beyond repair, old tools, and bits and pieces of mechanical parts bearing no identity in my own world filled the remainder of the forgotten corners. I wondered what happened to the apple-pie order I'd seen along the roadside, small farms seemingly raked clean of all debris, all surrounded with the rolling green hills of the countryside, littered only with the dotting of woolly, white sheep and cavorting lambs.

Fergus, Shannon's uncle, must have detected a hesitation in my step. He placed his hand under my elbow, saying, "Don't let the clutter bother you, Megan. Believe me, the farmhouse is in a temporary state, just as Jake is."

He knocked and then opened the back door. The aroma of freshly baked sweets wafted into the air around us. "Ah, Sally, hello," he said jovially as he stepped in, urging the rest of us to follow him. "We're here," he said as he inhaled deeply. "Hmm, something smells good."

Sally squealed in delight as her plump frame leaned heavily into the kitchen's wooden table and she rose from her chair. She scurried along the table's length and began smothering each of us with hugs and kisses, first Shannon, her niece and my friend, and then Shannon's Aunt Anne and Uncle Fergus. I watched nervously, but when my turn came, I couldn't help but laugh as she wrapped me up and buried me in her ample bosom. For one split moment, my feet dangled loosely, evoking childhood memories of rambunctious relative embraces. There was nothing unfriendly about Aunt Sally.

She released me and moved to the stove where she poured hot water into a ceramic teapot. "Jake told me you were coming. He's so excited. I told him I'd come help out," she announced as she waved her hand down the length of the table already laden with pastries. "He'd be here to welcome you himself, but he was a little late getting in. He's upstairs washing up now. He'll be down shortly."

She then led us into a worn but comfortable living room where Shannon and I busied ourselves exploring the old furnishings while Anne, Fergus, and Sally caught up on family matters.

Moments later, I sensed a warmth flood over me. I turned to see the man I presumed to be Jake standing across the room lavishing attention on Shannon and her aunt and uncle. His golden-brown hair, cropped short on the back and sides, spilled a few glistening tendrils onto his forehead.

As he hugged Shannon, his eyes peered over the top of her head and into the distance between us. I looked down, and then smoothed my hair and adjusted an earring, an earring not the least bit maladjusted.

Trying hard to hide my nervousness, I looked upward and kept my eyes riveted to the ceiling as my trembling fingers played at my earlobe. I could hear his heavy boots clump against the wooden floor in my direction. I folded my arms in front of me, trying to get a grip.

Taking a deep breath, I pried my gaze free from the overhanging light fixture and let it slide down over him. Khakis and denim shirt—a perfect match for his heavy, lace-up boots. A bit rustic. I don't know what I expected. He *was* a sheep farmer.

My eyes swept back up his torso. I detected a hard, well-defined masculine form underneath the country garb. As he came closer, his wide jawline and high cheekbones echoed a young Robert Redford, especially when he smiled at me.

He reached for my hand and cupped it in both of his, "Welcome. You must be Megan."

My heart did one of those flippy things as his gaze leveled to mine. I stood there staring at his penetrating emerald-green eyes, stunned by their clarity, knowing, just knowing he was a man of deep feelings; at that moment, I had an inexplicable urge to throw my arms around him. What had come over me? He certainly wasn't my type. Yet, something told me the feeling was mutual.

Embarrassed, I offered a weak hello, ducked my head, and turned away, pretending interest in an antique painting on the wall next to me. I stared at the youthful figures as they seemed to dance freely in the pastoral scene. I looked back at him and made a frivolous comment about how lovely his home was. He just stared at me, making no comment at all.

He turned away, and I suddenly felt very foolish. How could I have such an impulse for someone I'd never before set eyes upon and knew almost nothing about? To make matters worse, a momentary pang of guilt swept over me, reminding me of the fiancé I'd left at home.

Fortunately, Aunt Anne interrupted my mortification with an announcement that tea was served. Sally led us into the spacious but simple kitchen where the long, well-worn table was spread with antique cups and saucers ready for tea or coffee. Tiny egg and cucumber sandwiches, shortbread, and biscuits topped with sweetened clotted cream and strawberries offered up a feast for eyes and appetites. We filled our plates and then filed into the dining room, where we gathered around a cherry wood table with beautiful cabriole legs. Jake said his grandfather had hand-carved the intricate leaf design to perfection.

Later, Jake led us on a tour of his seventeenth-century home. Small alcoves and staircases led us up and down to picturesque but quaint rooms with rustic furnishings, all remnants of the past.

Two large bedrooms filled most of the upper floor, one totally masculine, strewn with an assortment of crumpled clothing, stacks of books, coffee cups with moldy dregs, piles of unruly papers, and odds and ends ready for the incinerator. Aunt Anne's brief history of Jake's past hadn't prepared me for the room's abandonment of a woman's touch, and Jake, laughing nervously, apologized as he led us to the second bedroom, an effulgent contrast, bright and meticulously tended, but cheerless with its stark white walls, white bed linens, and lack of furnishings or identifying belongings.

Above the bed, a painting of a frontal nude unabashedly conveyed the simplicity and power of the feminine. Yet, at the same time, her frailty and hopelessness pricked my gaze.

As I turned to face our host, wanting desperately to know more about the subject of the painting, but hesitating because of her revealed intimacy, a slight but sudden veil swept the brilliance from Jake's eyes. He turned away, ended our excursion, and led us back down to the kitchen for more refreshments.

I questioned Shannon's Aunt Anne later about the painting. She told me it was a self-portrait of Laura, Jake's deceased wife, one of the few reminders he allowed to remain in their country home after her death, the only visual reminder of her suffering—and his. Long after we left the house to walk out to inspect the surrounding grounds, the haunting expression of the woman in the picture hung over me, making me feel like a fly caught in a web.

Dry-stacked stone fences partitioned the green rolling hills into a checkerboard of patterns, each section claiming a herd of sheep, each woolly back marked boldly with red, blue, or green splotches of color, an indication of ownership. In the barn, men were busy inoculating a raucous gathering of sheep, while others prepared to dock the tails on the young lowland sheep. A worker explained that the sheep pastured on the upper slopes were allowed to keep their tails for warmth. There was no doubt in my mind where my sympathies went.

I inhaled deeply with relief when we left the stench of the weathered but rock-solid barn and stepped out onto a courtyard paved with rough, irregularly shaped *café au lait*-colored cobblestones. Horizontally stacked stones of all shapes and sizes enclosed the area, yet graciously allowed for a clear view of the lush green fields and meandering palisades of Shannon's forefathers.

Along the entire expanse of the west wall of the enclosure, a profusion of roses sprawled defiantly, saturating the air with a bouquet that made me dizzy from inhaling its sweetness. Jake picked a vibrant Gold Badge for Aunt Anne, a pink Caroline for Shannon, and a delicate white Iceberg for me.

As I stood gazing out onto the adjoining meadow, he walked up and slipped the flower above my ear, quietly stating, "I've always believed the rose to be the marrow of the garden, just as woman is, in a sense, the marrow of life. Without the rose, the soul of the garden is deficient; without woman, life has no heart."

As he turned and walked toward his visitors, I understood why my interest had flared when he'd walked in the room earlier that day. Strangely, I found myself longing for my world to become a part of his, if only for a while. I wanted a sneak peek at the tranquility of the ancient walls, the garden, the meadows, and I definitely wanted to connect with the tenderness of his heart. Yet I couldn't, for a moment, understand my thoughts.

In the evening, we bunched around a small table nestled in a corner of the courtyard, enjoying a glass of wine and a light supper Sally had left for us. Then Shannon's aunt and uncle called our visit to an end.

"Jake, we've really enjoyed the visit," said Aunt Anne, "but it's getting late and I do want to get home before dark."

"You're so right, my dear," added Fergus in his so-proper way, "and the girls must have time for their nightly ritual before turning in."

Shannon and I looked at each other and laughed. "Uncle Fergi, please," Shannon said as she rose from her seat and leaned down to kiss him on the cheek, "please, don't worry about us. Just give us a corner and we'll be fine. For that matter, Megan and I could stay here in the garden tonight with a canopy of stars and be perfectly happy."

"Well, that's settled," Jake responded good-naturedly. "I'll hustle up a few young lambs for pillows, some fresh moss for a mattress, and a blanket of heather to keep you warm."

"That sounds like perfection to me," I responded, "but that might be your misfortune. We'd probably be difficult to get rid of."

"Yes, we'd become pests of a different sort in your garden," Shannon added.

We all laughed, but the suggestion quickly became serious when Jake extended an invitation with more suitable accommodations. "Really, I would love to have the two of you with me for a while. You would liven up this old place."

"Well, it would be up to the girls," Anne said, her eyes wide as she looked first at Shannon and then shifted her gaze at me. "I'm sure they would enjoy it, but they don't have any of their things with them.

5

Maybe we should plan this for some later date." I could tell she wasn't keen on the idea.

Shannon put her arm around her aunt, giving her a gentle hug. "Why don't we let Megan stay the night? I'll go back to Inverness with you. Then tomorrow I can come back with our stuff. That is, if you'll lend me your car for a few days." I knew she was pushing it.

Anne looked up at Shannon, her eyes wide with surprise. "Well, I suppose I could if it's fine with Jake and Megan."

Jake nodded. "It's more than fine with me. Megan can have the extra bedroom, not quite as romantic as the garden, but there I can guarantee her safety from all creatures."

"That sounds wonderful ... if it's really okay," I said, wondering what Anne and Fergus really thought, yet eager to explore a world far from my own.

"It sounds like a perfect beginning for Megan and Shannon and their visit to the Isles," Fergus said, flashing me a smile.

Jake rose from his weathered chair with a perceptible elevation of spirit. "Of course, it's okay. Any objections?"

None were spoken.

Chapter 2

After we saw the others off, Jake showed me once again to the room at the top of the stairs and then to the bath, pointing out its simple but efficient necessities.

"Please make yourself comfortable. I need to check on a few things out at the barn, so I'll leave you for now. Feel free to roam, but I'll see you before turning in. Can you think of anything you need for now?"

"Well, there is one thing, if you don't mind. Do you have an old shirt I could borrow to sleep in?" I asked, feeling a bit uncomfortable asking for a piece of his clothing.

"Hmm, of course, no problem." He left the hallway where we were standing, entered his bedroom, and rummaged through a drawer. He walked back into the hall, holding up a pale blue cotton tee. "It'll come to your knees, but I promise you it's clean."

"It's perfect, thank you." I stood looking up at him, not knowing what to say next.

"Anything else?"

"Oh, no. I don't need anything. Anyway, I know you're anxious to get to your business. You've wasted enough of your time with me today. I'll be fine. I think I'll take a walk before bedtime."

"Sounds good. Well, I'm off. Enjoy your walk."

He sauntered down the stairs, leaving me reeling with excitement at the prospect of exploring the farm and the area around it.

Within minutes, I made my way downstairs and out into the courtyard where the remnants of our repast remained untended. Using a tray Sally had left on the table, I quickly scraped the leftovers and carefully stacked the cups, saucers, and plates and returned to the kitchen where I washed, dried, and, after exploring the cabinets, returned each piece of delicate china to its accustomed place.

I then left by the back door, where we had entered earlier that day, and picked my way once again through the littered patio. In the distance, beyond the disarray, I could see a meadow sweeping out into an endless expanse of nurtured life—field after verdant field dotted with peaceful, munching sheep. Its beauty sent a wave of exhilaration over me, reminding me of my young precocious nephew, who, standing on the banks of the Rio Grande as it flowed from the hills of Colorado, exclaimed loudly to my sister, "Mom, I wish I could grab some of it and stuff it in my pocket. Then I could take it out when we get home and see it all again."

We'd laughed then, but as I gazed across the broad sweep of land, I totally understood what he had felt—that unadulterated childlike appreciation for captured moments of the heart. If only I could allow myself the privilege of remaining a child at heart, not just for the moment, but forever.

I walked out onto a narrow dirt road that led from the back of the house, following it a few yards until it joined a stone fence paralleling its path to an end I couldn't see. I walked.

The sun had set earlier, and a misty twilight lit my way along the uneven but pleasant roadway. As I passed a ewe with her lamb, they both turned their heads to cast their round, black eyes on my strange presence in their bucolic kingdom, then turned away to resume their preoccupation with grazing. We were all at peace.

I walked steadily, a walk graciously relieving some of the tension that had seized me from the moment Jake had looked at me from across the room earlier in the day and again when he took my hand and still again when he slipped the rose behind my ear. Each time our eyes met, a jolt secreted itself deep inside me, sending shockwaves tingling down my spine and leaving me hungry for more.

I forced myself to focus on the moment in time—the breeze, the rustle of the leaves, the bleating of the sheep, the fresh air cooling my skin. Gradually I sensed the darkness crowding around me, and though I had no fear of real or imagined danger, I hoped to see Jake once again before turning in for the night.

As I came through the back door, I heard the tranquil sounds of bagpipes, and I followed the soothing sounds to the living room where he was reading, the melody soft in the background. I stood in the doorway, hesitating, not certain if I should disturb his quiet or just go unnoticed to my room. As I turned to make my way up the stairs, I heard his voice.

"Megan."

"Yes," I blurted out as I turned back in his direction.

"Come join me, please," he said, rising from his chair.

"Oh, I ..." I replied, feeling rather self-conscious, "I was just thinking I should let you have a moment to yourself."

"Absolutely not. A gentleman would not allow his guest to retire without a nightcap and a friendly word or two. Besides, you haven't told me about yourself. I've bored you and the others all day with my rustic way of life, and all I know of you is you're a friend of Shannon's."

"You didn't bore me in the least. I'm fascinated with country life. It's something I know little of. Besides, *my* life is rather boring."

"Well, let me decide that. Come on in and I'll fix you a drink. What would you like?"

"Surprise me. Give me what you're having."

"Are you sure?"

"Absolutely," I foolishly insisted.

"All right, Scotch on the rocks it is."

He handed me a heavy crystal glass filled with a few ice cubes and a golden-colored liquid, and then offered a toast. "To Megan, a welcome guest in my humble home, to your health and happiness."

"Thank you." I put the glass to my mouth and tilted it upward until the cool liquid met my lips, unprepared for its bite and the instant sensation of warmth as it trickled down my throat. I took a deep breath, trying to hide my surprise at its potency. "It's been awhile since I've had the pleasure of a toast."

No sooner had the words left my mouth than I remembered the toast my fiancé had made a few weeks earlier. I closed my eyes for a moment, trying to escape the memory, but I could almost see Mark's desperation as the cork popped and the potent liquid gurgled softly as it trickled from the bottle into our glasses.

"Here's to us," Mark had said a bit too loudly. "To us!" he repeated as he swung his glass up in the air in a toast, almost smashing into mine. But that was in the past.

I looked at Jake. He sat quietly, his eyes bright, offering me a relief from my thoughts.

"Toasting's a good tradition that has long been an expression of good faith, beginning, perhaps, with the Greeks."

"Really? With the Greeks?"

"Yes, they were wise as well as cautious about what they drank. Poisoned wine, you see, was an easy way to get back at your enemies. But don't fear. Even we Scots have outlived that strategy of getting rid of our enemies. We now just bore them to death."

"Not that again. Are you going to make me flatter you and the country life once more?"

"Any flattery at all is appreciated. Actually, any conversation is an improvement. I'm afraid I've been cooped up on this farm far too long."

"I'm sure that could be corrected." The words had no sooner popped out of my mouth than I realized their implication.

"In due time," he good-naturedly responded as he motioned me to a chair and sank easily into his own.

I attempted to settle into a worn, overstuffed throne of a chair across from him. Within seconds, an image of being swallowed by a giant marshmallow flicked in my mind as my weight poked like a finger into its soft spongy center. As I struggled to slip off my shoes and tuck my legs underneath me, its surface would rise to meet each movement. I felt foolish and helpless and began laughing in self-defense.

Jake rose and saved my drink, setting it on the table beside me. "I should have warned you. It's a very welcoming chair and takes getting used to. Do you need to be rescued?"

"No, I think I'm situated now, but I do know one thing. If I ever need a hug, I know where to come."

Jake looked away but not before a teary film reflected in his eyes. As he sat down again, I could see him struggling for composure. "Laura used to call it her hugging chair. I hadn't thought about that in quite a while."

"I'm sorry. Should I sit somewhere else?"

"No, no, no. I'm the one who's sorry. Things sneak up on me sometimes. Besides, you're trapped."

We laughed, but what I wanted was to wrap him in my arms and tell him how sorry I was for stirring up stinging memories. Instead, I looked down into my drink, sipping its warmth while stealing glances around the room, a room echoing a life of simplistic beauty.

"It's rather drab, isn't it?" he said, noticing my searching eyes.

"No, it's ... it's perfect. It's like reaching back in time. It would be a mistake to change it."

"You're more than kind, but probably right. And for that, you deserve another toast. Here's to a huggable lady."

"You seem to be an expert on the subject of toasting," I quickly interjected, wanting to avoid any reference to hugging or ladies—Laura or myself.

"No, not at all. It's just general information."

"Why the word *toast*?" I asked, desperate to keep the conversation flowing.

"Well, if my memory serves me well, that came from the Romans' habit of dropping a piece of burned bread into unsavory wine. It camouflaged its unpleasant taste. At least, that's one theory."

"If I had been a Roman lady, I think I would have refrained from imbibing in either unsavory *or* bread-soaked wine."

"A woman's wise choice, but men often fail to see the logic and look more to the pleasure of its effects. At any rate, that's my insight on the subject. Now, if I'm not being too personal, what brings you to Scotland?"

"It's really quite simple. I've wanted to make a change in my life for a number of years, and Shannon, who knows all my secret desires— well, not all of them—anyway, she offered to introduce me to authentic life in Scotland, and I accepted. End of story."

"I'll accept that for now, but I'm sure there's much more to your story."

"Details that would only bore you. You know, the Scots don't have a monopoly on boring one to death."

"That's possible, but not probable, at least in your case." He grinned and I knew he wanted to know more. But it would have to wait until later. Much later. We sipped our drinks in unison, and then, meeting my gaze, he asked, "How long are you staying in Scotland?"

"Oh, I don't know. I guess it depends. I want to stay long enough to do some exploring, see the sights, understand some of Scotland's mystique."

He nodded his head. "Ah, the mystique."

I felt strange—no, foolish—sitting there talking to a man who was part of that mystique. I laughed uneasily. "Do you think that's possible?"

He continued nodding his head and smiling, probably thinking I was an idiot. "Oh, the mystique is free for the taking."

At that point, I didn't know what to say. He just kept staring at me like he expected me to say more, so I added, "I want to try my hand at writing some travel pieces, but that's rather fanciful, I suppose."

"Not at all. You're in a good place to start such a venture. I dare say there are many areas worthy of exploration within a day's journey. I could even suggest some for you."

"That would be wonderful. I'd appreciate any ideas you have."

He tipped his glass up, swallowed, all the while his eyes twinkling, "I might even do better than that."

"How's that?"

"What if I took you on some excursions myself?"

"Really? You'd want to do that?"

"Absolutely. It's the weekend, my deserved time of rest. Besides, it's about time I tore myself away from here."

"Fantastic!" I let out a bit too loudly; I'd have toppled out of my chair if I weren't still trapped in its softness. I couldn't believe my luck. Then, trying to be more sedate, I added, "Where do you suggest?"

"Do you have any ideas of your own in mind?"

"Well, you might think this weird, but I'm interested in graveyards. But any place will do."

He was quiet for a moment as he stood and walked to a window overlooking the blackened night. "I think Scotland can offer a few graveyards. In fact, I know several sites you might find interesting. How about a prehistoric burial site?" he asked, turning to face me. "It's close by and would give you a taste for the many others scattered around Scotland. Does that sound like something that would interest you?"

I felt like jumping up and down and screaming in my excitement, but I answered with a simple, "I'm thrilled. I can't think of anything better."

"My pleasure. Now, off with you. Up to bed. I'll wake you early, so get your beauty sleep."

It didn't take much prompting. Eager for morning, I climbed the stairs, showered, and crawled under the covers. I couldn't believe my luck. A personal guide. Jake had been quick to offer his time, but being isolated out on this farm would cause anyone to be eager for diversion. And he just might be ready for some companionship. I'd find out more about him from Shannon later, but at that moment, I was ready to snuggle under the covers and get some shuteye.

As I pulled back the blanket, the mournful eye of the nude in the self-portrait above the bed caught my own. She was a lovely woman, but her pose and facial features—maybe it was the furrow of the brow—revealed an anguished spirit struggling to compose itself.

Chapter 3

The next morning I awoke to a light rap at the door, and Jake entered with a breakfast tray laden with scrambled eggs, thin slices of ham, red, plump strawberries, buttered toast, and a pot of steaming coffee, all served on swirl-rimmed white china edged with pink and yellow roses.

"Goodness. How can I possibly deserve this?" I mumbled, grabbing the sheet and pulling it up to my chin, trying to smooth my hair and hide what lay under his blue shirt.

"Well, you deserve something special for cleaning up our mess from yesterday afternoon."

"It was no trouble at all," I protested.

"Well, it wasn't your job. I'm the host here, mind you," he stated jovially as he set the tray on a small marble-topped table beside the bed. "Now prop up and prepare yourself for a hearty breakfast. You have some tough country ahead of you, and I don't want you running out of steam. By the way, I'm sorry to say that Shannon called earlier this morning. She can't return today after all. Aunt Anne needs her for a few days." He placed the tray gently on my lap, unfolded my napkin, and handed it to me. "However, Fergus will bring your suitcase this morning. I asked Shannon to have him leave it by the door if we're not here. I do hope that's satisfactory. She said to call if you need to."

He then asked if I needed anything else. Stunned, I shook my head, and he turned and headed down the stairs, saying he was off to give instructions to his farmhands and would be back in thirty minutes to collect me.

If I hadn't been in a hurry for breakfast before, I certainly was now. It was seven o'clock. Thirty minutes. Had I ever gotten ready in

14

thirty minutes in my life? Not wanting to delay our trip, I buried my disappointment that Shannon wouldn't be by my side and devoured the breakfast before me.

In record time, I walked down the stairs and into the kitchen with the remains of my breakfast. As I set the tray on the counter, I could hear Jake's footsteps on the cobblestones outside the kitchen.

He opened the door. "Ah, you're ready, are you?" he said as he walked in. "Well, let me get my keys and we'll be off."

He opened a drawer by the door, grabbed the keys, and then said, "Follow me." He walked across the kitchen and down a short hallway to a recessed area leading into a dark, damp room. I couldn't see anything until the light crept in as he pulled open two, large dilapidated doors.

"Hop into Old Molly, luv. She runs like a top. You should feel perfectly at home. She's solid American mechanism. A 1976 Ford Courier." He turned the key and the engine caught immediately. He hooked the gear into reverse, and we swept out of the musty enclosure and into the misty morning.

We drove into the heart of Inverness, past the city's massive cathedral, the museum and art gallery, and out again into the countryside, heading north along what he called Moray Firth. "You'll have to come and watch for dolphins sometime," he said. "Come in the evening. It's usually the best time to spot them."

He then turned east and wound past Smithton and Westhill and along the Culloden Muir, talking all the while about the cairns. He said they were several thousand years old and thought to have been burial chambers.

We made a right turn off the main road and pulled into a parking area. All I could see ahead was a thick area of trees swaying to and fro as the cool wind whipped them soundlessly. All was darkness within, as the sun hadn't broken through the clouds.

Jake had stopped the truck and turned off the engine. "Good," said Jake, "just what I hoped for. No one else here. You can experience this alone."

"Alone?" I questioned. "Why alone? Aren't you coming?"

"No, I'll wait here. It's just something you should see without being disturbed. Just go through the gate," he said, pointing out the window, "and discover it for yourself. Really," he repeated, sensing my hesitation.

"I'm more than happy to wait here. I brought some paperwork and a book or two." He placed his hand on the stack wedged between us.

Not particularly thrilled at the idea of roaming a dark forest by myself, I slid out of the truck and made my way for the gate, an antique turnstile of sorts. As soon as I entered the main portal, a smaller, narrower gate blocked my way, and I had to turn sideways to open it before I could enter. At the time, all I could think of was how I'd get out if I were in a hurry.

A small forest of gnarled trees rose from the rock-laden earth like specters waving their arms in the fierce winds. I shuddered, but then forced myself to move forward one step at a time, each step leading me deeper into the shadows of the ghostly phantoms. I wished Jake were walking next to me, then laughed out loud at my foolishness.

Woven from the many centuries of decayed debris of fallen limbs, leaves, and sphagnum, the soft earth sank like a richly nubbed carpet under my feet. The woodsy scent wafted up to fill my nostrils, carried by the simultaneous disturbance from my physical presence and the wind's sinuous movement. I breathed in deeply, delighting in the fragrance.

Tossing my notebook to the ground, I began to snap picture after picture of the gyrating trees as they stirred above me, the limbs swaying back and forth like worshipers with hands extended toward the heavens. Unable to capture the uppermost spectacle, I lay on my back and peered up into the maelstrom of nature. The yielding turf below me gently cushioned my frame, producing a feeling of comfort and calm.

I was struck by the paradoxical setting. Nature in all its grotesque pulchritude inspired absolute serenity—mine, at least. The apprehension I'd felt as I entered into the primitive space had been sucked from me.

I turned over and lay prone for a few minutes, eyes shut, my mind focusing on the incredible scene playing before me. Fearful I would lose the moment, I pushed myself up on my elbows, reached out, and grabbed my notebook, frantically scribbling every bit of description and sensation I could capture.

Pages later, I stood and began to explore the massive monuments to the dead, each one constructed from a ring of rocks and boulders. They reminded me a bit of ancient igloos, with a narrow walkway leading into a small circular chamber about six to eight feet across. I stepped soundlessly along an entry and ran my hand along the sides of the stones, reaching my fingers into the crevices, wanting to touch and know every inch within. As I paced around the interior, I began to feel a strange sensation, a longing to linger. My pace slowed to a standstill. I stood motionless, my hands caressing the smooth, cool rocks. Stones of all sizes had been layered intricately, each tier a foothold for the next. I don't know how long I wandered, fingering each crevice, hoping to poke into its secrets. Eventually, I became aware of the sound of the wind whistling above me.

I walked out into the open. The towering trees whipped above, casting flickers of sunlight and shadow. I spread my arms, leaning back, my face tilted toward the sky. Strange. I should be shivering. The scene was eerie, the wind cool. I was alone, yet I felt strangely at ease as I continued to inspect several other cairns, each one a replica of the first.

I then made my way to an immense boulder rising skyward in an expanse of open bare ground. Its man-crushing size loomed above me, reaching at least ten feet. I could only imagine how it had been placed upright so that it would tower above all the surrounding structures, providing a center for rituals. I knew I'd have to ask Jake for information about the grounds later.

Dwarfed by its massive form, I circled the giant, searching for a view offering light and shadow to its advantage. After taking a number of pictures, I placed my notebook and camera on the ground and stood before the stone, aware of the significance and power it must have evoked in its time. I inched toward it as I spread my arms and pressed my breast, stomach, and thighs against its uneven, rough surface. I leaned into the massive rock, my cheek resting on its hardness. I couldn't move. I didn't want to move. Contentment flowed through me.

I gradually pulled away, feeling a surge of euphoria. I laughed and did a strange thing. I began to dance among the trees, imagining myself a nymph, free and light as the air around me. I encircled a trunk, holding on with one hand and swinging like a child spinning around a flagpole. My body gyrated in my jubilation, just as the trees had gyrated above me. Aeolus's wafts seem to sigh in my ears, "Come ... fill me ... envelop me. Gorge me now with your love." I fancied something, maybe some spirit brushing against me, whirling around me, caressing me. I yearned to wrap myself in ghostly attire, to be one with whatever played around me, but my humanness resisted. Gradually, I became aware of a repeated sound, not a voice, but a kind of stirring, almost a whisper, "Megan ... Megan." I lay down again on the leaf-strewn ground to stare up into the swirling canopy. I listened intently but could hear nothing more than the rustling branches as they lulled me into a kind of restive reverie.

Suddenly, I realized Jake was waiting. I had no idea how long it had been. *Is he watching? How foolish I must look.* I hoped he was preoccupied with his work and unaware of my antics. Begrudgingly, I stood up, brushed off the debris clinging to my clothes, grabbed my notebook and camera, and headed for the truck. I tried my best to be nonchalant, as if I were the same sane, though quite jittery, person who had walked into those tranquil woods some time before.

As I opened the door to the truck, Jake looked up from his book. "Hey."

I didn't say anything, just set my backpack on the floorboard and climbed in.

"Well, how was it? Anything move you in there?"

I couldn't answer ... just stared through the dusty window glass in front of me.

His fingers cupped my chin and turned my head to face him, "You're flushed. You okay?"

"Yeah, I'm fine," I answered, knowing good and well I wasn't.

He dropped his hand, placed his book on the seat between us, and shifted his weight to face me. "So ... what do you think?"

I struggled for a moment, unsure how to express my feelings. Then with more exuberance than I intended, I said, "I think it was a gift ... the most amazing place I've ever been."

"Good. I want to hear more. You can tell me about it as we drive by the Culloden Battlefield. It's another place you can visit some time."

"Couldn't we stop today?" I asked.

"How much do you know about Scottish history?"

"Hardly anything," I laughed, feeling foolish.

"Well, I suggest you do some studying first. It would be worth it."

"I'm sure you're right."

"Besides, you have the cairns to think about for now," he reminded me. "You spent almost two hours in there. You must have really enjoyed it."

"Two hours? Really?" Stunned, I gazed into the woods and said, mostly to myself, "Yes, I did. I really did enjoy it."

"So tell me about it. Any special feelings?" he asked as he started the truck and began to back out.

"Yes, you could say so," I answered hesitantly, unsure how he would respond to my less-than-sophisticated antics. Yet, for all I knew, he had been watching me and had already formed his own idea about me.

He waited, and when I failed to continue, he said, "Laura used to come here from time to time. She said it affected her deeply each time."

"I guess you could say it affected me deeply, too. This may sound crazy, rather weird, but it was like a … an out-of-body experience."

At first, I did my best to avoid revealing too much to Jake, but eventually, I chatted non-stop, recapping the entire bizarre tale. When I was finished, he glanced over at me and said quite seriously, "I *knew* you were something special. Laura would have liked you a lot."

I figured he meant it as a compliment because I knew how much he had loved his wife; at least, that's what I had been told.

We drove slowly across the moor, viewing the Culloden Battleground from a distance. He talked endlessly about the details of the 1746 battle between the English and the Scots, but I was lost in another kind of world, a world new to me, a world writhing with … with something ethereal. And I had just been offered a peephole. I wanted more.

We stopped shortly before noon at a fish-and-chips shop in Inverness, and I gorged myself with the crispiest, freshest fish I had ever eaten. And the big, fat crunchy chips were unlike any fries I had ever had back home.

When I finished eating, I sat back and said, "Now here is something worth writing about. I could make my way across the land, hitting every fish-and-chips establishment that would let me in the door."

He laughed and told me I would have to do it on my own. He didn't have the stomach for it.

Chapter 4

When we returned to the farm, Jake headed out to the barn, and I climbed the stairs, looking for seclusion and time to think and write about my rather bizarre experience at the cairns.

I remembered momentarily fighting the impulse to dance around the trees, thinking anyone who saw me would assume I had gone mad. But I knew I had been alone with no one to pass judgment, unless, of course, Jake had noticed.

Yet I couldn't deny my actions had been strange. I could accept all of it, except for the whisperings. What I wanted to know was if they were just my own romantic but nonsensical notions or if they were some ghastly subterranean moans coming up from the cryptic stones? *Not likely.* I had to believe they were my imagination, brought about by a convulsion of sights and sounds, from misty shadows, thrashing trees and branches, whistling wind—all enough to caution me.

I thought of the Wordsworth poem I had read aloud to Shannon a few weeks earlier. I tried to remember his words over Burns' grave. "I shiver, Spirit fierce and bold …" I couldn't remember the rest. I went to the closet and pulled the small book from the side pocket of my backpack, and then lay across the bed and read it again.

When I finished, I knew his poem expressed a sadness I hadn't felt, but the line "As vapors breathed from dungeons cold" struck a chord. I just couldn't figure out why.

I looked up at Laura's picture above my bed. Strange. The furrows around her eyes seemed slightly different, maybe not quite so defined. *Ridiculous!*

I took a quick shower to remove any earthy smells I had collected while wallowing with the wraiths, dried quickly, put on some clean jeans and T-shirt, and headed for the barn, only to find it empty of human life. Disappointed, but glad to escape the stench, I walked out into the fresh air, scanning the countryside for signs of life beyond the grazing herds. Finding none, I crossed onto the meadow and gazed as mindlessly as the sheep before me. No wonder they had that far-off look in their eyes. The undulating hills, the verdant scent, the wafting breezes—it was enough to lull any living creature into dazed tranquility. I savored the moment and then returned to the house to spend the remainder of the afternoon writing, wondering all the while when Jake would return.

The door slammed a few hours later. "Megan," he called out. "Are you here?"

"Hey, yes," I answered, jumping from the sofa and making my way to the kitchen.

"Sorry to leave you so long."

"No problem. I've been trying to make some headway on my article."

He looked at me and smiled. "Good. I'm glad you were inspired. I was a bit worried you'd get bored and leave before I could get back."

"Now how would I do that?" I laughed. "You think I'm going to walk all the way back to town? Or just maybe I could catch a ram and play the part of Odysseus."

"Well, it has been done, and we do have to be resourceful around here, you know," he retorted in good humor.

Turning his back to me, he filled a large glass with cool water, drank thirstily, and then set the glass in the sink before turning toward me. "Got to go clean up, and then I'm taking you down to the nearest pub for some local color. Sound okay?"

"Sounds great. I'll be ready."

He clumped up the stairs in his heavy boots, and I hurried back to the sofa to collect my stuff before returning to my room to change clothes. I was anxious to make myself not only more presentable, but also more appealing, as this enigma of a man had my heart and mind racing, almost as much as my visit to the cairn.

I quickly pulled out a black-and-white crinkle-cloth tank with a jewel neckline and a black jersey skirt, perfect for such an occasion—

not for a trip to a pub in a Scottish farm community, but to flatter my figure and, perhaps, flatten his resistance. *There's something about him.*

My blond corkscrew curls fell in their usual puffed-out mass, still shiny from the earlier washing. I patted on some moisturizer, dabbed on some eyeliner and shadow, a bit of cheek blush, and a touch of lip gloss. *Much better!*

As I inspected myself in the mirror, the bathroom door opened and Jake walked across the hall into his room, closing the door behind him, but not before I caught a reflection of his trim but muscular back and towel-draped hips. *Ah, yeah, much, much better.* I giggled to myself. And in the next instant, I had an urge to strip and join him. I could see myself, walking buff-bare into his room, sliding silently next to him, pulling his towel slowly away, letting it slip from my hand onto the floor, and then pulling myself up to him, just as I had leaned into the stone at the cairn. I would be able to feel the same hardness I had felt when I had abandoned my inhibitions and pressed myself into a spiritual realm I had never before entered. I could feel the same explosion of energy, only this time it was physical. I could feel my blood coursing through my body, the tingling, the hunger, the headiness. I closed my eyes. *Oh my god, how could I have such thoughts? I don't even know him.*

There was a knock at my door. "Megan, are you all right?"

Startled, I forced my eyes open and turned from the mirror to see him standing in the doorway, clean and smart looking in a fresh pullover and khakis. "Oh ... you startled me. I was just ... daydreaming, I think, but I'm ready," I fumbled.

I picked up my purse and headed toward the doorway. He stepped aside, and as I passed, he placed his hands on my shoulders, turning me to face him. Then he tilted my face up to his, just a breath away. "You look flushed. Are you sure you're okay? You're not sick, are you?"

For a moment I wanted to say I was ill, feign weakness, and fall into his arms, but I knew melodrama was for the movies. Instead, I looked up into his beautiful face and said, "Now where is this place you have in mind?"

He took me by the hand. "Come with me. We're going to put you in the middle of country folk. There's no better place to reap the local flavor than in a pub. Everyone who matters in our little community goes there nearly every evening. It's the way we entertain ourselves and keep from going sheep-shearing mad."

So we were off, bouncing down the rocky road to town in Old Molly, leaving behind all my fantasies.

The pub bubbled with chatter, laughter, and clinking glasses. A fireplace in one corner glowed warmly, throwing flickering shadows against the wooden walls that were laden with Scottish landscapes, old signs, dirk daggers, sporrans, and a hodge-podge of kilts and other accoutrements.

Jake led me up to the bar where he ordered Scottish ale for the both of us, and then, with a mug brimming with the amber liquid in hand, we looked around for a table for two. Finding none available, we joined a group already sitting in a corner by a fireplace.

We introduced ourselves and squeezed onto a bench across from three backpackers from England. Two of the trio were sisters, the third a young man who obviously had eyes for one of the girls. I assumed they were lovers. They filled the next hour with stories about hiking across Scotland and then, after finishing their meal, bid us good-bye with hugs and handshakes and headed out the door, leaving Jake and me sitting side by side, staring at all the empty places around our table.

At that moment, another crowd entered. I glanced around the room, and just as I spotted a table for two, Jake stood and extended a helping hand. I climbed over the bench, and we took our places across from each other in a secluded corner.

"Um, nice," I said, thinking how handsome he was with his bronzed face and curly golden brown hair.

"Yes, it is," he nodded and tilted his mug for a long draft. "Well, what do you think of the Scottish pub?"

"I love it. Absolutely love it. It's so warm ... and friendly."

He then leaned with one elbow on the table, his eyes leveling to mine. "Do you realize that we have been under the same roof for almost forty-eight hours, and we don't know much about each other? At least, I don't know much about you. And I don't know what you have been told about me."

"All I've been told is you're Shannon's favorite cousin, and—" I paused, feeling uncomfortable speaking about his wife. "And that your wife passed away about a year ago. I'm so sorry. I know it's been hard."

He nodded, looked away from me, took another drink, and then resumed talking. "She was a wonderful woman. I miss her every day."

"Tell me about her."

"Maybe someday I will. Right now, I want to hear about you. Tell me about your life in Texas."

"You're kidding. There's not much to talk about," I said, hoping to avoid any discussion leading to my fiancé.

"Really, Megan, I'd like to know something about you. I must say, anyone who takes long baths in my tub needs more than just a name."

"Okay, you're right," I laughed. "Where should I start?"

"Wherever you're comfortable," he said as he leaned back in his chair.

I started talking, telling him about my family and teaching, but stopping short of revealing my relationship with Mark.

When I felt I had said enough, I took a sip of my ale and said, "See, I told you there's not much to my life. That's why I had to get away … why I had to make a change."

"So you came to the middle of sheep country thinking it would enliven your life?" he asked mockingly.

"Well, actually, that wasn't part of the plan, but now I'm here, I'm glad."

"And why is that?" he asked, as though doubting my sanity. "You're not going to tell me that you're really interested in sheep?"

I couldn't help but laugh. "Yes, and no. Yes, I enjoy looking at them and the countryside, but, truthfully, when you get up close and personal, they do smell a little."

"Yes, so they do, but it's part of the mystique … the barnyard experience. You can't have one without the other."

"I guess you're right. I guess I'll have to suffer the good with the bad. It's kind of like life, don't you think?" I added.

"No doubt," he said, nodding his head. He was quiet for a moment and then asked, "So what else do you like about Scotland other than sheep from a distance?"

I sat staring at him, embarrassed. How truthful could I be? In the beginning, I had been just a tag-along visitor feigning interest in the farm, but my la-di-da attitude had quickly been upended when I set eyes on him. Nevertheless, I really doubted I could be so bold as to tell

24

him the truth. What the heck was I going to say? I raised my mug once again, sipping the cool liquid, searching for a truthful answer, one that wouldn't make me feel like a flirt.

"Hey, don't go to sleep on me. Am I that boring?" he asked, leaning forward and waving his hand in front of me as if to break a trance.

"Honestly, I'm trying to decide what to tell you."

"Maybe I can help you," he interjected.

"Really?"

"Yes, really."

"Okay, go ahead. I'm waiting. What is it I'm really interested in?"

"Me," he stated flatly, raising his eyebrows and giving me a cocky smile.

"Am I that transparent?" I gasped, rather surprised and embarrassed.

Leaning back in his chair again and trying to look serious, he answered, "Actually, no, I was just, ah, teasing you."

We stared at each other awkwardly and then burst out laughing. I was definitely embarrassed as he continued, "But I like the idea, and, if I may be truthful, I am rather interested in you."

At that point, I finally started breathing again. "I don't know whether to believe what you're saying or not. Are you teasing me again?" I asked.

He slowly shook his head. "I'm serious about being interested. Is there any reason I shouldn't be? I think we both felt the attraction when we met. Am I right?"

"But how could you know what I was feeling? Are you psychic or something?"

"I think it's just a matter of stating the obvious. We both felt something, but you turned away, shutting me off."

I looked at him in amazement. He held my gaze for a few moments and then continued, "Do I scare you?"

"No, not at all. It's just that ... well, I'm more afraid of myself, I guess."

"Afraid of what?"

"I don't know. Maybe of just doing something ... rash."

He smiled, picked up the candle in front of him, and waved it slowly back in forth in front of his face, whispering as if telling a secret, "Be wary of the meadows. They're terribly tempting."

25

"Now you are making fun of me," I said, suddenly feeling foolish for talking so openly to him.

"Maybe," he stated matter-of-factly as he replaced the candle and then enveloped my hand in his, squeezing it lightly. "Try to relax and enjoy your time here. It's a calming place. It's worked for me."

"I've noticed already, especially as I've been drinking this ale."

We clicked glasses, toasting our friendship, and then he surprised me by saying, "I'll bet you have suitors knocking your door down at home."

"Not actually," I admitted.

"Then you must have a serious relationship with someone." He gave me a moment to respond, but when I didn't, he added, "I'm right again, aren't I?"

I nodded. No more cat and mouse. This was a man who was on the level and wouldn't be easily fooled, not that I wanted to fool him, but, for some strange reason, I couldn't keep any secrets from him. So I began to tell him all about Mark.

Jake listened attentively as I spread the details of my story before him like empty words in a dream, and when I finished, he leaned forward, covering my hand as I nervously fingered the cool edge of my mug. "So you've run away, coming all the way to the land of lambs to escape making a decision?"

"That's pretty bad, isn't it?" I said, feeling foolish. "I should have told Mark something more definite."

"In a sense, I think you already have. And he certainly doesn't seem willing to wait."

"No, he was pretty put off by me. And I didn't give him anything definite to go on. Even now, I don't know what I really want. I just know if I tell him I don't ever want to get married, it would be a horrible blow. He has spent so much time and energy on our relationship."

"I would imagine *you* have also dedicated yourself to him," he said, but I could tell it was more of a question than a statement.

"Of course. It's just terribly difficult."

"Do you still love him?"

My heart suddenly jumped to my throat. I couldn't speak for a few moments, but then I began in a rush, "Perhaps ... no, I care a great deal for him. I've known him since I was twenty, Jake. That's a long time. We've grown so close and spent so much time together—planned so much. Even though I'm miles away, he's in my thoughts continually. It's not that I don't want to think about him." I paused, realizing that wasn't exactly true. "Well, actually, I guess I'd hoped I could just escape for a time and give myself a breather from stressing out over making a decision that would affect me … us, possibly forever. I wanted to clear my mind so I could decide what it is I want … what I *really* want. I'm not sure that makes any sense at all."

Then Jake said something that made me feel as if I'd been slapped in the face: "You don't want to give up a good thing, but you want to have the opportunity to find something you might want more."

I looked at him and understood immediately the meaning between his spoken words. "I've never allowed myself to think of it that way. I guess I haven't been totally honest with myself or Mark. He's been so good to me and waited so long, and I've left him with so little to go on."

"A bit selfish, don't you think?" he questioned in a somewhat fatherly way.

"Thanks, I needed that," I laughed, with tears in my eyes.

"You know, Megan, it's not that you have done something so terribly unforgivable, but you might want to do some serious leveling with yourself and with him."

"But I didn't tell him to wait for me."

"Did you tell him not to wait for you?" He paused, and then added, "Or did you?"

"No, I guess I was too focused on *my* uncertainty to even think of being fair or honest. I'm so ashamed," I whispered. I couldn't believe someone I'd only recently met had dug deeper into me than I'd been able to do for years.

"No need for shame, but you owe him the truth, whatever you decide that is."

I knew he was right. He'd uncovered a nagging truth I'd kept shoving back into the corners of my mind.

"I'll talk to him soon, but for now let's change the subject. Let's talk about you."

"I have a better idea. Let's have some steak-and-ale pie. Have you had any of Scotland's finest pub food?"

"No, I haven't," I said, not really having the stomach to eat after uncloseting my pathetic skeletons.

27

"Well, tonight's the night. Steak-and-ale pie it will be. I'll be right back. I'll put in an order."

Jake made his way to the bar while I struggled to calm my nerves. I couldn't understand how he had gotten into my personal life so quickly and how he had forced me to face reality within minutes. It was uncanny. And I still knew so little about him but felt bound and determined to change that before the evening's end.

I was disappointed when he returned to the table with a young farmer neighbor and his wife who pulled up chairs to join us at our tiny table for the remainder of the evening, but my discontent was quickly replaced with enjoyment of their jovial company.

On the way home, we rode in silence. He said no more about Mark, and I didn't press him again about his wife. The pain he still held in his heart was not something I wanted to disturb now, but I hoped in time he would allow me to intrude upon it. Until then, I was awestruck by the man next to me.

Chapter 5

The next two days passed quickly. Jake and his brothers had to meet a deadline for a market delivery, and although he worried about leaving me and offered to give me a ride back to Aunt Anne's, I assured him I would be fine on my own. I told him I needed more time to write. The truth was I didn't want to abandon the premises. His premises. Not yet. Besides, I detected a hint of relief when I turned him down.

I created a private place for myself in the garden by dragging the small table we had used for supper a few nights earlier to the edge of an arbor of showering roses, placing it just inside a veil of shadow. A weather-beaten chair and a borrowed sofa pillow completed my space.

I spent the majority of the next two days writing and rewriting my article. I figured there was no time like the present to put pen to paper—well, fingers to laptop keys.

Evenings found me padding on the cropped grasses of the lea, bare feet and toes drowning in the soft tuft. I felt the child in me smile with each step, each private step, so mine, so alfresco. Miles and miles of elbow room, so exposed, yet so hidden from all humanity. No sound except the slight whisper of wind as it wound its way through my hair, whipping carefree strands almost silently around my ears.

The first night alone, I read a book I borrowed from his shelf. On the second night, I danced to the mournful sounds of Scotland's pipes. Step, step, arabesque. I knew I was rusty. Step, step, élevé. *Can't wait until he's back.* Assemblé. Assemblé. *Beauchamps would be incensed.* I can't say my dancing ever impressed anyone except my parents, but even they didn't fuss much when I said I wanted to quit.

Jake returned that second night, filling the doorway with a baffled look on his face as I swished one foot and prepared for a jump. I attempted to camouflage my movements by squatting on the floor in hopes he would think I was searching for something, but my sudden change in direction propelled me forward and left me splayed out flat in front of him, my nose pressed hard against the rough planks of the ancient floor and my eyes tightly closed in embarrassment and wishful thinking. *If only the din from that one small cassette hadn't concealed his arrival, I could have welcomed him in a more appropriate manner. I could have ...* The possibilities were endless. But the reality was I lay prone before him, wondering what my next move was. A dreadful silence hung between us. I just knew he was contemplating either laughter or uncommon concern.

After a few seconds, he knelt beside me, placed his hand on my lower back, and then traced the path of my spine with his fingers until they met the nape of my neck. There he began a gentle massage while we both took a few moments to gather our thoughts.

He was the first to speak, his voice soft, "Hmm, you seem to be in one piece. Are you okay?"

I pulled my knees up, rolled onto my side, and pushed myself into a sitting position. "Never felt better," I quipped.

"Do you make a habit of such welcomes?" he asked, brushing my hair back from my face, the corners of his mouth twitching ever so slightly.

"Oh, I've always been rather good at impromptu," I quipped. "There's no telling what I could have done if I'd known you were here."

"I'll keep that in mind. Come on, let's get you up." He pulled me to my feet and led me to the sofa, easing me down. He then turned down the stereo and sat across from me. I could only imagine what he was really thinking.

"You okay?" He leaned toward me.

"Yes, I'm fine, just a bit of an ego bruising."

I was hoping he wouldn't ask what led to my fall because I'd have to tell him, but he did, and then, of course, I did. He just gave me a curious look and said he'd love to see me dance, but I'd best be careful about dancing solo again.

He talked briefly about his trip to market and then asked for a run-down of my time alone on the farm, that is, other than my "reeling," as he called it. He seemed pleased to hear of my progress on my article and took a copy up the stairs with him when we turned in for the evening.

As I came down the stairs the following morning, I was surprised and delighted to see Shannon sitting at the kitchen table, drinking coffee with Jake. He glanced up as I entered the room and flashed me a grin, a grin I found intensely stimulating.

"Here she is now—our writer in residence," he said as he pulled out a chair next to Shannon, placed another cup on the table, and filled it with steaming, strong coffee.

I hugged Shannon and sat down. "Why didn't you let me know you would be here today?" Before she could answer, I added like a clucking mother, "And where have you been? You left me all alone," pretending an innocence I knew I didn't possess.

"I hardly think you've been alone. According to Jake, you two have been quite busy."

Jake looked at me and winked, "Well, we have had our moments, but I did abandon her for a few days. I invited her to help out, but she chose to spend her time roaming the meadows or writing." He chuckled and added, "I just can't understand why she would prefer listening to her muse over shepherding the Cheviot."

"She's nuts that way," Shannon said as she rolled her eyes at me.

"But I know *you* love the little lambs," I said, looking at Jake. "You're so devoted, and the look in your eyes when you come in after working all day. You're just plain dazed by the barnyard bouquet, but oh so content." I pinched my nose and grimaced. There was no way I was going to let him get off easy after teasing me.

We all laughed, but I saw a sudden flush cross his face. He looked at Shannon and then back at me. "Yes, I suppose you're right. It is good work. Not exactly difficult, but it is time consuming. Keeps the mind from thinking too much."

I immediately knew my statement had pushed him back into his secret thoughts of Laura. I was embarrassed and stared down into my coffee.

Shannon must have noticed too and wittingly changed the subject.

"You asked where I've been. Are you still interested?" she asked good-naturedly.

"Tell us about it while I fix breakfast," Jake said as he opened the refrigerator.

"I'll help," I suggested, and the three of us gathered around the counter.

By the time we finished eating, Shannon had shared the details of a hiking trip from Inverness to Culloden, a trip she had taken with two cousins from Glasgow. "And," she stated excitedly, as she ended her tale, "they invited us to come visit them the last few days of their vacation."

"Really?" I responded coyly. "I don't know if I should impose on more of your relatives." The truth was I wasn't sure I was ready to abandon Jake.

"Sure you can," he said. "We Scots love visitors, and you would find Glasgow an exciting city. There's much to see and do there. You should go."

"Oh, so you're trying to get rid of me," I taunted.

"Come with us, Jake," Shannon pleaded. "It would be such fun." And to me she said, "Megan, Ashley told me there are all sorts of museums and art galleries. We'd love it. I know we would. Besides, she told me the shopping galleries are fantastic."

"Sign me up." I was definitely a patron of the emporium, even if it meant just window-shopping, and that's about all I could do unless I started generating some cash flow. Besides, a few days of shopping and sightseeing wouldn't be so bad, especially if Jake went along.

"So, are we *all* going?" she asked, looking at Jake.

Jake got up from the table, stacked a few dishes, and then said, "I'm afraid I need to stay here right now. Duty calls, you know. You two will have to manage without me."

I felt let down. I didn't want to go without him, but Shannon would be disappointed if I didn't accompany her. We tried persuading him, wanting desperately to change his mind, but, in the end, he stood firm. We would be going without him.

Jake left for the pens, and Shannon and I began making plans. She had collected a number of travel brochures in Inverness before returning to the farm, so we sat at the kitchen table and made a list of all the places we wanted to visit.

After we studied the material and made our wish list, we walked down the narrow road behind the house. The morning sun, blinding but dazzling, fell around us, fading the usual brilliance of the meadows. A cool breeze countered.

Shannon's stride easily outpaced my own, so keeping abreast of her was difficult. I found myself almost sprinting at her side. Mark had always referred to her legs as "glorious gams." No denying it.

She talked nonstop about her backpacking experience, and we both marveled at how different our lives had become in the past weeks.

As we headed back to the house, I rehashed the details of my visit to the burial site, omitting the strange happenings, and then filled her in on my ensuing struggle to complete my article. "I finished it, though," I told her. "It's ready to mail, so I guess we can do that in the morning on our way to Glasgow."

"Fantastic. I knew you could do it. I just can't wait to see it in print."

"Neither can I, believe me. I'm a little nervous about it. If I don't get published, then my journey may come to an end a bit sooner than I anticipated."

"It'll happen. Don't worry. Just think. You've taken a chance. It's just a matter of time."

"I hope you're right."

"Trust me," she said in her "I-believe-in-you" teacher attitude.

"Thanks, Shannon. I needed to hear that. Sometimes I wonder about being here, especially staying with Jake. And, by the way, you did go off and leave me all alone with him. Why did you do that?"

"Oh, I just had a feeling about you two. I think you both need each other. He's all alone, and you're a solitary oyster when it comes to men right now."

"Shannon, I ... I still care about Mark. I've never said I didn't. I'm just not sure if I want to make it a permanent thing, at least not until I have some breakthroughs career-wise."

"Okay, I'll accept that, but tell me about you and Jake. It's obvious you two have a thing for each other."

"Now, how can you tell that, may I ask?" I knew precisely how she knew. Just as she always knew—an uncanny knack.

She stopped in front of me, grabbed me by the shoulders and shook me playfully. "Do you think I was born yesterday, girlfriend? How could I not tell? You two were drinking each other up at the breakfast table. So what's going on?"

33

"Actually, nothing's going on."

"Oh, please. How could it be nothing? Level with me."

"Well, I mean there's nothing *serious* going on. He's been great. He took me to a burial site. We've had a few meals together. He works with his sheep. I write. He works some more. I write some more, and I take some long walks."

"And some cold showers, I bet," she added, urging me to say more.

I laughed at her, "You're not getting anything else out of me, Shannon."

"He's handsome, isn't he?" she broke in.

"Yes, definitely handsome." We continued walking. "But it's much more than that."

"So, there haven't been any sparks?" she urged me on.

I looked at her and shook my head, "Now you're getting nosy. Besides, there's not much to say, other than he's different from anyone I've ever known ... even Mark. I can't explain it."

"And?" she encouraged.

"And, nothing," I answered, getting a bit put off by her questions. She and I had been friends for a long time, and all the years of sharing our private thoughts had given both of us free rein on digging into each other's business. "It's just difficult to tell you how I feel about him right now."

"Why? Because he's my cousin?" she asked.

"Maybe ... partly ... but the other part is Mark. I've had to do a lot of soul searching. I can't understand why or how I can be attracted to someone else so quickly. I'm really surprised."

"Yeah, but there is something between you two?"

"I don't know if there is or there isn't. Right now, I'm having a difficult time deciding where I am in my feelings about Mark, so I suppose you could say my conscience is bothering me."

"The old guilt factor has raised its ugly head?" she asked, already knowing the answer.

"No doubt. That seems to be the story of my life." I paused, and then continued, "No, it's more than that. I just have some decisions to make, and until I do, I don't know how I can possibly move on."

"Megan, I would never try to influence you, but I can tell you that Jake comes from a wonderful family. Remember, I'm part of it.

And even though I haven't seen him since I was a kid, I know he's a good man ... a wonderful man—other than having an odd penchant for sheep farming, not that it's a bad thing. Besides, he's intelligent, well educated, and respected in the academic world; at least that's what Aunt Anne told me."

"How's that?" I questioned.

"Well, she told me he's been teaching for some time."

"That's strange. I told him I was a teacher. He didn't say anything about his teaching, but I guess that explains why he seems a bit out of place here. Where does he teach?"

"At a college in Edinburgh."

"Really? Why isn't he there now?" I asked, surprised he hadn't told me. *What else didn't I know?*

"From what I understand, he seemed to just lose heart after Laura died. He came back to the farm to try to pull himself together."

"Do you think he'll go back to teaching?"

"I don't know. Why don't you talk to him? Ask him."

"I've tried to get him to talk about himself, but he always puts me off and starts questioning me about *my* life," I explained.

"Well, if you ask me, he needs to talk to someone, and it might as well be you. He's been through a lot of pain, and he's not over it yet. I can tell your being here has made a difference. He's got a sparkle in his eye, one he didn't have when we first arrived."

"I've noticed," I said, rather confident I was the reason. "But," I continued, "he's thrown me for a loop. I've always felt my relationship with Mark was unshakeable, that I would never care for anyone else, and here I am, not even a full month into my search for *myself*, and I've discovered another man I think I could love as much as Mark ... or maybe more. That just doesn't seem right, much less possible."

"Megan, I know you're attracted to him, but attraction and love are two different things, don't you think? You really don't think you know him well enough to have fallen in love already, do you?"

"Crazy as it seems, yes, unless he's hiding a wicked side from me. And by the way, just to make it perfectly clear, there hasn't been anything serious between us, nor do I have any intention of going in that direction right now, not that I'm not interested, but ..." I trailed off.

Shannon stopped walking and burst out laughing, "Oh, Megan, you do have it bad. So, you've been having thoughts about him, have you?"

We both laughed, and I raced down the road ahead of her, like a kid with a secret, yelling back, "You're not getting any more information from me, not even if you torture me with a shepherd's staff." I suddenly felt relieved I'd shared my secret with someone else. I'd let it out. It was real.

She quickly caught up with me, and we ran until we were both exhausted; we then collapsed on the dense grass growing along the outside of the pastureland, grass that had escaped the hungry mouths of the ever-grazing sheep. We lay there for a few minutes until we could breathe without effort.

"You know what, Megan? We are out of shape. There's been too much of the easy life in the last month."

"Too many fish and chips. I think I can see fins and potato eyes growing between my ribs."

"Come on," she said as she jumped up and pulled me to my feet. "Let's go back and get you packed. I've got to call Ashley to let her know we'll be on our way in the morning."

Chapter 6

We spent the remainder of the day in a frenzied state, packing, studying and restudying the brochures, and adding to our list of destinations. That evening, we cooked dinner for Jake. Shannon chatted endlessly about Ashley and her friends. Jake listened politely, nodding and smiling from time to time. He was unusually quiet.

We said good night a few minutes after eleven, and Shannon and Jake went up to bed. I sat on the couch deep in thought about the little piece of myself I had discovered in the last few weeks. It was small, but it was something. More than anything, it was a feeling, an exuberance of spirit. *If I only knew what to do next.*

Within minutes, I decided to call Mark. Now was the time. I couldn't put it off. I realized moving on could also mean breaking off.

I placed the call, knowing Mark would still be awake.

His familiar voice answered the phone, "Hello?"

"Hello, Mark," I said, my voice shaking in nervousness.

"Megan?"

"Yes, it's me," I said, dreading what I would say next.

"How are you?" he asked with more excitement than I expected.

"I'm fine. How are you?"

"I'm missing you. I'm really missing you, Megan."

There was an awkward pause before I forced myself to continue. "I know. Me too," I said out of guilt, but knew immediately it was the wrong thing to say.

"When are—" he began.

"Mark," I interrupted, knowing I had to get to the point before he said too much. "I have something I need to say. I'm sorry I have to say it on the phone, but I thought it would be better than a letter."

"Megan, don't do this," he said, clipping his words.

"I have to be fair to you. I really am sorry, but it's best."

"So, who is he?" he asked flatly.

"Mark, I really don't want to hurt you, but I think it's best. I just—"

"Where are you, damn it? Where the hell are you?" he yelled.

I pulled the phone away from my ear, fighting the impulse to hang up, but knew I had to get it over with. "Scotland. In Scotland. You know that."

"Okay, so where in Scotland?"

"With Shannon's family." It wasn't a lie, but not quite the truth either.

"What if I need to reach you? What's the number there?"

"I don't know the number, Mark."

"Well, find it. Look in the phone book."

This time I lied. "There doesn't seem to be one here."

"You've got to be kidding. So ask someone."

I didn't answer.

"I guess no one else is there," he said, mocking my silence.

"Mark, I gave you Anne's phone number and address. You can call or write me there if you need to." Only part truth.

"There? Where the hell are you, Megan? But I guess you don't have the answer to that either."

"Just write me, Mark."

"Write you?" he snapped. "I'm not much in the mood to write you."

Silence hung in the air like a dirty secret—mine. I knew it was time for me to 'fess up to what we both knew.

"Mark, I'm staying out on a farm, and I'm writing. I finished my first article. I'm sending it to New York tomorrow." I was warming up to the truth.

"And what are you doing on a farm?" he demanded, making no mention of my article.

I knew what he really wanted to know, and, as much as I wanted to separate myself from his question, I couldn't and wouldn't. I desperately wanted to be on the other side of the issue.

"I'm staying with one of Shannon's cousins. It's quiet here and there's so much to see, so many places to write about."

"Okay." Silence again.

I gritted my teeth. "His name is Jake—"

"His name is Jake," he repeated. I couldn't believe his calm.

"Yes."

"I see."

I could hear him take in a long heavy breath.

"Mark, I—"

"It's okay," he broke in. "Let's not make it any worse than it is. You certainly didn't leave me with much hope when you left. I don't know what I expected."

"Mark, it's about being honest. I know it's not much—"

"That's where you're wrong, Megan." He paused a moment and then added with incredible control, "It's a bit much."

He was right. I could say more, but it wouldn't make a difference.

"I'd better go," he stated flatly.

"I'm sorry, Mark."

"Me, too." He paused a moment and then added, "Maggie's missing you," referring to my cocker spaniel I'd left behind with my mother. He wanted to make me feel guilty. He succeeded.

"Oh, Mark," I whispered into the mouthpiece.

"Good-bye," he said quietly and then I heard the click of the receiver.

"Good-bye," I whispered to no one. I lay on the sofa, muffling my sobs in one of its faded pillows, wishing I could deaden the pain for both of us.

Gradually, the tug-of-war gripping me for so long began to wane. The chimes on the clock sounded midnight as I made my way up the stairs. Jake's door was closed, his room quiet and dark.

I quickly undressed and pulled a gown from my suitcase, easing it over my head. Exhausted, I lay down with my back to Shannon, expecting sleep to come quickly.

I heard the clock chime once for half past twelve. Then again for one o'clock. I rolled slowly from the bed and crept down the stairs and out into the courtyard. I could smell the fragrance of the roses in the soft breeze as it curled around and under my gown, thin, white cotton lifting and swirling with each breath of the airy night. I closed my eyes, rubbed my hands up and down my chilling arms, and drew a deep breath, the only sound except the wafting of the wind as it fingered my gown and whispered in my ear. *I would miss the farm. I would miss—*

"Megan."

"Oh—"

And in a hushed voice, Jake said, "Sorry, I didn't mean to frighten you. I was walking. I saw you." He walked up behind me, unnervingly close. I could feel his warmth. "You look beautiful standing here in the moonlight."

"I … I didn't know you were out here," I stammered. "I just couldn't sleep. I guess I'm excited about the trip tomorrow."

"I couldn't sleep either."

"I better get back in. It's rather chilly out here," I said nervously, aware of the flimsy fabric dancing around me in the dark.

"Please don't go. Stay here with me," he said as he turned me to face him and wrapped me in his arms. He pulled me close, his hands on the small of my back. Gradually, he relaxed his grip. "I'll keep you warm."

He tilted my face up to his and kissed me softly on the lips. I laid my head on his shoulder, comfortable and strangely at ease. My restlessness had vaporized the moment he took me into his arms.

"I've wanted to do that since the first moment I saw you," he said in a hushed voice.

"I think I knew that," I whispered.

"Did you?" he asked as if amused.

I was silent. He was calm and relaxed.

"Maybe we've been avoiding it," he suggested.

"Maybe."

I stood perfectly still. This was a moment I had yearned for since the day I met him. His arms around me, his breath on my cheek, his strength pressed against me. I stood still, waiting for his next move. Then, quite suddenly, his grip loosened and he stepped back.

He disappeared into the house but quickly returned with a blanket.

"Here. Let's wrap this around you."

My heart sank. For an instant, I had thought he might spread the soft woolen tartan under the stars, pull me down with him, and make love to me. But it wasn't that at all, and I felt like a silly little girl, a silly little disappointed girl—and, once again, I was amazed at my thoughts.

40

He led me to a bench nestled under an ivy-covered arbor. Little moonlight faeries danced across us as we moved beneath its trellis. "Sit down," he whispered softly, as if not wishing to awaken the woman inside me. "Let's talk."

"About what?" I asked, pulling the blanket across my lap.

"About what you're thinking."

"I'm thinking I must be dreaming."

"Because—"

"Because you led me to believe ... to believe ..." I couldn't tell him. I couldn't say what I had been thinking.

"I led you to believe what?"

Embarrassed, I looked down at my hands gripping the edges of the blanket as if afraid of losing hold. I looked back at Jake. He had no idea I was having lunatic thoughts. And I had no idea where they came from. I had to come up with something more sensible than making love with someone I barely knew or, for that matter, who barely knew me. So I said, "I just thought you were going to desert me when you went back in the house."

He laughed and sat looking at me with an unassuming expression. "Now why would I do that?"

I smiled and said, "Well, just maybe because it's cold out here and it's way past bedtime."

"And because, perhaps, you don't know anything about me."

I started to tell him I knew all I needed to know, but in an instant, I knew he was right. What was I thinking? Shannon was right when she said I hadn't known him long enough to fall in love, much less to make love. What I was feeling was lust, and this whole thing could be such a mistake.

"And what are you thinking?" I asked, trying to pull myself out from under the spell he cast around me.

"Well, strangely, I have an urge to protect you. You've been here with me less than a week, and I can see a young woman who is struggling with personal issues that weigh heavily on her heart."

"But why would you need to protect me from myself?"

"I don't know. I can't explain it. It's almost as though I'm somehow responsible."

"Jake, that's insane. And this is all rather embarrassing." My confusion whirled inside my head and suddenly plunged deep into the pit of my stomach. I felt sick. Faint. Taking a deep breath, I struggled to steady myself, "It's the second time today I've set myself up for embarrassment."

"What do you mean?"

"Oh, just something Shannon and I were talking about earlier."

"Do you want to tell me about it?"

"No. I think you know more than enough about me. I think it's time I learned what's going on with you."

"Okay, that's fair. Where would you like me to begin?"

Remembering his words to me the night in the pub, I said, "Well, in the words of a very wise man, begin 'wherever you're comfortable.'"

"Fair enough. Okay. I'm forty-three years old." He paused as if to let that fact sink in and, perhaps, to gather the courage to continue. "I have a doctorate in history, and I taught for fifteen years before my wife died of cancer a year ago."

"I'm so sorry, Jake," I said, remembering the agony expressed in Laura's self-portrait.

He nodded, looking down at the ground as he bent over, elbows on his knees. He looked up at me and continued slowly, "She was a brave woman ... a beautiful, wonderful woman whom I have missed beyond belief." He paused, took a few long breaths, and then continued, "After she died, I had a difficult time. I just couldn't stay in our home without her, nor return to the university where we had shared an office and our professional lives."

"So you came back here to the farm?"

"My brothers were still here, and it was easy to slip back into the life I left as a young man. I had to make a change. Everything in Edinburgh was about her. That's where I met her, where we both finished our degrees and started teaching, where we built our home and wanted to raise a family."

"You never had children?"

"No." He was silent. I could see him swallow hard. He leaned back in his chair, his shoulders hunched forward.

"What did she teach?" I encouraged, knowing he needed the release.

"She taught French literature. She loved it and was so good at it. She was always so full of life, and she gave her all to it. She used to have students over sometimes on the weekend in the early afternoon ... and they'd sit around the living room, some on the floor. They'd talk for hours about whatever they were reading. She had to chase them out sometimes. She gave meaning to all of our lives. Even when she was sick, some of the students kept coming ... just to sit by her bed for a few minutes.

"They must have loved her."

"And she loved them. Eventually the pain got to be too much and she went into the hospital. A few would still visit and just hold her hand. The day after she died, a dozen or so came to the house. Each one of them handed me a letter. They had written about her, her dedication, her love of literature, her humor ... the way she would prod them, encourage them. Some of the letters were funny, others sad, but all seriously earnest about the respect and love they had for her. I knew she had made a difference. Even if they hadn't brought those letters, I would have known. It was important to her."

He looked at me with tears in his eyes. I wiped away mine.

I didn't know what to say. I felt inadequate. No wonder. When he was kissing me, he must have been thinking of her.

I turned toward him and wrapped my arms around his neck, hugging him gently, nuzzling close within the curve under his chin. We sat that way for a while, comfortable in each other's presence. No tension. No question as to what we were feeling ... sadness for his loss and, perhaps, gladness for a friend.

In his ear, I whispered, "I don't want to go tomorrow, Jake."

His reply was simply, "Good."

I sat leaning into his chest, the warmth of our bodies fading into each other like the blending of colors on an artist's palette. His arms pulled me in tightly. Now he was holding me and not a ghost.

"Thanks for being here, Megan. I don't know how it came to be or why, but you've made a difference."

"I haven't done anything."

"You've done more than you realize. I know it sounds strange, and I certainly don't mean this in a disparaging way, but you've been a distraction, a rather beguiling one, I'd say. And tonight, well, tonight you've sent my heart racing again. It was very difficult not to make an ass out of myself."

He paused, pulled back just enough to see my face. I closed my eyes and he kissed me lightly. "You've brought joy back into my life. I've found reason to look forward to tomorrow again."

He stood up, pulling me with him. His strength pressed into me, leaving me breathless.

"Can you feel it?" he asked, hugging me close.

"What?" I asked, trying hard not to laugh.

"My heart is pounding," he whispered. "Feel it," he said as he placed my hand on his chest.

I wanted to do more than feel his heart ... much more, and the thought scared me. I turned, pulled the blanket tightly around me, and headed toward the house.

Remembering his statement from earlier in the evening, I said, "Well, we know each other better now."

"Hey, you!" he called playfully. "You are a minx."

"Really?" I stopped to look back at him. "That's what Mom used to call me when I was a little girl."

"Well, she was right, but I don't think she'd call you a little girl anymore."

"Probably not. No. Probably not." I smiled at him and shook my head more at myself than at him. "Good night, Jake."

"Get some rest. We have some planning of our own to do tomorrow," he said, still standing where I had slipped from his arms.

"And some explaining, too," I added.

I reentered the house and climbed the stairs to the bedroom where Shannon was sleeping soundly. I slipped into bed beside her and the rhythmic breathing that quickly lulled me into a deep sleep of my own.

As I dozed off, I said a prayer of thanks. I was thankful I'd finally been truthful to Mark and been lucky enough to meet a man who was wiser than I. That evening, I'd learned just how vulnerable I was. Somehow, fortune had smiled on me when I met Jake. I'd been so eager for intimacy, and he had spared me and himself an incident that might have changed our friendship. But I'd been lucky. I now had an intimate friendship that was more than a sexual encounter. I was learning ... on my own.

Chapter 7

The next morning I woke to kitchen noises and the heavenly aroma of fresh bacon frying. Shannon's side of the bed was empty, her suitcase was gone, and a note had been pinned to her pillow.

> Hey, Sleepyhead,
>
> Couldn't bear to wake you. Talked to Jake. I'm glad you took my advice and got him to talk to you. He's lucky to have you as a friend. He needs you. I'll be thinking of you while I'm seeing the city. Have fun. Be back in a few days—maybe.
>
> Love,
> Shannon

How she could collect all her belongings and get down the stairs without waking me was beyond my understanding. It was nine o'clock. I hadn't slept late since I was a teenager.

I quickly dressed in jeans and T-shirt, brushed my teeth, washed and creamed my face, and added a few minor touches of color before heading down the stairs to join Jake in the kitchen.

"Good morning," I said cheerily.

"Good morning to you. I was about to come drag you out of bed."

"I wish someone would have before Shannon left. I really wanted to talk to her."

"I told her to wake you, but she said not to bother you. She said you needed your beauty rest."

"Well, that sounds like something she would say. And it's true. I do," I agreed.

"Only because you were a night owl last night."

"Very kind of you. When did you get up?"

"I've been up for a few hours. It's part of the farmer's life."

He placed the crisp bacon on a paper towel and began cracking eggs into a bowl. "Shannon told me you two have been friends for a while. Sounds as though you have a close friendship."

"Very close. I guess she told you we teach at the same high school. We even have rooms next to each other at school. Well, I guess you could say *had* rooms next to each other."

"As a matter of fact, she told me that and much more."

"Uh-oh. I definitely should have been awake and down here defending myself. What did she say, or should I ask?"

"Nothing that you need to be concerned about. Now sit down and have some coffee while I finish the eggs."

"You should let me do that."

"Why? You don't trust me?" he teased.

"Oh, yes, believe me, I do trust you. I think you are the most trustworthy person I know."

He stood in front of the ancient oven, a shabby apron tied around his faded jeans, his shirt untucked, sleeves rolled to his elbows.

I wondered how he looked standing before his classes. I imagined he'd keep his hair shorter, no curls trailing down his forehead or neck. And definitely there would be no beard stubble. He would be closely shaven and dressed in a smartly cut suit or just maybe he would be wrinkled and disheveled from head to toe. But he didn't strike me as the absentminded professor type, even as he stood there in his mismatched getup.

He looked at me and grinned, pointing the spatula at me. "Now, relax, my lady, don't worry about a thing. It's all under control."

He turned off the burner, took two plates from the cabinet, and scooped out the steaming eggs from the cast-iron pan.

"Okay, you win, but please don't make a habit of this. You'll spoil me."

"That's the idea, but it's going to take some clever doings."

"What do you mean?"

"Well, look around you," he said, as his arm swept a semicircle around the room. "You're sitting in a rustic farmhouse, surrounded by flocks of sheep, civilization's a jolting ten-mile ride away in a bucket of bolts, and you ask what I mean? Now, you're cleverer than that."

"What makes you think anything else would be *more* than this?" I asked seriously.

He tilted his head to one side, his mouth forming a funny cockeyed line that said, *You really don't mean a word of what you just said.*

"Don't give me that look. I'm serious. I'm in love with this place," I blurted out. "I'm in love with this house, the meadows, the sheep, the air, with—"

Jake placed the plates of scrambled eggs, bacon, fried potatoes, and toast on the table and stood before me, his washed-out apron edged with cavorting lambs still wrapped around his waist.

"You love what?" he asked in a hushed voice, his eyes searching mine.

"I love … your *apron*," I said, looking down, grabbing the frayed corners, and spreading the cloth before me. My heart thumped in overtime, making me breathless from what seemed to be miniature explosions under my breast.

"You can wear it next time," he said, winking as he took it off and crossed the room to hang it on a hook on the wall.

I grabbed my fork and looked down into my plate. My face burned with embarrassment. Not knowing what to say to make the moment return to normalcy, I decided to continue where we left off before I gushed like a lovesick twerp.

"Well, I turned down a trip to an exciting city with my best friend. That should say something about my feeling for this place."

He refilled my coffee cup. "Maybe you're going to gain another best friend."

"I think I already have, but if you keep feeding me like this, my friend may decide differently."

"I'll keep that in mind," he said as we began to eat. "Oh, Shannon said to tell you she took your manuscript and will mail it for you."

"I guess she knew I was ready to toss it."

"Nonsense. You know you don't mean that?"

"I know … and I really am glad she took it. Now I can just focus on my next article."

47

"Good idea," he said, smiling at me.

By the time we finished the dishes, we had mapped out our week. Jake suggested, and I quickly agreed, that we continue to focus on ancient stone circles and cairns.

He then weighed me down with a stack of books he assured me would be fodder for thought. I knew one thing. They would keep me occupied into the wee hours of the night.

I had often heard of the fickle finger of fate, but if I had harbored any doubts before, I knew then my life was entwined with something more than luck. Good fortune is made by good choices, sometimes bold choices. Even so, I guess we just get lucky sometimes.

Chapter 8

The next week passed quickly. We rose early every morning, loaded picnic basket and books into the truck, and headed toward a new destination: an ancient burial site, an old fortification, even Hadrian's wall. I spent most of the days taking pictures and writing, while Jake read volume after volume of British history. Although I was content with my days, the mysterious events of the cairn continued to cripple my mind. I couldn't move past its haunting.

At noon we'd unpack a cold lunch onto our makeshift writer's nerve center, a blanket spread on the ground of our chosen ancient kingdom of the Scots, our dominion for the day. We'd eat and dabble in dreams and reality. We'd banter with each other unmercifully—throwing gibes, taunts, grapes, nuts, or whatever was at hand—to keep from taking ourselves too seriously, especially when a lull in academic thought would seduce our senses, drawing our eyes together in silence, quickening our already stirred desire. At times, Jake would stretch out to doze in the afternoon's hush, leaving me to wrestle with private thoughts. Eventually, we'd return to our academic dallying, a term we adopted during the days Dionysus hung heavily on our lids. At other times, we'd walk, leaving our work behind.

It was good to be the student again when Jake would lay down his book and interrupt my thoughts with bits and pieces of history of the ancient grounds. His words came easily. He was at home in these remnants of the ancient world.

He would pace around a gigantic burial stone looking it over, rubbing his palms up and down its surface, fingering its crevices, as if examining a fine racehorse, his enthusiasm overflowing into his speech. I could see the teacher in him. He would excite students even though they were sitting in a cold classroom. He was a natural. His words would fill their minds, but, more importantly, his enthusiasm would inspire their souls.

By the end of the week, we ended our daily excursions, welcoming the thought of spending time with our books and notes in more comfortable quarters. I'd curl up on the sofa across from his easy chair, and he would drop a stack of books at his feet and meticulously thumb through the pages marked with sticky notes, pausing to write pages of his own. We made a grand pair. From time to time, one of us would interrupt the other with a tidbit of information that had to be shared, but most of the time we worked in silence.

In the evenings, we would sit out in the courtyard enjoying the rose-infused breezes and a glass of wine. When the rain chased us indoors, we'd nestle in our usual places enjoying the languishing embers in the fireplace and carefully delving into each other's thoughts.

Through the weeks, our relationship evolved as we shared an intimacy transcending the ordinary. We explored each other's psyches, desires, hopes, and dreams. Jake was open and honest, speaking of his heartbreak and loss following his wife's death. I listened—quiet and patient.

Although we cautiously held our emotions at bay, sensuality floated like a musky fragrance between us. We made love with words, thoughts, and ideas, a mere intimation of what lay below the surface of our minds and hearts. I think we both knew sexual involvement would be too easy, almost child's play. Something extraordinary had begun to develop between us and had become far too compelling to interrupt ... at present.

One night after dinner, he said, "You know, after Laura died, I didn't believe I would be thinking about the future again. I didn't think about what I wanted. So many of my dreams were fulfilled with her. Then when I lost her, nothing mattered anymore. But I can feel that changing for me."

"I'm glad," I told him. "When did that begin to happen?"

"I'm not sure. Maybe during our visits to the ancient burial grounds. It was a gradual process. Day by day I felt some relief."

"Do you think getting away from the farm affected you?" I asked, thinking of his self-imposed isolation.

"That's part of the reason, I'm sure. I've kept myself quite removed from civilization for a good bit of time. But when we were out there on the highlands and I was rambling about the ancients, I experienced a kind of renewed pleasure." He laughed and added, "But I know I must have been boring you again."

"No, how can you say that? Not only was it fascinating and valuable to me, but I loved seeing you so excited. You were definitely absorbed. You're a marvelous teacher, Jake."

"You're an easy audience," he teased me.

"Well, I'm interested."

"You've been more than just an audience to me, Megan. Our time together has been very therapeutic, and I've even begun to think I might return to teaching again."

"That's wonderful. I know that's where you belong."

"You mean the sheep won't miss me?" he asked, his crooked grin playing on one side of his lips. I wanted to kiss them.

"They will, I'm sure," I forced myself to joke, "but I'm sure they would welcome a visit from time to time, and I know you'll miss the farm more than you might think."

"It's been a good place to be, and you, Megan, have played an important part in my … healing. Before you came, I … I didn't know if I would ever feel whole again."

At that moment, the chimes struck twelve midnight. He stood and crossed the short space between us to the sofa, reached out for my hand, and pulled me up to face him. "Megan, I want you to come with me."

I lowered my forehead against his chest, feeling a frenzy of sensations. I, too, had noticed his change and watched with interest as he became more animated and eager to talk about his studies.

"Come with you? Where?"

"To Edinburgh. I've been in contact with the administration, and they want me back this fall. I'll have to go soon, and I want you with me." He tilted my chin up to him and kissed me gently on the lips. "Come with me."

He pulled me closer. His kisses became urgent. I eagerly welcomed them, yet each time he kissed me, I felt myself sinking into oblivion. *I can't do this. I can't let this happen. Not now.* I pulled away and lay my head on his chest, hearing and feeling his hastening breath, an echo of my own. Then his arms tightened around me, almost brutally, pulling me further into his responding body. My own desire was welling up inside of me. *What am I doing? I can't let this happen.* I knew I had to be in command of my life. Once I gave in to him, I would be engaged in a battle—with myself. I wanted to be sure. *I must be sure.*

The phone rang. Startled, he loosened his grip, and I pulled away and crossed the room.

"Let it ring," he commanded in a voice resonating throughout the room.

"I'll get it. It may be Shannon." He stood staring at me, rebuffed, bruised.

I lifted the receiver. "Hello," I said in a barely audible voice.

On the other end was Sara, assistant editor for a travel magazine. She told me she had received the article I'd written about the cairns and had shown it to the senior editor, and if I could expand my coverage to include similar sites, and add more pictures as well as a bit more human interest, then they would consider publishing it. She apologized for calling so late, and we hung up.

I didn't know whether to be excited or disappointed. I sat down on the sofa next to Jake and gave him the news.

"That's terrific," he said, his voice flat, obviously not thrilled the news had come when it did.

I sat still, not knowing how to react, just knowing dreams were hard to come by. My eyes were brimming, ready to overflow. His arms encircled me. I tried to still my heart from the intensity of the previous minutes.

"It is?" I questioned.

"Absolutely, Megan. You'll come with me to Edinburgh, and I'll introduce you to a colleague of mine who knows absolutely everything there is to know about the publishing world. She'll guide you through the process, and you'll write an article they won't be able to refuse."

"Oh, Jake, I don't know. You've already done so much for me. And I'm not sure I should."

"I don't know why not. Besides, we're friends. That's what friends are for."

"That's asking a lot of your colleague, don't you think?"

"Don't fret about that. Linda owes me. Besides, you already have everything you need in the way of additional information. Our trips have seen to that."

"Jake, I'm beginning to believe you're psychic. Did you know I needed to work on my article?"

"Just a hunch, nothing more."

"Why didn't you tell me?" I asked.

"It was not for me to say. And how would you have felt if I had told you it needed some final touches?"

I had to smile at his choice of words. "Oh, I might have been a little hurt."

"And," he added, "you would have been upset with me."

"Umm, maybe upset with myself."

He spoke more about Edinburgh, dangling all sorts of carrots. Before I went up to bed, I told him I would sleep on his suggestion and let him know in the morning. If I decided to accompany him, it would be my decision, not just his—and on *my* terms. I didn't want to be plagued with thoughts of my own weakness—again. I'd been through enough of that with Mark. I'd let him direct my life from the moment I met him, up to the point of marriage. He manipulated me. And I let it happen because I loved him. And feared losing him. And I didn't plan on being weak-kneed when it came to Jake ... if I could help it.

My relationship with Jake had, to this point, been on a level above what I had experienced with Mark. Maybe that wasn't fair, but it was true. I had to continue to be cautious, even if I felt Jake was the one I wanted to complete my life. On the other hand, that wasn't what this part of my life was supposed to be about. In spite of the temptation to allow him to sway me, I knew it would have to be on my terms. And our proximity wreaked havoc on my will.

Chapter 9

I woke early the next morning. No smell of coffee or breakfast. I hurriedly dressed and went down to the kitchen. It was quiet. Jake's bedroom door was still closed, so I figured he was, at last, getting some much-needed sleep.

I made the coffee and looked in the refrigerator for breakfast makings. Three eggs, a bit of cheese, a few cups of milk, a part of an onion, and a tomato were the only worthy remnants. *That will do*. I scrounged through the cabinets and found flour, baking powder, salt, and shortening. I could make a few biscuits, something I hadn't ever done, but I had watched Mom make them hundreds of times.

After cutting the shortening into the dry ingredients, I gently stirred in the milk. I knew the importance of not over mixing the dough. "If you want mouthwatering, light biscuits, treat them tenderly," she always said, and her advice never failed to produce a mouthful of pure heaven. After rolling out the soft mixture and cutting rounds with a fruit glass, I placed the pan into the oven and began the omelet. This *pièce de résistance* would have a Mexican flavor, one I was certain Jake would enjoy.

I waited until the warm aroma of crusty biscuits began to fill the kitchen before pouring the egg mixture into the pan. I then set the table and poured myself a cup of coffee.

"Jake, it's time to get up," I called up the stairs, hoping I would elicit a response. None came.

A few minutes later, I took the biscuits out of the oven and removed the sizzling omelet from the fire. "I'm going to come up there and pull you out of bed!"

Hearing no movement, I ran up the stairs and knocked on the door. No answer. "Jake," I whispered, then laughed. I'd been yelling loud enough to wake the dead.

I cracked the door a few inches and peered into the cool darkness of his timeworn sanctuary. I could see the outline of his muscular form as he lay on his side, his back to me.

"Jake, wake up. I have breakfast ready and waiting. It's going to get cold."

No response. I walked into the room and crawled onto the bed and placed my hand on his shoulder. "Jake, are you—"

In one fluid motion, he turned and engulfed me in his arms, pulling me down across the warmth of his chest, his bare skin damp and feverish against my own. His lips began a soundless search of my flesh, while his hands gently served as their guide. My breath caught in my throat. I tried to resist, but his arms were unyielding.

As he began exploring beneath my clothing and tugging to free them, I fought my own natural urges and forced my arms up from beneath his, placing my hands on his chest. "Stop this right now, Jake. Stop it now," I said with a severity shocking even me.

He froze, and then released me from his grasp, his hands freezing in midair, fingers extended as if they had lost their purpose. "I'm sorry," he offered stiffly and rose from the bed, wrapping a blanket around his hips. "I lost my head." He hesitated and then continued, "I was dreaming of you, and I wanted you. Forgive me, but this is getting difficult."

I stood in the doorway looking at him, not knowing what to say. So I said the only thing releasing me from the moment, "Just get dressed and come downstairs. Breakfast is ready."

With my legs trembling, I walked back down the stairs, hanging onto the banister as my knees buckled beneath me. I sat on the bottom step, trying to sort my feelings. I yearned to have him hold me, to make love to me, but it couldn't happen like that. I wouldn't let it. I wanted more. And at that moment, I wasn't sure what that was. Maybe *more* was just a fantasy.

In a few minutes, I heard Jake's steps at the top of the stairs, so I shook myself out of my frenzy and headed for the kitchen. I emptied the cold coffee from my cup, poured some fresh, and sipped it cautiously, keeping my back to him as he walked into the room.

He stood by the table, keeping his distance, "Megan, I'm truly sorry. I had no right to ... to do that. Please forgive me."

I wanted to be angry with him. It was all I could do to meet his gaze. I blinked as I looked up at his suffering. "There's nothing to forgive. You haven't done anything wrong. You just let me know you really care for me, that you feel for me the way I feel about you."

"Then why didn't you make love to me?"

I couldn't answer.

"Seriously, if not now, when?"

"I don't know. I don't know when or ... if ever."

He looked at me for a moment as if trying to unravel a puzzle lying fragmented between us. "You're right." He turned from me, placed both hands on the counter, and stared down at the floor.

I filled his coffee cup and handed it to him. "It's okay."

I then walked to the stove, picked up two plates, filled each, and then offered him one. "Sit down and eat," I said, embarrassed by his shame and wanting to take him in my arms and kiss away his pain—a thought I immediately squelched.

We ate in silence. He then rose from the table and walked out the back door. As he was about to close the door, he looked back at me with the same wide-jawed grin that had first set my senses spiraling out of control. "By the way, those biscuits melted in my mouth, and the eggs were good, but they would have been much better if they hadn't been cold." He quickly shut the door before I could respond. I breathed a sigh of relief. I knew we were still friends.

The incident had been awkward, yet I knew it *might* happen ... no, I knew it would happen. We ached for each other. Mentally I had been rehearsing my response. I had a choice. I could become involved with him and take my chances as to the outcome or I could attempt the near impossible—resist him and stay focused on moving ahead in search of the elusive hatchling of my mind. Maybe my desire for a different kind of career would amount to nothing. Maybe it *was* just a dream, but how in the world would I figure myself out unless I stayed focused? Besides, I didn't want to give myself to him unless I was sure.

After cleaning the kitchen, I poured another cup of coffee and walked out of the back door to discover the source of some racket. Jake had pulled a cart into the middle of the open area and had begun tossing all of the junk—broken garden pots, old tires, useless tools, and other bits and pieces of worn country life—into its belly.

As he bent to collect shards of broken glass bottles and bric-a-brac, he looked up at me. "I thought it was time to get rid of some of the trash cluttering the periphery of my existence. Laura's nurturing spirit has gone to waste. It's a sad little piece of her legacy ... so little it took to create and so much to destroy." He looked up at me and smiled, then continued, "When we came here in the summer to take a break from school, she would fill the back of the truck with plants and, within a day, the whole place was screaming with all manner of color. I guess I've neglected it."

"Would you like some help?" I asked, wondering if this was the time to interfere with his thoughts.

"No, I think I've just about cleaned up the worst of it. Just need to get this place back in order before I leave."

"When do you think you'll go?" I asked, hesitant to pry, unknowing of his sentiments toward me after our morning encounter.

"Three or four days, I'd say."

"Not much time to say good-bye to all of this."

"No, but this," he said as he threw a chipped clay pot into the cart, "is something I've needed to do for a long time. I've been ignoring *it* as well as other things in my life."

"Don't you think that sometimes we have to do that just to make it through difficult times?"

"I'm sure, but there comes a point in time—"

He didn't finish. He pulled off his gloves, stuffed them in his pocket, and sighed deeply before continuing. "I've loved it here, and I'll always miss her. Maybe someday I'll come back and it will be easier."

He tossed the last evidence of broken refuse into the cart and reached out for my hand. "Let's go for a walk."

"Let me put my cup in the kitchen. I'll be right back."

I hurried into the kitchen, placed my cup on the counter, and took a deep breath, exhaling slowly. A sudden flood of contentment rushed through me, washing away the doubt tinkering with my reason. This man had awakened my senses in a way I had never experienced before, but I knew my decision to refuse his advances was the right one, at least for now. Why the difference between my relationship with Mark and my relationship with him, I wasn't sure, but I felt carefree, neither bound nor tied to an idea of what our relationship should be. Each day was an eye-opener.

I walked back out into the cool morning air to join him just as he returned from carting away the last remains of his morning work. He took my hand, and we began to walk out of the newly cleared yard and onto the road tracing the outskirts of the meadow. After a few minutes, he led me to a dry-stacked wall cutting a serpentine path across the lush Scottish grassland.

"Come on," he said as he helped me over the barrier. "Let's walk and enjoy Scotland's finest meadows. No use staying on the straight and narrow when greener pastures beckon."

"Oh, my," I laughed, "aren't you getting poetic. Shades of Marlowe, I do believe."

"Familiar with him, are you?" he said as I slid from the fence and into his arms.

Our momentary bodily contact jarred us, and we stood unmoving and silent. "Isn't everyone?" I whispered, my lips brushing the salty skin of his tanned neck.

Slowly he released me and we resumed walking. "I suppose so. Can you quote a few lines, Ms. English teacher?" he asked.

"Oh, I think I can do that," I answered, enjoying the challenge. "Over here," I said, leading him back toward the stacked-rock wall we had just crossed. "You sit there on the ground," I said, pointing a few feet away, "and I'll climb up here. I think it was this very spot where Marlowe spoke to his love."

"I doubt this was the spot, but it couldn't have been too far away," he encouraged as he held me by the waist while I struggled to find my footing on the rocky surface. As I slowly stood, he released me and walked a few feet away where he sat on the ground and grinned up at me, the green of his eyes reflecting the vivid grasses surrounding him.

"Okay," I said, standing above him. I closed my eyes and rehearsed the lines in my head. He waited quietly.

I remembered only a few lines, but I was having too much fun to let that minor detail ruin the moment. I then opened my eyes, spread my arms out with palms up, and spoke with intended melodrama:

> Come live with me, and be my love,
> And we will all the pleasures prove,

That hills and valleys, dale and field,
And all the craggy mountains yield.

I looked down at him. His eyes sparkled with amusement. I continued,

There we will sit upon the rocks,
And see the shepherds feed their flocks,
By shallow ... falls—

"By shallow rivers, to whose falls," he corrected me, and then we continued in unison, "Melodious birds sing madrigals."

I stood silently, unable to concentrate. He was leaning back on one arm, legs apart and bent, looking up at me in silence. His grin had faded and his lips were drawn tight as if he were about to say something of importance, but the words wouldn't turn loose from his lips. I knew we were both grappling with our emotions. I felt my face flush. I wanted to descend my rustic stage and let him take me in his arms. Instead, I shocked myself and blurted out, "Applause, applause!"

He shook his head as if he wondered why in the world he put up with me and then slowly began to clap until he was playing my game. "Bravo. Bravo."

I climbed down. He pulled himself up from the ground and took my hand, and we continued our journey over the highland, enjoying all the pleasures surrounding us—the crisp morning air, the cooling breezes, the expanse of green, the romping lambs, and the strengthening bond of our amity. I knew we understood each other's struggle.

During our walk, we talked about his plans to return to teaching, and I told him I had decided to go to Edinburgh with him, but I thought it best to get my own apartment. He was pleased about my decision, and although disappointed that I wouldn't be staying with him, quickly offered to help me in my search for a suitable place to stay.

Chapter 10

Some time later, we returned to the farm, exhausted but exhilarated from our outing. We eagerly quenched our thirst and then sprawled wearily at the table. Jake sat across from me, regarding me in his quiet manner. I waited. I knew he had something to say. I leaned back into the hardness of the straight-backed chair.

"You mean a lot to me, Megan. I hope you know that."

"Yes, I think I do," I answered, unsure of what would follow.

"I realize you have your priorities, and I shouldn't disrupt what you have going."

"You're not a disruption, Jake. *You're* the one who has allowed me to intrude. You've been a godsend to me."

"You definitely have strength of character. I really admire you for that."

I smiled at him, momentarily wondering if I was losing ground with him, but I knew I had to stop thinking that way. "Well, it hasn't been exactly easy staying focused."

"Me, too," he said, getting up from the table. "You're sure you want to get your own apartment?" he asked, changing the subject. "I have plenty of room."

"I'm sure," I answered, with a knowing grin. "I think having my own place will help me keep my priorities straight."

"That's what I'm afraid of," he said with a chuckle. "No, really, I'll do everything I can to help you get settled. I have some ideas already where we might look for a room. In the meantime, is there anything else you would like to do around here, any place you would like to go before we head to the city?"

"I was thinking of returning to the cairns. I really find it fascinating and would appreciate a second look." Inwardly, I was panicky at the idea.

"Why don't you take the truck tomorrow? I need to take care of closing down the house, and I have some phone calls to make. If you go without me, you can take as much time as you want."

"That would be great. Are you certain you won't need the truck?"

"Positive. It's yours for the day."

"Great. That should work. And speaking of phone calls, I need to call Shannon to let her know of my plans."

"Of course. You'll find Aunt Anne's number in the book by the phone. I'm sure she'll have the number where you can reach Shannon. Maybe she can join you for a while in Edinburgh."

"I hope so. I'm not sure when she's planning to return to the States, but it should be soon, and I would like to spend a bit more time with her."

"I know she would like that. In the meantime, I still have some cleaning up to do around here. I'll be out at the barn if you need me."

"I'll come out and give you a hand when I'm finished talking to her," I said, hoping he would refuse my offer. Shoveling barn refuse didn't have much of a hold on me.

"Why don't you just stay in and take it easy. I know how you really feel. You're not fooling me."

"I'll tell you what. I'll work on the kitchen. It's the least I can do."

"Sounds good," he agreed as he headed toward the back of the house. "See if you can salvage something for lunch. If not, we'll go into the village. I know of a splendid pub where intimate conversations are the main attraction."

"Now that you mention it, I'm sure the refrigerator is empty," I called after him.

"Good. I feel a big appetite coming on." And he shut the door behind him.

After giving the kitchen a good scrubbing and throwing practically all food items away, I made a fresh pot of tea, poured a few cupfuls into a thermos, added lemon, and set out for the barn.

I was surprised to see the pens empty, the feeding bins scrubbed, and the ground raked into neat little grooves. Jake was in the storeroom tossing cans, bottles, syringes, and empty vials of medication into a trash bin.

"Take a break. You've been out here for hours. I made some fresh tea," I called out to him.

"Well, Megan, my girl, you came just in the nick of time. I was about to call you to come bail me out of this mess."

"Well, it's my pleasure to be of service," I replied with a curtsy. "Take off your camouflage," I said, nodding at his gloves and heavy apron, "and let's sit out in the courtyard one more time."

"Go ahead. I'll be right behind you. I need to finish this."

"No, I'll wait right here to keep you company," I said, setting the thermos on a shelf and joining him in his cleaning frenzy.

We worked in silence. I was glad to be there by his side, even in the barn.

After tea, Jake returned to his work, and I pulled out my article, gathered up my newest notes, and began revising. At first, the work seemed nothing but drudgery, but as each word emerged on the page, I felt myself lose all concept of time.

Hours later, Jake stuck his head into the living room. "Hey, do I smell smoke?"

"Oh, I didn't hear you come in. Are you finished for the day?"

"Yes, I am. Going to shower. If you can take a break, I'll meet you out back in a few minutes."

I looked over at his handsome, sweaty face and said, "Deal."

We spent the remainder of the afternoon in the courtyard. He was pensive as he talked about his life in Edinburgh, yet I knew he reveled in his return. He said a young student had been house-sitting for him during his absence, but would soon be moving to an apartment in the city near his new job.

We both lay sprawled on a tartan, lazing in unison until twilight nestled around us and the damp fingers of the breeze brushed in and out of the spaces between us. From time to time, his hand would reach out and he'd stroke my cheek or brush my hair from my eyes. Our conversation faded into random comments, his laced with tenderness, mine with caution.

In time, Jake slept. I tried to join him but couldn't take my eyes from the movement of his chest as it rose and fell in time with his breath. I rolled to my side so my face brushed his shirt and inhaled the fresh cotton smell mingling with his own. I was intoxicated. I sat up and read.

When he woke, he rolled toward me and said, "A nice way to end the day, eh?"

Yes, perfect, I thought, but I sat silently beside him, hesitant to say the words aloud and intensely aware of the magnetism between us.

"I suppose we better find something to eat," he finally suggested. "I've worked up an appetite lying here."

"Me, too."

Jake folded the blanket and we entered the house as we made plans for the remainder of the evening.

Chapter 11

By the time I woke the next morning, Jake had already set out for his final chores. The house was quiet. I dressed for my return trip to the cairns and organized my backpack—camera, film, notebook, pens, water, jacket. I bounced down the stairs and into the kitchen, scanning the cabinets for two small packages of shortbread I had found during my cleaning frenzy the day before. I tossed one into my backpack and placed the other on the cabinet where Jake could find it in case he came looking for something to eat.

He left me a note on the table, telling me his brother was picking him up and they would be out all day, but he would return in time for dinner. A "P.S." stated he had placed a map on the front seat of the truck to make sure I didn't lose my way. Feeling like a silly schoolgirl, I folded his note and tucked it safely away in my bag.

The truck was parked in the back drive, keys lying on the seat with the map he had meticulously sketched. My heart raced. I couldn't believe I was on my own to drive to the cairns. I couldn't decide if my excitement sprang from this liberty or the anticipation of revisiting the ancient grounds.

Jake's directions took me along the same route the two of us had taken on my first visit. The traffic was light, and I arrived at the cairn without any mishaps, feeling quite confident and exhilarated.

The sun's brilliance splayed across the terrain, confusing me at first. I expected the somber setting of my initial visit—darkness and mist casting a gauzy veil, casting its mysterious spell even in the morning hours. Instead, the dazzle of sunlight filtered through the spindly branches and played whimsically over the stones' contrasting textures, colors, and shapes. All metamorphosed.

As I maneuvered the entry gate and entered the expanse once again, I marveled at the transformation before me. Each step I took offered a virginal view, each one as stunning as the next.

I crisscrossed the terrain that had enchanted the myriad lives of Scots for centuries and visually scoured the area for the most spectacular view. When I reached the boulder that had captured my attention and imagination on my first visit, I set my backpack on the ground, secured my camera around my neck, and began snapping pictures of the chromatic performance capering before me.

After using an entire roll of film and feeling confident I had more than enough photos for my article, I returned my camera to my bag and began to explore the cairns once more. Nothing had changed except the weather.

I retraced my earlier path, weaving my way to the site where I had lain in the cool, dark bracken. I lay down once again, my mind combing through the disparity of feelings and sensations my two visits had conjured.

I had been overwhelmed on my first visit with unfamiliar grounds, bleak weather, airy voices, and whimsical movement—all a mystery, then and now. Yet the experience had awakened a sensation both tantalizing and delectable.

I stared up into the sky and marveled at its dazzling brilliance, such a contrast to the chilling dampness and eerie whisperings of my first trip. Even so, the awe remained. It was too perfect, too easy to love … just like Jake.

I wondered about the whisperings I had heard during my first visit. Were they a chintzy trick of my emotions? *They were real to me. I heard them. They belong to me.* Maybe I'd been hoodwinked into playing the fool, believing they were real. Real or not, I knew something in them stirred passion in me. And I wouldn't let my own doubts ruin the effect. *No doubting yourself, Megan McEller. No tarnishing the silver. Jake, this is what you have done to me.* Or maybe it's what I've allowed …what I've determined for myself.

After lying there for some time with my eyes closed and my thoughts wandering like gypsies on the run, I suddenly felt a tremor beneath me. I sat up and listened. "Silence" echoed in my mind. I lay back down, attempting to squelch my panic. *Be calm. It's just your imagination.* I couldn't hear anything. No birds calling, no wings flapping, no stirring … nothing.

I don't know how long I lay there, but I suddenly realized I had been asleep. And strangely, I now lay on a boulder, not on the ground where I had been earlier. My spine and head pressed mercilessly against the hard surface. My legs and arms were spread wide, my face streaked with tears and perspiration, and my pelvis arching in slow, undulating movements toward the sky. I was wet and whimpering.

Bewildered, I gradually pulled myself out of my delirium. *Have I been dreaming? What's happening to me?* I managed to gather up my belongings and almost tiptoed my way toward the exit, not wanting to disturb *whatever* had cast its spell on me.

I climbed in the truck and locked the doors. My hands trembled. I fumbled with the keys, dropping them on the floorboard. As I reached to retrieve them, I shoved them under the seat and knew I'd have to get out of the truck to search for them. For a few moments, I gripped the steering wheel, unable to let go, shutting my eyes, not wanting to see the scene before me. The sky had turned dark and the wind whipped the treetops above me. Nothing else moved. I knew I'd have to take my chances, so I flung open the door, jumped out, leaned down to peer under the seat, and spotted them. Within seconds, I locked the doors again, turned the ignition, and sped away.

As I retraced the narrow road leading from the cairn, I kept telling myself *it was just a dream* and kept repeating those words until the beating in my chest resumed a more normal pace.

I pulled onto the main highway relieved, but I needed to stop. Strangely enough, I longed to write. Within minutes, I drove through a village where I noticed a small restaurant tucked on the side of a hill just off the main road. Perfect. I could surround myself with the hubbub of normal human activity.

Once inside, I began to relax. I found a small table in a corner and ordered lemonade. I wasn't hungry, but felt shaky and parched after my experience or, as I told myself, after my dream. I pulled a notebook from my bag and began to write. My first word was "Silence." *What is that all about?*

I clutched my pen as it continued to scratch out words of its own:

Devouring hush, dull thou the living brow,

And bid the sweet consume each breath's decay;
Yank the gasping sighs from th' lover now,
And scorch the canker where it seethes today;
Beware the mask of clouds that hides the crime,
With hideous rack and bonds of blackest doom;
The rose with thorns will prick before its time,
With all its beauty spoiled and love entombed;
But hear the noise that deafens all the dreams,
To spread madness cloaked—seduction's friend;
Make haste, O Sweet, abandon all that seems
To awe with touch, a kiss, the bitter end.
      If weak and feeble minds delay to choose
      Then grieve for all the pain it dreads to lose.

The pen's movement stopped. I waited, expecting it to dash off another line. But it lay inert in my trembling hand. Mine again. I tossed it on the table and struggled for composure. I wanted to scream, wanted to run away from this town, from the cairn, from the farm … and from Jake. I looked across the room. Only a handful of customers shared the room. No one seemed to notice my distress.

I looked down at the words written on the notebook in front of me. What did they mean? Was it something lying secreted in my mind? Something I had read long ago and it just happened to pour forth at this time? I didn't think so. I knew it had written itself. It read like a poem, a sonnet. I read it through twice, then a third time, trying to make sense of anything. *It's all so confusing. Where did it come from? Are these my thoughts?*

I sat staring at the poem, thinking until I could stand it no more. I picked up my belongings, paid my bill, and walked into the late morning air. *Maybe my muse broke through today. Maybe this is my purpose. Poetry. Who would have thought?* I began laughing … hysterically. *Making a living might get a bit difficult.*

With the unsettling lines running through my head, I headed toward the historic Culloden Battlefield. I needed time to think before returning to the farm. I walked the trails along the battle's progression. I tried to recall the history Jake had so patiently told me, but chilling words kept running through my mind: *devouring hush, gasping sighs, blackness cloaked.* Jake's history turned into fragments. *Love entombed?*

A small group of children, being led by their teacher, blocked the walk at one point, and as I made my way around them, I eavesdropped on the teacher's story of the Scots' failed attempt to overtake their enemy. Some children listened wide-eyed with wonder, some whispered their own stories to one another, while others played along the stone-lined path of the battle scene, clueless. I wanted to warn them to pay attention, pay attention or they were going to miss something. The same as I had. Was I like one of these kids who played on the sideline? *I* certainly didn't know what was going on.

After an hour of exploring the area and examining a number of the engraved stones that memorialized the fallen clans, I drove back into Inverness. By then, my stomach was rumbling. I parked within the city center, slipped on my backpack, and began walking into the bustling life. Stopping at a small market, I purchased a turkey sandwich and a cold bottle of water, and then walked along the River Ness.

I crossed a footbridge over the river and onto a grassy knoll where I sat staring into the serenity of the open spaces. It was difficult to eat but easy to sit mindlessly ... too confused to think.

Eventually, I gathered my belongings and walked along the banks of the Caledonian Canal, breathing deeply.

By the time I completed my return trek along the riverside walks and viewed several historic buildings up close, it was four-thirty. *Time to head back to the farm.* My day in the heart of one of the oldest settlements in Scotland had been unbelievable. Almost unearthly.

Chapter 12

Not needing the map, I drove back to the farm in plenty of time to dress for dinner with Jake. I parked the truck in the drive where I had found it, gathered my belongings, and climbed awkwardly down onto the rutted earth. I entered the kitchen through the newly tidied entryway, placed the keys on the kitchen counter, and sprinted up the stairs to my bedroom. Jake was nowhere in sight.

After drawing a bath, I stripped off my clothes and peered at my back in the mirror. It was bruised. Tiny cuts and bits of blood dotted my spine. It hadn't been a dream. I climbed into the tub, anxious to wash away the sour dampness clinging to me like an unwanted embrace, but needing more than anything a relief from the uncanny feeling overwhelming me since my visit to the cairn.

As I scrubbed away traces of my day's romp, I heard the back door slam, followed by the tramp of heavy boots on the stairs. They paused at the bathroom door, and Jake called out, "Megan, your escort has returned. Are you ready to go wet your whistle?"

"I will be soon," I yelled back. "Almost finished."

"No hurry. Take your time."

I could hear him walk back across the hall and into his bedroom, shutting the door behind him. I knew he would be exhausted from a full day's work and would be anxious to clean off the grime of his labor, so I hurriedly rinsed my hair and shut off the water. I climbed out of the tub and dried, using the one towel I had set aside for my last few days in the country.

Wrapping it around my damp torso, I peeked out into the hallway to make certain his door was closed and then hurried into my room, yelling that the bath was free as I shut my door. Cool air from the open window welcomed me, relieving the steamy warmth from the hot bath. I let the towel drop to the floor as I stood enjoying the soft breezes and the green, rolling expanse spread below me.

In the next moment, I leaned out of the window and yelled, "Hey, you. Hey, you sheep out there chewing and gazing, and gazing and chewing. Here I am. Right here. And guess what? I am lucky. So very, very lucky." They didn't bother to look.

Strangely, in spite of the day's bizarre happenings, I was exuberant—and suddenly startled at my actions. I retrieved the towel from the floor, wrapped it around me, and wondered what had come over me. I wasn't sure. Whatever it was, I knew more was to come. Something was going on. Something about this place. I knew it had to be more than my feelings for Jake. *What is it?* Each morning since my arrival, I'd awakened with a quickness of breath. My adrenaline was flowing. Something new had taken hold of me.

I sat down at the small dresser and began the ritualistic ordeal with my hair, detangling, scrunching big handfuls while drying with my head hanging between my legs, and then adding a dab of smoother to take out the frizz. After a time I gave up and began scrutinizing my face. Country life agreed with me. My cheeks were rosy and my skin clear and radiant. I applied just a hint of eye color and lip gloss, then dressed, choosing a skirt with an asymmetrical ruffled hem, a lightweight, sleeveless tank, and a silk embroidered jacket with mandarin collar, all in shades of periwinkle blue, the dressiest outfit in my wardrobe.

I want to look snazzy. I dug to the bottom of my suitcase, finding a pair of black sling-back heels and a small black purse. I slipped on the shoes, dropped lipstick, comb, and tissue into the purse, and, last of all, secured an eclectic necklace of glass, metal, wood, and beads around my neck.

As I stood back from the mirror and studied my reflection, I wondered if I really was lucky. Surely, it was more than that. Sacrificing the known for the unknown was risky business, but choices did make a difference. And maybe that was what I was doing—creating my own luck through my choices. Whatever it was, I felt I had discovered a few things about myself that were definitely news to me.

Unfortunately, my hair lay limp—shiny and curly, but limp, so I pulled it together at the nape of my neck and secured it with a large silver hair fastener. *Hmm, I like it, and I think Jake will too.*

Satisfied, I picked up my purse from the bed and went downstairs, my heels clicking against the wooden steps. As I reached the landing, I could hear the melodious sounds of bagpipes rising from the stereo. Jake was standing across the room looking out the window, his back to me. He didn't turn when I came in, so I stood quietly a few feet from him, enjoying the tranquility of the pipes.

As the last strands of "Shenandoah" faded, he turned. His breath caught, his ready smile hidden. His body swayed ever so slightly.

"Don't move. Don't say a thing. Just let me look at you."

He stood staring at me a few seconds, and as the triple rhythm of "Mull of Kintyre" filled the room, he walked up close, gathered me in his arms, and began waltzing me around the floor. We were fluid. I felt every ounce of my being streaming with his with every step, every turn. It was as though I had danced with him all my life. As the last note sounded, exertion and desire conspired, and we stood wrapped in each other's arms perfectly still, breathless.

"The Lord of the Dance" broke our reverie. He took a step back. "Oh, my, girl, whits fur ye'll no gin by ye," he said. I figured he was making an effort to keep the moment light.

"I'll take that as a compliment," I said, not having the faintest idea what he meant.

"Oh, it's just something I feel in my bones, something my mum always told me. It means, 'What's meant for you will not pass you by.'"

"I'll take your word for it," I laughed.

"No, believe it."

"Well, I just hope what's meant for me is good. Otherwise, I'm not so anxious to know what it is." I couldn't help but think about my visit to the cairn.

"As dedicated as you are in finding what you want, there's little chance you'll miss it. I'm sure of that."

"Thank you, Jake. You have no idea how very much that means to me."

"Well, we better leave if we are planning to eat anytime tonight. Bring a jacket. It's cool and it looks like rain."

I hurriedly returned to my bedroom, grabbing my jacket and collapsible umbrella, made a few hasty adjustments to my hair, and then descended the stairs to join him at the back door.

71

He picked up the keys from the counter and relieved me of my jacket and umbrella. "Let me carry those for you. You won't need them right now. It's rather nice out, cool but pleasant."

As we walked out the door, the wafting breeze slipped into the folds of my skirt and billowed the hem around my thighs. I wondered how wise I had been in choosing silk for a trip to the highlands. Having lived in a hot, humid climate all my life had not prepared me for the change.

"Geez, isn't this July? It's much cooler than I expected."

"Do you want to change? We have time."

"No, not really. I'll be all right once I get in the truck."

He helped me up into the cab, closed the door, and made his way to the driver's side. He slid effortlessly up onto the seat beside me and turned the ignition, and we were quickly bumping down the road once more, stomachs growling but spirits high.

By the time we arrived at the restaurant, crossed the mezzanine floors, and were seated at our table, the chimes of an antique clock across the room sang out eight o'clock.

"This room is beautiful," I said, gazing at its grandeur.

"It is, isn't it? It's a result of some intensive restoration efforts."

"Well, it's really worth the drive over here just to see it. I only hope the food is good."

"I'm certain you'll enjoy it. They're known for using only the freshest ingredients. I've had some wonderful meals here in the past."

"I guess you and Laura came here together."

"Many times. In fact, other than tonight, those were the only times I came. She loved the food here. It has a French flair and is presented beautifully."

"I can't wait. I'm starving," I said in anticipation.

Jake chose a full-bodied red wine our waiter recommended, but I opted for a white, as reds tended to give me a headache, and within minutes, we were sipping and making plans for our move into the city. Jake had one more day of work at the farm, and I told him I would continue my efforts inside the house.

We shared a small appetizer of mushroom, red onion, and peppercorn bruschetta along with another glass of wine, and then enjoyed our meal—salmon on a bed of penne with basil and white wine cream sauce for me and a robust Angus-beef steak for Jake.

Around nine-thirty, we walked out the door, ready to enjoy a leisurely stroll while window-shopping along the brightly lit city streets. Jake stopped in front of a kilt maker's shop and pointed out his clan's plaid. I told him it would be an honor to see him in full dress, and he told me I would undoubtedly have the dubious pleasure if I stayed around for a while.

On our way back to the truck, I delighted in scouring the window of a hat company that had a hodgepodge of headgear—Juliets, berets, pillboxes, wide-brims, cloches, stocking caps, skullcaps—displayed artfully on an assortment of racks, shelves, and hooks, all in a medley of colors—reds, pinks, blues, greens, yellows, purples—an eye-crossing feast.

"It's just too bad that they're closed. I could definitely use something with a Scottish flair. They have so many choices," I marveled as I rubbed my hands up and down my bare arms.

"Are you cold?" Jake asked, and then slipped off his jacket and draped it over my shoulders as we walked into the evening.

"No, not really," I lied, feeling foolish I had left mine in the truck. "But yours feels good. It's so warm. Now you'll be cold."

"No, not in the least," he said, wrapping his arm around my shoulder and pulling me close.

"I'm enjoying the walk. There's so much to see."

"I dare say you will truly enjoy Edinburgh, then, and you'll have all the time in the world to explore the city."

"I'm looking forward to that. I'm also anxious to meet the professor you said might help me with my writing. What's her name?"

"Linda Scott."

"Well, that's a nice Scottish name."

"It is indeed. I think you'll like her. She teaches a number of writing classes and really works with her students. Many publish."

"I could just enroll in one of her classes, couldn't I?"

"It might be simpler if you sat in on a class or two. She wouldn't mind, and it's a bit late to enroll. If you stay on for a while, perhaps you can take a course."

"Maybe," I responded, knowing only time would tell.

Chapter 13

We returned to the truck just as a light rain dotted the sidewalk, but as we left the city lights behind, a downpour slowed our way. Jake was quiet as he concentrated on the dark, narrow roadway in front of him, so quiet I could have easily nodded off to sleep had the rush of wind and rain and the intermittent lightning not unnerved me.

When we arrived, he guided the truck slowly up onto the wet grass bordering the house. As he opened his door, he handed me my umbrella and said to give him a few seconds to unlock the back door to the farmhouse.

Within moments I saw him standing inside, waving me in, so I shoved open my door, raised my umbrella, and pressed the button that magically spread its portable roof. I stepped out of the truck, slamming the door behind me. The wind and lightning had subsided, but the rain fell in a hushed shower. I walked a few steps and then stopped and spread my hands in front of me, letting the cool wetness pool up in my palms. I turned, reopened the passenger side door, lowered the umbrella, and tossed it on the seat. I began stripping off my clothes and flinging them on the seat. I'd always wanted to do this. Clad only in the goose bumps that had quickly risen to the occasion, I stepped out on the squishy, waterlogged grass, tilted my head back so I could face the sky, and drank in heaven's spilling droplets. Something like skinny-dipping.

Jake stared at me a few minutes, no doubt thinking I was crazier than he had originally thought, then yelled that I better come in as I was going to be struck by lightning. I laughed and called him a chicken but decided he was right when I heard a clap of thunder overhead.

After I retrieved my castoffs from the truck, Jake met me at the door with a towel and an expression showing his approval, although he tried to deny it, saying, "Has anyone ever told you you're nuts?"

"Not until now," I assured him, "but now you've told me, I think it feels pretty good to be nuts. I may explore the possibilities more often."

"Running around stark-naked in a thunderstorm?" he mocked.

"Whatever it takes. I'm just disappointed you didn't join me."

"I thought it better not to. I was in enough trouble watching you from the doorway."

"Well, as you told me, we're friends, and what are friends for if not to go through a little trouble?" I teased, then moved out of the kitchen and up the stairs.

"Come back down for a nightcap when you're presentable," he called after me.

"I will. I need to be warmed up. I'm freezing!" I yelled back.

After toweling dry, I slipped into a gown and a soft terrycloth bathrobe I found hanging in the closet. I removed the clip from my damp hair and combed out the tangles. I felt wonderful. So alive.

When I entered the parlor, Jake was sitting quietly with his eyes closed. As he heard me enter, he looked up and smiled and took a small glass from the table beside him and handed it to me.

"Just a bit of brandy to take the chill off, my lady."

"Mmm, thanks."

"A toast," he said, raising his glass to me.

I raised my glass to his and waited.

"To the craziest girl that's ever crossed the threshold of this lowly farm."

"And to Jake," I chimed, not having the slightest idea what I was about to say. "To Jake, the most ... noble of men ... on any Scottish sheep farm."

"Hear, hear! We are a lucky pair, are we not?"

I sat next to him, pulling my legs up under me and snuggling down in the sofa's deep cushions. "You may be joking, but today I thought about being lucky."

"What do you mean?" he asked.

"Well, when I got back from my little jaunt, I had a feeling of ... oh, I don't know ... of such happiness, like being on top of the world.

You know, how you feel when you're a kid and you're playing outside from morning until night. It's the best. And then suddenly you hear your mom calling your name, saying that it's time to come in. That's when you wish time would stop and you could go on and on in your own little world."

"You're afraid *this* is going to end?"

"Exactly."

"Don't let it end."

"Is it that simple?"

"It could be. What do you think you would have to do to keep it from ending?"

"I don't know. I think that's part of my fear. I keep battling with myself. I keep questioning what I want."

"Don't you think you have to question yourself from time to time?" he asked.

"Do you?"

"Of course I do, all the time."

"When was the last time?" I asked him, curious as to what in his life was a problem, that is, other than the memory of his wife.

"I question myself about you."

"Really?" I said, astounded.

"Yes, really."

"In what way?"

"Sometimes I wonder how I could possibly care so much for a young woman I hardly know, especially when I think about Laura and how much I loved her. And that wasn't so terribly long ago."

I wanted to tell him I'd been having the same thoughts, but I didn't. I just sat there, suddenly nervous, anxious for the bantering to resume, but our conversation had taken a serious turn. I could feel my face flushing and the perspiration bead on my upper lip. "It's hot in here," I snapped as I stood and walked to the window, pushing it open. The rain had stopped. A cool breeze brushed against my face.

I turned back to him. "My being here has been difficult for you, hasn't it?"

"No," he said without hesitation. "If anything, you've made life easier … better. You've made me want to start over again. I've told you that, but I can't help but question my feelings for you."

"As you said, we have to question ourselves from time to time, or no telling what we might do. Maybe do something ... like, like ..." I stuttered, wanting to say *fall for a crazy American girl,* but, instead, I finished, "do something crazy like running around in a rainstorm."

"Well, you really should add the naked part." He set his drink on the table and walked up to me.

I placed my glass on the windowsill and looked up at him.

"Megan, it has become quite clear to me I'm crazy about you. I don't know what our future holds because I know you have your own agenda, but I want you to know I think I've loved you from the moment I saw you."

"And you're causing me to have one of those *nutty* urges again."

"Well, I'm not sure what that entails, but I'm ready for anything."

I wrapped my arms around his neck, and he embraced me tenderly, kissing me long, but unhurriedly. He then took my hands in his and looked at me thoughtfully, "What are you thinking?" he asked.

"Do you remember when we first met?"

"How could I forget? I walked up to you right about here, where we're standing now, and after a very brief encounter, you turned away from me."

"Yes, you've already reminded me of that, but I had to turn away. I was fighting one of my wild urges. When you took my hand in yours, I wanted to throw my arms around you and just hold on. Foolish. A perfect stranger. I was embarrassed by my thoughts."

"You've gotten over being embarrassed," he teased.

"That's a good thing." I led him back to the sofa and sat down, pulling him down beside me. "I need to talk to you, don't I?"

"I think that would help our situation considerably." He folded me into his arms.

"I think ... no, I know I'm crazy about you, too. I just don't know if I want to, you know, commit to anything more right now."

"I'm aware of that," he said, nuzzling his chin against the back of my head.

"And I know I've completed part of my journey since I've been here, but I want to be able to finish what I started. Otherwise, I'm not sure if I'll be entirely happy. I would always wonder."

"And I think you should complete your journey. I won't get in the way. But remember, Megan, your entire life is a journey. There is no way you will discover the whole picture of who you are until the journey's at its end. And I would say you probably have fifty to sixty years to figure that out. That should be ample time."

"I understand what you're saying, really, I do, but I think it has something to do with being independent."

"Weren't you independent before you came here?"

"Well, I was in a way, but I was so tied to Mark."

"Did that stop you from knowing who you were?"

"It seemed to. I can't explain it. Maybe I was in a rut, doing the same thing day after day. I don't know."

"I'm a patient man. I love you. That will do for now."

I turned to look at him and once more wrapped my arms around his neck and kissed him. He enclosed me in his and pulled me up across his lap, holding me close, his muskiness filling the air.

He smiled. "So, you like to dance, even in the rain."

"Hmm, yes, especially when you're watching."

"Don't you think that's cruel and unusual punishment?"

"Whatever do you mean?" I quipped. "Don't you find it pleasurable?"

"To an extent."

"Would you rather I abandon such impulses?"

"No, but I think you need to be honest."

"About what?"

"About what you really want."

"And what would that be?"

"I think it's rather obvious."

"You do, do you?"

He looked at me intently. I knew. He knew. My chest felt tight as my breath quickened. I brushed my lips against his weathered cheek as I said, "I so want you." He pulled me further into him. I could feel the rise and fall of his chest.

"Megan," he whispered into my ear, causing a wave of sensations. My breath caught.

Cradling me, he stood. I slipped out of his arms and tugged at his shirt, pulling it out of his slacks. As I unfasten each button, my kisses traced the hard curves of his moist flesh. He stooped to lift me again, but I resisted.

"Wait," I said. I unbuckled his belt.

He freed the tie wrapping my waist, and then gently slid the robe from my shoulders.

We stood a few moments in the soft light, his hands warm and gentle, stroking first my cheek and then wandering down until his fingers played eagerly along the curve of my thighs.

My eyes were closed, but I could feel his movement to the couch. He removed his shoes and slipped out of his clothing. Then he was standing against me, kissing me long and hard, his hands sliding down my back and onto my buttocks, pulling me inward. Suddenly, in one swift motion, he draped a tartan over his shoulder, scooped me into his arms, and headed out the door and into the courtyard. As he neared the stone fence, he lifted me over its side onto the soft turf below, setting me and the tartan free. He then climbed over, spread the blanket, and lowered me to its fuzzy warmth.

He placed a small red rose under my nose. "Can you smell it?" he asked as he flicked it back and forth under my nose. "Its scent is like yours, sweet and delicate." His breath warmed against my neck, setting loose a chill that traveled down to my toes. "The light of the moon unveils its beauty just as it does yours," he continued as he edged over me, his lips pulling on my nipples, then traveling down my belly to find my warmth. I arched against him, wanting more.

We made love until the stars faded and the mindless sheep turned to stare. The roses that clung to the wall next to us moved back and forth in the breeze as if in tune with our frenzy.

A few days ago, I had thought it would take forever to figure out what I wanted. What a difference a day makes.

Chapter 14

When I woke in the morning, I felt him against me. In spite of the
blankets he had piled around us, the cold crept silently under their
edges. We had spent our first night in the meadow surrounded by
nature. I snuggled closer. His arms laced around me, pressing me into
the bend of his body. Slowly I turned to face him, staying locked in his
arms, nestling my face into the curve of his neck. Salty. So good. I bit
his earlobe.

"What was that for?" he said sleepily.

"I just wanted to make certain that you were really here beside me,
and I wasn't dreaming."

He turned on his side and drew me close. "If it's a dream, I don't
ever want to wake up."

"Me either. I think we should forget Edinburgh and just hole up
here until the cows come home."

"Well, they probably already have, and the sheep, too. Thanks for
reminding me that my day is not my own. We'll have to postpone
such reverie until tonight. If I don't finish today, we will be here for yet
another day." He kissed me, and then stood and headed for the fence,
his bare buttocks stirring me again.

"I guess that means I won't see you until tonight," I said, sitting up,
the cool morning air teasing my nipples into hard knots.

"Sorry, luv, but starting tomorrow, without fail, we will be off on
an adventure of our own making. Until then, your time's your own."
After grinning and blowing a kiss, he headed for the house.

His long stride across the meadow slowed as he came to the fence.
He turned and looked at me as I said, "I'll be around here cleaning
up."

"Not a chance." He scaled the fence and turned toward me again. "This old house can wait for another time. I'll leave the keys to the truck on the counter. I want you to fill your day with whatever makes you happy, and I'll see you tonight. Besides, if you stay around here, you'll starve."

"You've talked me into it, but I really don't know where to go."

"Take the highway out here and head north. See what you discover."

"Aren't you going to tell me what's out there?"

"No, it's my surprise for you today."

"Not even a hint?"

He laughed and looked down. "I think I have a really big surprise for you behind this fence."

"Really? Show me."

"I don't think I have a choice," he said, as he hiked himself once more over the fence, revealing one of the most erotic transformations of nature.

"Oh, my, I had no idea," I said, trying unsuccessfully to stifle my laughter.

"Well, you do now," he whispered as he draped his warmth over me and transformed my laughter to cries of joy.

As he lay by my side minutes later, I asked, "And my other surprise?"

His laughter filled the air as he rose up on one elbow and leaned over to bite my lip gently. "You're relentless. I've just given you my prized possession, and you want more. You're insatiable." He stood up and looked down at me. "I'm not telling you anything," he said, and then headed for the fence.

"Not even if I twist your arm?"

He turned back to face me. "Okay, you win. I won't stand for any abuse. Your hint is that it's a treasure."

"I thought you just gave me that," I yelled as he scaled the fence and headed toward the door.

"Well, that's all you get." As he entered the house, he turned to look back at me. "You are sensational."

"You were, too."

"That's not exactly what I meant," he smiled, "but now that you mention it, you were magnificent."

"Oh, you're always going to stay one up on me, huh?"

"If I can, but it won't be an easy task. I'll see you around five or so."

"Right," I replied as I picked myself up from our love nest, wrapping the blanket around me.

I joined him at the top of the stairs, we kissed one more time, and he left me with instructions on driving safely and something about controlling my urges, as he didn't want to bail me out of Scotland Yard.

I dressed quickly, grabbed the keys from the kitchen counter, and headed out the door. On the seat of the truck was a note from Jake. It read: "Second hint: You'll love it. Wish I were with you. Love, Jake. P.S. You were better than sensational."

I hadn't yet reached the highway when I met another car coming my way. I slowed a bit so we had room to pass on the narrow lane leading away from the farm, and as the driver's silhouette flashed at my side, my heart jumped to my throat. *Ohmigod, it's Mark.*

I had a momentary urge to stomp on the accelerator and flee, hoping he was a figment of my imagination. Instead, I slammed on the brakes and smacked my nose on the steering wheel. As blood trickled down into my mouth, I rummaged unsuccessfully for tissue, something to stifle the flow. Suddenly, my door opened and Mark's big hand reached in, holding a neatly folded handkerchief.

"We have to quit meeting like this," he whispered in my ear as he leaned over and kissed my cheek."

"What are you doing here?" I asked, shocked at the cutting edge in my tone.

"To find out what *you're* doing here," he said with what I knew was a great deal of control.

I shut my eyes and leaned my head back, applying pressure to my aching nose. I could hear him stand up, shut my door, and move away from the truck, the gravel crunching under his feet. Seconds later, he entered the passenger side and slid easily across the seat. Without hesitation, he gathered me into his arms.

"I guess you're surprised to see me?"

"I suppose you could say that," I said, lowering my gaze from the truck's ragged ceiling and turning to look at him. "Why didn't you let me know you were coming?"

"Somehow I thought it would be better to surprise you."

"Well, you *did* that."

As I stared at him in disbelief, I realized I had to do something—fast. I didn't want to take him back to the house. Not now—not until I had a chance to talk to him—so I told him to pull his car off the road, and we could take a drive. We could talk.

As he got out of the truck, the note Jake had written slid with him out the door, landing at his feet. He stooped to pick it up, looked at it briefly, wadded it, and threw it into the seat.

"So just how sensational were you, Megan?"

I felt paralyzed as I gripped the steering wheel, trying desperately to think of the right words to say. But there were none that would make a difference. "I'm sorry, Mark. I didn't want you to find out this way. I wanted to tell—"

"Bullshit!" The words spit between his clench teeth. "Bullshit! I don't remember anything about you fucking someone else when you called me."

"Mark, please. I wanted to tell you, but it's so—"

"So *what*, Megan? What is it? You tell me. I'm listening."

The silence was excruciating. It was all I could do to look at him, much less find the words that would ease his pain. I felt shame, not for making love to Jake, but for what I was doing to Mark, even if I was having the time of my life doing it.

"Please get back in, Mark. Please," I begged.

His hands gripped the open window frame as if he were trying to steady himself. Suddenly he turned loose of the door, kicked the side of the truck, shook his head, and headed for the rental car. I couldn't let him go. Not like this. I jumped out of the truck and ran after him, wedging myself between him and the door.

"Mark, give me a chance, please."

As I looked up at him, his body seemed to sag. I could hear him take in a deep breath. He rocked forward a little and shut his eyes, and then his arms came up around me and pulled me to him so tightly I couldn't breathe.

"I love you, Megan. I think I've loved you from the first day I met you. I've always thought you'd be mine forever."

His grip loosened, and he opened the car door. "Yes, we need to talk. Get in."

I slid under the steering wheel, and he climbed in behind me, started the engine, and did a u-turn. Knowing Jake would be concerned when he saw the truck by the side of the road, I told Mark I wanted to get my backpack. I hurriedly went back to the truck, grabbed the wadded paper and a pen from a side pocket of the pack, and scribbled, "I'm fine. It's Mark." Leaving it on the seat with the keys, I returned to Mark's side as he gunned the engine and we sped down the road.

When we returned to the farm later in the morning, he let me out on the road where the truck remained undisturbed by my absence. I walked around to his window and kissed him lightly on the cheek. He sat there motionless and unresponsive. At least the rage was gone.

"I'll call you, Mark. We'll get together again before you leave." I knew it was a stupid thing to say.

He shrugged his shoulders. "I don't think so." He sat for a few moments, then look up. "But if you ever need me, call." He gave me a weak smile and a nod and pulled away.

I felt a strange mixture of depression and relief rolling around in my chest and stomach. We'd known each other twelve years, years that had bound us together. Far too long. For me. I knew he'd be all right in time. And, hopefully, we'd managed to break through the pain and anger and reach an understanding of sorts.

I threw my backpack on the seat of the truck and then eased behind the steering wheel, pressing its hardness to my chest, hoping to numb the sadness that had come with the knowledge we were no longer a couple. I was ashamed I had harbored the idea for years and had prolonged my move, but I knew Mark had never considered the possibility. He had looked so shocked when I told him I'd been with Jake for weeks, living in an isolated farm house. And the issue of sex? He wanted to know about that. "When did it start?" And when I told him it had happened only the night before, he looked at me in disbelief.

I tried to explain that I really hadn't planned to get involved with Jake. I just wanted to know him. I told him about Jake's wife and how he struggled with her death. His response was, "So you ... you feel sorry for him?" I told him that of course I felt sorry for him, but that wasn't why I slept with him.

He wanted an excuse for what he called "my madness," but when I didn't supply him with one, he seemed dazed. When I tried to touch him, he pulled away. He asked if I was in love with Jake, and I told him the truth—I was serious about him.

Without meaning to, I had caused Mark a great deal of pain. I suppose it happens all the time when two people get involved. Something goes amiss in one of them, like me and my missing piece, and little by little, that love affair isn't enough. Maybe I fell in love with the idea of being a great writer who travels the world and lives a romantic, adventuresome life, or maybe I realized I wasn't finished with myself, and I just didn't want to start something I wouldn't want to finish—especially a marriage.

The day we met …

I was sitting alone at a table, bent over a bagel and a steaming cup of latté, reading Franz Kafka's Metamorphosis. *At the exact moment I swallowed a mouthful, Kafka's bug—beetle, cockroach, whatever— attached itself to the picture of the lady with the fur hat, and I choked. The java, bagel, fur, and bug wound into a loathsome knot in my throat. I struggled a few seconds, gasping for just enough precious air to generate a cough. It didn't happen.*

I looked around frantically, hoping someone would notice my predicament. An older man sat with his face buried inside a newspaper, and two women across from me laughed hysterically in their own private moment. I wanted to cry out for help, but the grappling at my throat muzzled all sound, and damn if anyone paid any attention. I practically lay on the table, clawing at my throat, begging for God or even Glenda the Good Witch to wave her magic wand in my direction.

Just as I sucked in what I thought to be my last breath, someone grabbed me firmly around the waist, lifted me from the floor, and jabbed with a quick, intense motion that spewed the bitter liquid and soggy bagel free. As I began coughing, taking in tiny gulps of air, the ceiling resumed its normal position and my feet made contact with terra cotta. The grip around my cradled waist loosened, and gradually I became aware of my liberator. He set my rag-doll form on a chair, propping me up by holding my shoulders back and then leveling his face with mine. We were eye to eye as he kneeled directly in front of me.

"Are you breathing? Shake your head," he ordered.

I nodded and attempted to wipe the tears streaming down my face.

He handed me a napkin, not the monogrammed handkerchief of romance stories, saying, unromantically, "Cough into this."

I complied out of necessity, making all sorts of noises as I sucked in each breath and then hacked it back out. Gradually, I began muttering words of thanks and apologies, fighting for composure.

"Are you okay? You look kind of dazed," he said, breaking into my fluster.

I picked up my backpack and began rummaging through it, trying desperately to regain a sense of normalcy and pretend nothing of consequence had happened. I wanted to say, Oh, I just nearly choked to death, but I'm okay. Instead I spewed, "Thank you so much. I'm really better. I just can't thank you enough. Thank you so much."

He ignored my dither. "I'm just glad I was here to help. My name's Mark Hamilton. I'm a student here."

I just stared at him, giving him a weak smile.

"I suppose you're a student," he continued. "I noticed the book you're reading. No wonder you choked. Do you mind if I sit down?"

"Please ... yes, I am. For my lit class. Can't thank you enough. You saved my life. I feel so embarrassed. I was just sitting here reading, and, well, you know the rest." I rattled foolishly, as he straddled the chair across from me.

"Thanks, I think I will," he said magnanimously.

Mark had been my savior from the first moment we met ... the answer to what I thought were my prayers, my family's prayers ... my Adonis from that moment on, that is until that wave of discontent swept me away from what I'd always known.

After our "breathtaking" meeting, we studied together, laughed together, cried together, slept together, and then fell in love. Well, not exactly in that order. And only later was I willing to admit what a lie I'd told him that first day, what a meaningless phrase—*I promise not to impose upon you again.* Yet I'd done just that from day one. I must have turned into an imposter.

But that was twelve years ago. I picked up the wadded note from its spurned place on the seat next to me and smooth its creases to look at the words that had confronted Mark with more clarity than my words could have ever conveyed. I folded and slipped it into my backpack.

I started the truck and drove away from the house once more. I knew I could hole away with my thoughts or finally let go. I chose the latter. The second I allowed myself the freedom, I felt the groundswell of guilt, which had consumed me for months, dissolve into a bittersweet balm, easing both my mind and heart.

When I saw the sign pointing the way to Urquhart Castle, a thirteenth-century fortress, I knew I had discovered one of several surprises of the morning. I pulled into the parking lot and headed into the spacious, modern visitor center. I was eager to learn its history, but the café was my first stop. I ordered a blueberry muffin and orange juice and sat at a large plate-glass window, enjoying both the rugged allusion to ancient splendor and the deep blue of Loch Ness as it bordered the crumbled walls.

After making a quick pass through the gift shop, I headed toward a wall display tracing the castle's past. I picked up a flyer with information in a nutshell and walked out the door and along the lengthy stairway leading to the fortress. I spent the remainder of the morning exploring the remains of the once-majestic walls and trying to imagine life within the ancient rooms.

In spite of a blustery wind, I boarded a boat for a ride on Loch Ness. A search for the famed water beast seemed mandatory. Only a few other passengers had come on board, and all were sitting in the main cabin, protected from wind and splashing waves, but deprived of an unlimited view. I sat with them for a few minutes and then asked the guide if I could sit on the upper deck. He responded, "Yes, my luv, but you might be blasted by the elements."

I told him I would take my chances and climbed the narrow stairway to the top, where I was rewarded with an unobstructed, breathtaking vista of water, rolling hills, and sky, but challenged by wet sprays and cooling winds. Undaunted, I sat quietly, caught up in the beauty around me, the elements soothing my spirit, but chilling me to the bone.

When we arrived on the other side of the lake, I checked on the times for a return trip to Urquhart and set out in search of a good bowl of warm soup and an outdoor view. A small café with alfresco seating satisfied both of my needs, and I was soon spooning up the remainder of a delicious homemade onion soup while enjoying the splendor of life blazing around me.

Content, I paid my bill and spent the next hour wandering through the shops along the narrow streets. I discovered a hat boutique much like the one Jake and I had seen on our night out. There was a wonderful assortment of Scottish headgear, and after I told the salesman I really needed to see how they looked on a handsome man, he agreed to model a few. He spent a good twenty minutes modeling for me, and, in the end, I purchased tams for both Jake and me.

With only fifteen minutes remaining until my return trip, I walked out to the pier. My wait was short and in no time, I claimed my vantage point on the upper deck but had to share it this time with a crowd of sightseers.

By the time we arrived at Urquhart, I was anxious to return to the farm, so I made a quick stop at the visitor center and then made my way to the parking lot and into the truck. It was after four, and I wanted to beat Jake home.

Knowing there was no food at the house, I stopped at a small village market on the return trip and bought cheese, bread, tomato, onion, pepper, and a few slices of ham. I searched for a bottle of red wine for Jake and was pleasantly surprised to find a few small bottles. The storeowner assured me they were good. I thought it funny how simple a meal could really be. Our last dinner at the farm would be light and relaxing out on the patio under the evening stars. Perfect.

A little after five, I parked the truck in the drive, gathered my bags, and entered the house. It was dark and quiet. After washing my hands, I pulled out a cutting board and began to chop the veggies into tiny pieces. Placing them in a bowl, I added olive oil, garlic, salt, and pepper and stashed the concoction into the refrigerator along with my Chardonnay. The clock chimed five thirty.

I set two small bottles of red wine on the table where they could be opened shortly before dinner. I then put on some music and walked up the stairs to the melancholy sounds of Scottish pipes.

I bathed, washed my hair, wrapped the terry robe around me, and lay on my bed, aching with exhaustion. Intermingling thoughts of both Mark and Jake made me restless, but eventually I drifted into sleep.

I don't know how long I slept, but when I woke, all was silence. After a few moments, I realized darkness surrounded me. I sat up and listened. Nothing. Getting up, I turned on the light and walked to Jake's bedroom. It was empty. I returned to my room and picked up my watch from the dresser. Seven thirty-five. How strange. Maybe he came in, saw me sleeping, and decided to let me rest. I quickly dressed and ran down the stairs calling his name. No answer.

I walked out of the house and almost ran to the barn. Nothing but shadows and the creaking noises of aging timbers. My breath quickened and my heart raced. *Calm down. He's probably here somewhere. If not, he'll be here soon.*

I went back inside, turned on the light in the kitchen, and set out some plates and wine glasses for our late supper. Deciding to slice the cheese and bread, I opened the refrigerator to see not only the items I had purchased, but also a small roasted duck, a leafy green salad, and another bottle of wine, my favorite.

"Oh, good grief, where are you, Jake?" I said aloud to no one. I called again, only louder this time, "Jake!" Still no answer. *This is crazy. Where is he?*

I looked again in the parlor, thinking he might be asleep on the sofa. The room was quiet and lifeless. I walked back to the kitchen and out the back door once more, deciding this time to check the courtyard around the side of the house.

A hint of light from the stars played on the white roses as the breeze gently rocked the vine, the only movement. I picked two double white roses and tucked them behind my ear, turned, and began to walk back to the house. I heard a sound, like a sigh, then again and again. I stood motionless, listening carefully as I traced the rhythmic breathing.

In the dark, next to the rock wall across from the display of roses, Jake's large frame lay sprawled awkwardly on a garden bench. He had propped his feet on a chair in front of him and had, obviously, dozed off while reading. A magazine lay in his lap.

I walked over to him and sat down on the end of the bench, twined my arm around his, and lay my head on his shoulder. A fresh, soapy scent from his skin mingled with the fragrance of the rose. I smiled, took a deep breath, and whispered, "Yes, I am lucky, so very, very lucky."

He stirred. His feet moved from the chair. "Oh, my," he groaned, "this is no way to sleep." He released his arm from mine, stood with magazine in hand, and stretched. "How did it get so dark? I thought I just came out here," he said as he extended his hand and pulled me up to him. "I have a feeling we both took a long nap."

"I think you're right, but from now on, would you do your napping inside?" I said with a look of pretended admonishment.

"Napping hadn't been in my plans, but I saw you snoozing on the bed and wanted to let you rest before dinner. Speaking of which, we have quite a feast in store," he said, giving me a gentle squeeze.

"I know. I saw it a while ago. Until I opened the refrigerator, I had no idea you were at home."

"Home, hmm. That sounds nice."

I slid my hands under his shirt and felt his warm, bare skin. "I just thought you hadn't returned from working, but when I saw the duck and the salad, I ... well, I finally looked out here. It was so dark, it's a miracle I saw you. If you hadn't been snoring so loudly, I would have had to eat without you," I teased.

"You wouldn't dare."

"Yes, and I would have drunk all the wine in my sorrow."

"There's no need for that. I'm here."

"Yes, I can tell," I said as I ran my hands down his back and then snuggled into his arms.

"Besides," he continued, "I would have called if I had been delayed. Remember that."

"I'll write it down and get you to sign it."

"No need for that. It's a promise."

We sat silently for a few moments and then I told him of Mark's surprise visit. He listened patiently, and when I finished my drama and even told him of my promise to see Mark again before he left, he asked me if I was okay. When I told him I was more than okay, that I was fine, he said, "Yes, yes, you are fine," and kissed me on my cheek. As he pulled me to him, a thorn from the rose behind my ear pricked against his mouth. He jerked back. "I think your ear just bit me. Ahh, a double rose. Don't you know better than to tempt fate?"

"Tempt fate? What do you mean?"

"You haven't heard the tale of 'Tam Lin'?"

"No, tell me," I begged eagerly, sensing the magic of the moment.

"It's an old folk tale about a young boy named Tam Lin who was stolen by the fairies. All the young girls of the land were warned not to enter the woods alone because if he happened to find a girl there, she would fall under his spell. Years went by and one day a young girl decided she would go in spite of the warning. She entered the woods and found the fairy well where Tam Lin was believed to have disappeared. She hadn't been there long when Tam Lin arrived and asked her why she was there and why she had picked his roses. She told him they were hers to pick as the land belonged to her father."

"What was her name?" I asked, interrupting his tale.

"I don't know. We'll call her Megan," he said. Then he continued with his story, "So Tam Lin and Megan spent the day together enjoying the forest. She returned home, but after a few months, she decided to return to the well where she hoped to see him again. He didn't appear until she again picked two roses from the bush. After they talked for a while, he asked her if she would be willing to save him from his life with the fairies, which, of course, being a high-spirited young girl, she said she would. He told her to return at midnight on All Hallows day, and when she saw him riding by with the fairies, she should grab hold of him for dear life and not let him go, in spite of any fearsome thing that happened, until she felt a burning hot iron in her grasp. Then she was to throw him in the well.

"So at the appointed hour, Megan returned. As Tam Lin passed by her on his white horse, she grabbed him by the waist and pulled him down with her. The fairies screamed, and then she found herself holding onto all manner of vile creatures—a newt, a snake, a bear, a lion, and even a burning-hot iron, but she hung on and threw Tam Lin into the water of the well as he had told her."

"And I assume the spell was broken and the two young people lived happily ever after?" I asked.

"That's right."

"What a horribly wonderful story. And I think I'll be more careful about wrapping my arms about your waist from now on. I don't know if I could be so brave as to hang onto monsters," I said, teasing him.

"Well, you're hanging on to monsters now."

I looked at him in disbelief. "What do you mean? I don't have any monsters."

"Well, call them what you may. Monsters ... creatures ... your own personal demons."

"How can you say that? I don't have any *demons* either."

"Demons ... doubts," he explained. "In the real world, they're all the same."

It suddenly hit me that something about this story seemed all too familiar. And then I knew why. The dream I had had a few nights before Shannon and I left home had left me breathless ... as though I had been on a wild ride. I remembered hanging on to a man's waist, struggling desperately to keep myself from being flung from the security I felt as I clung to him.

"Are you okay, Megan?"

"Yes, just thinking about the story ... and my ... doubts."

"I'm sorry. I didn't mean to upset you. Maybe we better go inside," he said as we walked hand-in-hand toward the house. "Now, what would you like to do first?"

"First?" I questioned, leaning my head, sans rose, onto his shoulder.

"Don't act innocent."

"Well, I am hungry."

"And I'm starving."

Chapter 15

The next day we were loading the truck when the phone rang.

"Jake!" I yelled from the back door. "Shannon's on the phone and she wants to know when she can meet us in Edinburgh."

He placed a box onto the bed of the truck, looked around, and shrugged, "Tell her to give us about four or five days. Today's Saturday, so make it ... about Wednesday or Thursday, but to call before she comes."

"Four or five days? Why so long?" I asked, puzzled.

"I'll talk to her. You finish putting these small bags in the truck. I'll be right back," he said as he headed for the door.

I had a feeling there was more to this exchange than Jake was telling me, but I knew I'd get more out of him when he returned.

As I loaded the last of our luggage on the truck, Jake walked up from behind and scooped me into the air, whirled around in a circle, and then hugged me tightly to him, my feet dangling off the ground.

"Okay, mystery man," I demanded, "what's going on? Why four or five days? I thought we were going to be in Edinburgh tonight."

"So much for surprises," he replied with a bit of exaggerated disappointment in his voice. Then, with a trace of a grin, he added, "If you must know, I'll tell you, but are you certain you really want to ruin the surprise?"

I decided to go along with him. "I guess it's not really necessary. After all, it's only half ruined. That's not so bad."

"Good. Now, let's get on the road." He looked around. "Anything else?" he asked.

"I've already double-checked for my stuff. What about you?"

"Anything I leave behind, the mice can have."

"Ugh!" I exclaimed. "I never saw any."

"You're not supposed to. They're like ghosts. But now that we're leaving, they're making plans already," he said with an evil grin.

"Whatever!" I called back to him as I returned to the house.

He followed me in to take one last look around, and then we headed for the truck. As the motor revved, he looked over at me. "Are you ready?"

"Not really," I said, and meaning it. "I miss it already. I love it here."

"We'll come back," he assured me as he gave Old Molly some gas and released the clutch, "For now, well, just hold on."

"That sounds like a threat," I said as we jounced down the road.

"I think you'll like what you see," he responded.

And he was right. As we drove farther into the highlands, I was mesmerized by the flood of heather across the hills. Each mile offered a treat, whether of wooded hillsides, bubbly springs, or quaint villages.

After several hours, we were both ready for a slower, up-close-and-personal view.

"I hope you'll like the hotel," he said as he turned into a wide drive leading to what seemed more of a castle than a hotel.

"Oh, Jake, this is lovely—like a fairy tale. Have you been here before?"

"No, but one of my colleagues has spoken of it quite often. He says it's quite nice even though it is an antique. It has an old flavor."

"I would say so," I agreed as I leaned out the window. A tower loomed at one end of the baronial building. Several turrets crowned with crenellations projected from the wall of the tower. "Rapunzel, Rapunzel, let down your hair," I chanted, fascinated by my storybook surroundings.

"Rapunzel is nowhere to be found in Scotland, I'm afraid," Jake said, breaking the spell.

He parked the truck, gathered our belongings, and led the way into a splendid foyer opening into a drawing room smelling of tobacco and Scotch. Setting the suitcases down, he told me to relax a moment while he registered. While he was gone, a waiter offered me tea and shortbread. I couldn't resist. I was still sipping and munching when he returned.

"Aha, celebrating without me, I see," he said, sitting down next to me. "Take your time. I may have a cup myself."

"You could starve before they come. Close your eyes and open your mouth," I commanded.

He laughed, closed his eyes, and readied himself for a bite by baring his teeth and dropping his jaw.

"Hmm, you're so good to me," he mumbled as he bit into his crunchy prize.

"Well, I'm no match for you, Jake. This place is fabulous. I'm so excited, so happy," I said, leaning over and giving him a quick kiss on the cheek.

"I think it's time to find our room. If I'm to have kisses, I'm not going to settle for a paltry peck."

Standing, he took my cup from my lap and helped me to my feet. We located the elevator, filed in with our suitcases, and dared a much more fervid kiss as we rode a few floors.

"I think you're horny," I whispered as I pulled away and gathered my belongings.

"There you go … being a minx again. I wonder if your mother really knew what she was saying when she called you her 'minx.'"

"You can rest assured she had only the best of intentions."

The elevator stopped. "After you," he said, as the door opened. "To the right. It should be down toward the end of the hallway."

We wandered down the dimly lit corridor until we spotted room 29, where Jake jiggled the large iron key in the antiquated keyhole until the door slowly released with a groan from its casing. The room was spacious and echoed its heritage with Scottish plaids, antique furnishings, and window casements stretching to the ceiling. I unlatched one and pushed it wide to reveal an idyllic storybook setting, a scene like one I'd often seen on the colorful pages of my childhood collection. I stood mesmerized, inhaling the fragrant mountain breezes and looking out over the rolling countryside.

Jake wrapped his arms around me, pulling me close. "A beautiful sight, isn't it?"

"I've never seen one better."

"It's my opinion you never will."

"Spoken like a true Scot."

"And you're a beautiful sight, a beautiful, beautiful sight," he whispered in my ear. "And there will be no more sightseeing until I explore every inch of you."

"Sounds delightful," I responded, looking forward to beginning a long evening.

Chapter 16

For the next three days, Jake hauled me back and forth across the highlands as we roamed through castles, wallowed in the scents of flower gardens, marveled at the beauty of medieval churches, sought headstones of famous persons in graveyards, clambered up mountains, and even poked around a few tourist shops. We ate on a rock on a hillside, on a blanket in the meadow, on a bench in a village, in a cozy pub, in a small but picturesque café by a lake, and in another of Jake's favorite restaurants.

Some mornings when I'd lie in bed next to him and hear his slow, steady breathing, a twinge of apprehension would mingle with my elation. I had managed to escape from the dreariness staking its claim on my life, but I wondered if tedium could or would return. At this point, I didn't see how, but I supposed anything could happen if I let it.

I thought of the times when I was about six or seven years old and would tell Mama I was bored. She'd say, "Life is what we make it; always has been, always will be." She said those were the words of Grandma Moses, and since grandmas were wise, she believed them wholeheartedly. She made a believer out of me, too, because if I said I was bored once too often, she would find some godforsaken task for me to do, like cleaning out my drawers or closet, or even scrubbing a garbage can.

I can't say life was ever really boring, even when I was with Mark, because I was always busy. I kept myself that way. I guess Mama's warnings made a believer out of me. Besides, I didn't want Mama sneaking up on me and hearing me complaining. No way.

I knew plenty of people who bellyached about what they called their *miserable* lives, who complained about getting up early every morning to go to the same *boring* jobs. Most of these same people returned home at five o'clock just so they could sit in front of the one-eyed monster night after night, week after week, and year after year. Sometimes I thought they should go … go paddle a canoe or something, anything that would get them off the couch.

That reminded me of Daddy. He used to get mad at Mama sometimes when she would try to tell him how to prune a bush, or wind the hose, or even peel an apple. He'd jerk away from her intruding hands and say, "Go paddle your own canoe, woman. I can handle mine just fine." Mama would walk away shaking her head and then come in behind him when he wasn't looking to straighten up his mess.

And now as I think about it, I guess most people make a few wrong strokes when they're trying to paddle their own canoes. I suppose that's just the way life is. Perhaps someone else will even have to come in behind them to help out, but, eventually, if they keep trying, they'll get it right. And that was definitely what I hoped I was doing—getting it right.

Chapter 17

After three days of our happy meandering, Jake cranked up Molly and we turned south for Edinburgh. The trip passed quickly as he talked of his beloved homeland, and as we entered the capital city and Jake drove down Princes Street, I knew he hadn't been exaggerating.

"It's another fairy tale, Jake. I can't believe it's so beautiful."

"I doubt you will be lacking for entertainment in Edinburgh," Jake assured me. "It's a city that has a tendency to spoil its inhabitants."

"It's fantastic. Just fantastic," I said as we drove slowly alongside a maze of colorful storefronts spilling out streams of laden shoppers.

"And," he emphasized, "you'll find art, history, theater, restaurants, castles, gardens ... anything your heart desires."

"Do you ever get overwhelmed?" I interrupted.

"Well, no. There is the peace and quiet of home, you know. And if you get lonely for village life, you can find one a few miles down the road, along with beaches, bird watching, and long walks."

"It's wonderful, Jake."

"Well, we could drive around all day. I think it's time to head to the house."

With our brief tour ended, he drove out of the city and into a peaceful residential setting.

"How do you ever find your way around?" I asked after we had driven for some time. "It seems we're going in circles."

"Oh, an old dog always knows his way home," he said as he turned slowly into a drive winding its way through a stand of flowering trees and shrubs. As we came out of the dense foliage, I was surprised to see a stately home rising before us. Manicured gardens lined the wide, circular drive leading to the front entrance where Jake pulled into a covered area adjoining the front entry, stopped, honked the horn, and opened the door.

"Last stop for today," he said, sounding relieved. "I don't know about you, but I am ready to put my feet up and stay awhile."

"Goodness. This is your house?" I asked, dumbfounded my farmer friend could possibly lay claim to anything so palatial.

"Why? Don't you approve?"

"Of course, I approve. I'm just surprised. I just wasn't expecting anything quite so ... so, uh—"

"Grandiose?" he interjected and laughed.

"I guess you could say that," I responded, looking at him as though I were seeing him for the first time.

"Ah, Peter," he called out as a young man came rushing out of the front door.

"Hello, Professor, so very glad to see you again. It's been a long time."

"It has, hasn't it?" he said as he walked around the truck, shook his hand, and helped me out. He then placed his arm around my waist and pulled me to his side. "Megan, I want you to meet Peter Wallace, a very good student and friend of mine. Peter, this is Megan McEller, the woman I told you about on the phone. She has come to Edinburgh to explore the area and, hopefully, put up with me."

Embarrassed, I shook his hand. "It's nice to be the topic of conversation."

"I'm delighted to meet you, and rest assured, the professor shared only the best."

Jake tossed the keys to Peter, asking him to park the truck in the garage, and we gathered our bags and entered the heavily carved double doors. As we stepped into the foyer, I was stunned at the magnificent setting—marble floors, crystal chandelier, a staircase sweeping grandly to a balcony that crossed the expanse of the second floor.

"It's beautiful, Jake."

"Come on, I'll show you around the lower level," he said and led me on a tour that left me wondering what else I didn't know about this man.

A half hour later, the three of us gathered in the kitchen for refreshments while Jake questioned Peter about university news. After politely inquiring about my background, Peter then began to update Jake on his new job.

When I yawned and stretched, Jake stood and walked up behind me. "Come with me," he urged and gently pulled out my chair. "I'll be right back," he said to Peter.

"So nice to meet you, Megan. I hope I'll see you again soon," Peter said as he rose and slightly bowed.

"Of course, so nice to meet you," I offered, feeling self-conscious.

Jake picked up my suitcases and led me up the massive staircase, down a wide hall, and into an immense bedroom that shamed the castle-like hotel of our wanderings.

"I thought you might like to have some time to yourself. I know you're tired," he said as he drew me into his arms and began to kiss me softly.

"I am," I replied, happy for the chance to be alone with my thoughts. "I think I'll lie down for a while." I pulled away from him and walked to a window overlooking a lush, manicured garden.

Sensing my mood, he walked up behind me and folded me into his arms. "Is something wrong, my luv?"

I turned to face him and buried my head into his chest. "I'm just so overwhelmed with all this."

"With all what?"

"Your home ... its ... opulence. I had no idea, Jake. Why didn't you tell me?"

"Tell you what? That Laura had family money? What difference would it have made?"

"I don't know. I just thought you were—" I laughed and snuggled into him.

"That I was a simple country farmer?" he grinned and hugged me tightly.

"Yes ... well ... not entirely."

"Well, I'll have you know I have talents other than sheep shearing, and you better not forget it."

"I have no doubt about that."

"Don't let these trappings fool you. I am a simple man with an uncomplicated background, and I'm in love with one absolutely fascinating woman."

"Who's that?" I teased, beginning to feel more at ease with this man who had more layers to him than I had thought.

"If you don't know, then we really do have a problem," he said under his breath and then kissed me on the top of my head. "If Peter wasn't downstairs, I'm afraid you wouldn't get much rest."

"Tell him to leave."

"Do you want me to?"

"Yes ... but no. That would embarrass me. I'll be waiting for you. Take your time."

"Okay. You pamper yourself while I go down and settle with him and see him off. I'm certain he's anxious to get on his way." He crossed the room to the door, gave me a wink, and added, "I'll only be a few minutes," then shut the door behind him. Instantly, it opened again. "By the way, behind that door," he said, pointing across the room, "is an extraordinary *salle de bain*. Enjoy. I'll return shortly."

I sighed deeply, longing to crawl into the sumptuous covers of the four-poster bed, close my eyes, and escape from all the questions crowding my head. Instead, I rummaged through my suitcase once more for something presentable to wear—something clean—slipped out of my travel clothes, and stepped into a marbled walk-in shower, fumbling with the faucet until I finally discovered its secret. I didn't know if I would ever adjust to British plumbing, but indulging in the extravagance surrounding me wasn't difficult.

As the pulsating jets relieved my stiffness, I let my mind run back over the events of the past few weeks. Meeting Jake had been a stroke of luck. He had unearthed something deep within me. I felt transformed ... complete ... peaceful. Almost like floating. And then I thought of Mark's surprise visit, and my heart sank.

As I rinsed off and reached to turn off the overhead deluge, Jake stepped into the shower behind me.

"Leave the water on," he said as he pulled me to him. "I thought you might need me to wash your back."

"I would love it," I whispered as I turned to face him. His hands traced down the curve of my hips and thighs, wrapped below my knees, and lifted my weight against him and the wall behind me.

Light still shone through the open window when I awoke. I turned over to find the bed empty beside me. Slipping out of bed and into the cotton jogging suit I had pulled from my suitcase hours before, I traipsed back into the bathroom, brushed through my hair, and made my way down the staircase and into the foyer.

I walked into the kitchen first, thinking Jake might be exploring options for dinner, but all was quiet and undisturbed, the adjoining rooms the same.

I crossed to the other end of the hall, where I found a door ajar and could hear Jake's voice. He was talking to himself. I entered on tiptoes. His back was to me as he sat at his desk, bent over a page-filled notebook that had his full attention. After thumbing a few pages, he scratch out a line or two, then continued writing. Feeling like an intruder, I retraced my steps to the door. I had almost pulled it closed, when I heard him call my name.

"Megan, don't go," he said as his empty hand motioned me back into the room.

I eased into a comfortable chair, and, as I sat waiting, my eyes traveled over him in fascination. In place of his usual khakis and cotton denim shirt, he wore what appeared to be an expensive pair of slacks and a long-sleeved silk shirt, tucked and belted. Fine black leather shoes had replaced his heavy boots, and a Rolex watch boasting a number of diamonds shone from his wrist.

I looked down at my faded sweatpants, at my hands that desperately needed a manicure, and at my bare feet that signaled my naïveté. My freshly scrubbed face had nary a hint of makeup, and my hair lay limp as seaweed on my shoulders. I fidgeted, wanting desperately to run back up the stairs to start over again.

"Glad to see you up," he said, placing his pen on the desk and breaking into my insecurity. "Did you sleep well?"

I fidgeted, not knowing if it was my appearance or his that had me wishing for a way to escape his gaze. "Yes, I must have. I didn't hear you when you left."

"I woke about an hour ago. I didn't want to disturb you."

He closed the notebook, opened a file drawer to his left, and placed it inside, shutting and locking the drawer. Standing, he dropped the key into his pants pocket and meticulously placed the pen he had been using on its pedestal. He then slid his chair under the desk.

As he crossed the room, I marveled at the man who tended the sheep and shoveled the barn, who wandered the meadow with a small-town girl and applauded her feeble recitations, and who spoke of Old Molly as though she were a part of the family.

He stopped in front of my chair, reached for my hands, and gently urged me to stand. The top of my head eased under his freshly shaven jaw as he held me to him. I didn't move. I didn't want to move, and I didn't want him to do what he usually did next, but, of course, he did. He titled my head back, and he looked into my clean, shining face. I shut my eyes and then inwardly winced at my childish attempt to hide behind closed lids.

"What?" he asked. "Why such a look?"

"Oh, nothing. I just thought of ... of how much I clash with this place," I only half lied.

"Megan," he said and then paused and extended his arms, moving me away from him and taking a long, exaggerated look at me, from my head down to my toes and then back again. "You're perfect. I wouldn't have you any other way."

"Liar!" I fired back, even though I appreciated his flattery and kissed him eagerly to prove it.

"Would you like to go back upstairs?" he asked, picking me up with an easy effort and walking to the door.

"Aha! The truth at last. You want me to go back up there. You think I'm ugly."

"Of course, I'm in love with a witch, an ugly old witch."

I grabbed his neck with both hands and squeezed with mock rage.

"Oh, she's snarling mad," he said, putting me back on the floor. "Now go on up and put on another mask if you must. This one has worn out its welcome."

"I would, but I'm painfully hungry, and I might just pass out if you don't feed me soon," I teased.

"Well, that would be a shame. What would you like?"

"Anything. You know I'm not picky."

"Name it. Tell me what you want."

"Okay, let me think. Uh, lobster or any little thing," I kidded.

"No, the lady's not picky. Just wants lobster, so lobster it is."

"Really? You're serious?"

"Shouldn't I be?"

"And I guess you would expect me to change before we go out?"

"Why should you? We will be dining at home."

"Really? You just happen to keep lobster on hand?"

"No, but I do have ways and means."

"I don't doubt that," I said, and then reflecting once again on my appearance, I hastily added, "Still, I do think I'll go up for a few minutes."

"Not a problem. Take your time. I'll be about."

He turned, heading toward the kitchen, and I escaped up the stairs, hastening to spill out the contents of my little bag of tricks that usually managed to performed miracles.

Classical music emanated from secret hiding places as I ventured back down the stairs twenty minutes later, confident my change of clothes and primping had improved my chances of meeting his gaze.

Strangely, I felt constrained. The house with its high ceilings and ornate embellishments chilled me, a contrast to the comfort and warmth of the farmhouse. And the disparity between the man waiting for me and the one on the farm puzzled me. Or was it me? Was I the one who had changed? Obviously, old Ms. Panicky had started to weasel her way in. Why should I suddenly feel ill at ease? Why couldn't I just enjoy the moment? *Okay, calm down and take this one step at a time. Assume that all is as it has been, that is, other than the surroundings.* Maybe I did have demons.

I entered the formal dining room with its grand table, chandelier, silver candelabras, and china settings. The lights were dim and candles glowed in the semidarkness.

Jake appeared from the kitchen. "We have time for a glass of wine. I have a chardonnay for you, ready and waiting." He took me by the arm and led me into the kitchen and out the side door onto a spacious courtyard.

"I see your love of roses doesn't stop at the farm," I said, admiring the beauties eagerly climbing the trellises surrounding us.

Jake wrapped his arms around my waist. "Love of nature cannot be isolated any more than our love can be confined. Otherwise, we would be prisoners."

I thought about the meaning his words had for me and how this man seemed to have an uncanny ability to read my mind. "I have never felt more liberated than I have since I've known you, Jake. I feel like, somehow, being with you has released me from myself. Do you know what I mean?"

"You tell me. From what have you been released?" he asked, squeezing me lightly.

"I don't know if I can even put it into words. It's something inside of me, something I feel, something that has finally been ..." I paused, searching for the right word, "unshackled. I think, maybe, it's freedom, freedom with no expectations except my very own. Does that make any sense at all?"

"I think it makes sense to you, and that's what's important."

"Then it makes no sense to you?"

"Of course I understand what you're saying," he said indulgently, "but it's most important *you* understand and make sense of it. That's important because you're a poser, Megan, someone who cross-examines life and then questions and re-questions every move you make. And what I've come to appreciate about you is your demand for answers smacking with logic ... as well as impassioned meaning."

"Impassioned meaning? I like that. Now, counselor, exactly what do you mean?"

"Megan, the mind is very powerful, much more powerful than we realize. Every word that has been uttered to us and by us, every word we have read and written, every word we have thought, and even every word we think we have forgotten has stamped its impression onto the fabric of our being. The complexity of our makeup is so multifaceted it's no wonder we become muddled sometimes."

"Hmm, *muddled* is definitely the way I feel sometimes. You know, the night before my dad died, he told me to always listen to my heart. Then he reached out and tapped a finger against my forehead, and said, 'The noggin doesn't always know what it wants.' I remember looking at him and wondering what exactly he meant, but he didn't explain. He just clasped my hand and pressed it to his chest. He was weak. His hand shook, but I'll never forget the beating of his heart against my palm. It was slow, pitifully slow. Then he closed his eyes and slept. That night, he died in his sleep, and I never had the opportunity to talk with him again. He was such a good man, Jake. I miss him."

"I can tell. And his words to you should be quite clear."

"What do you mean?"

"You said he took your hand and placed it on his chest. Think about it," he said, looking down at me as I stood locked in his embrace.

He pulled back. "Give me your hand."

Releasing me, he slid his hands down my shoulders and arms, and then took my hands and pressed them into the warmth of his chest. "Tell me what you feel," he said, looking down at me and holding me close.

As I leaned against him, I could feel the rhythmic beating of our hearts as they pulsated repeatedly against our intertwined fingers.

"It's as though our hearts are speaking to each other."

"The heart is a strong communicator of who we are."

"It sounds so simple. Why haven't I thought like this before?"

"Because you've been listening to life with only your mind. You must remember to listen with your heart also."

"That must be what Daddy meant when he'd tell me to mind my heart. He knew. He knew me. When I think back to all the times we spent together, just the two of us, from the time I was a little girl, I realize how well he must have understood me."

I buried my head into Jake's shoulder, fighting back the tears with little success. He held me close, our hands still trapped between us as he slightly swayed as if to rock away my grief.

When I raised my head, Jake wiped my tear-streaked face and kissed my swollen lids. "And that, my luv, is the impassioned meaning. Does it make more sense now?"

"Everything makes more sense."

Later, we had our lobster dinner that had been timely delivered to the front door, complete with white-wine butter sauce. With each bite and lick of my fingertips, I marveled at not only the goodness of life, but also how important expectations could be in our lives, especially when they are our own. I had playfully asked for lobster and got it. Sometimes it's that simple. Sometimes all we have to do is ask … or … we can just take what's given.

That evening I truly realized the connection of the mind to the heart. I learned I couldn't isolate one from the other, but I also learned the importance of a balance between the two. The scales would tip from time to time, each situation would have to be weighed, and the rest was up to me.

Later in the night, in the arms of my shepherd-professor, I thought of how far I had come and wondered how much farther I would go. Staying here—even here—would be so easy. Both my mind and my heart told me so.

I thought again of Daddy, of the times he saved me from adrenaline-producing nightmares, from monsters in the dark, from lightning flashes and thunder rumblings. I thought of the quiet nights when we sat side by side in the wooden-slatted swing he had built for Mama, and how he talked of constellations with strange names like Ursa Major and Ursa Minor, of Corona Borealis and Cassiopeia, and of others I can no longer remember. I know now that somewhere they're in the recesses of my mind; their imprints last although the words escape me.

I remembered how he sometimes let me stay up late with him to watch *Saturday Night Live* while everyone else slept. Sprawled on the floor in our pajamas, with pillows under our heads and popcorn between us, we'd revel in our stolen moments with "Coneheads," "Samurai," "Cheeseburger, Cheeseburger, Pepsi," and Todd and Lisa and the Blues Brothers, laughing hard at human folly and foolishness.

As I dozed off, I realized it had been a dozen years since the two of us had shared such a moment, but the memories of our happy times played before me with high-definition intensity. They were mine to keep forever.

Chapter 18

As promised, Jake made an appointment for me to visit with Linda Scott so she could fill me in on the gaps in my writing. I worked frantically, and with her encouragement, e-mailed a set of articles to my editor and waited in eager anticipation.

In the following days, Jake began spending more time at the college, renewing friendships, straightening his office, and developing his plans for his classes in the fall. At times, I'd roam the city on my own, but when I longed for his presence, which was more often than not, I'd accompany him and spend the day holed up in a corner of his office, working on a new article. When I tired of that, I'd peer over his shoulder and into all junctures of higher learning, trying desperately to absorb more of his world.

One evening, Jake and I drove into the city and walked the Royal Mile, stopping to eat in a small bistro. On another, we drove out of the city, stopping in a historical village to walk the cobbled streets. He tempted me with promises of weekends to be spent romping in the ocean and blazing our private trails along its shores. Neither of us mentioned the apartment.

A week after our arrival, Jake left for the university early in the morning, leaving me with a promise of an early return. Thrilled to have time to myself, I dug out my notes from a recent excursion and began reviewing them. The phone rang.

"Hello," I said, wishing I had just ignored its summons.

"Hey, girlfriend," Shannon chimed.

"Shannon, we've been wondering when you were going to surface again."

"Well, my time's running out before my fateful return to reality."

"When are you going back?"

"In ten days. I purchased my ticket today, and I thought I'd better check with you to see how you're doing."

"I'm fine. How are you?"

"I'm okay. It's just ... well ... I ..."

"What? You what?" She didn't answer, and I repeated, "What's wrong?"

"Megan, I know about Mark. That he came over here to see you—"

"Really?" I broke in. "How do you know?"

"I've talked to him."

"Oh, well, I think we worked things out. I told him the truth. He took it hard, but he seemed okay when he left. The only problem is I told him I'd see him again before he leaves, and I really—"

"Yeah, he told me what happened. I feel kind of bad since I introduced you and Jake. I feel like it's my fault."

"Shannon, it's not your fault or anyone's fault. Besides, I love Jake like I could never have loved Mark."

"I know. I could tell. You two seem to have something special."

I changed the subject, "Okay. So he called you?"

"Who?"

"Mark! You said Mark called you."

"Yes, he called Aunt Anne's and got my number. We talked. He was so upset, Megan. I felt sorry for him. My friends had me invite him here with us. He didn't have anywhere else to be. I hope you don't mind. I don't want you to be angry."

"He's there with you now?"

"Well, not this very minute, but he's here in Glasgow. I told him about visiting you two. I think he's interested."

"I can't believe that."

"Well, let me put it this way. He didn't say he wasn't interested."

"That means he's thinking about it."

"Yeah, well, I don't know what to do. I'm not so sure it's a good idea. He's still upset."

"I'm sorry you have to deal with that."

"It's okay. I just don't know exactly what to do."

"If he decides to come, we'll deal with it," I said, doubting Mark would consider such a visit.

"You're not angry he's here with us, are you?"

"Of course not. Actually, I'm relieved. I've been feeling pretty awful about his coming all the way over here."

"Yeah, well, I—"

"As I said, I told him I would see him again before he left."

"Why did you say that?"

"Who knows? I wish I hadn't."

"Do you think Jake will mind if he comes?"

"Minding and liking are two different things. Personally, I'd rather Mark didn't, so I hope he'll think about it." Of course, I was hoping Shannon would convey the thought to him. "But I know Jake's expecting you."

"Yes, but there wasn't anything about Mark in the deal. And I hate to leave him in Glasgow by himself. So you think Jake wouldn't mind?"

"No, but ..." This conversation wasn't heading in the right direction, and I was wondering why I had suddenly gone brain dead. I really wanted to see Shannon, but having Mark under the roof with Jake? That didn't seem wise.

"Are you sure?"

"Absolutely ... without a doubt," I said, gritting my teeth.

"Sounds like you know Jake pretty well."

"I'm working on it."

"Have you decided what you're going to do?"

"I'm working on that, too."

"You don't sound very sure. I hope this isn't a repeat performance."

"That's tacky." But I knew what she meant. I had taken my time trying to make up my mind about Mark. Twelve years, to be exact.

"I'm sorry."

"It's okay." I knew I had a penchant for vacillation. "So when are you coming?"

"Well, do you think it would be all right if I bring Mark and a few other friends? On Friday?"

"I'm sure it will be fine, but if there's any problem, I'll have him call you."

We ended the conversation, and all I could think was *Damn, I'm nuts!" I should have talked to Jake first. We could have thought of something ... a lie ... anything but this.*

After an hour of mumbling to myself, I managed to resume my work, and it wasn't until Jake came in the door hours later that I raised my head.

Chapter 19

In anticipation of our guests, we immediately made a list of needed groceries and supplies and headed for the market. With that done, we furnished the guest bedrooms and baths with fresh linens and toiletries and then headed for the kitchen, having felt the rumblings of hunger.

Jake sliced freshly baked bread and piled the hefty portions high with ham, cheese, tomatoes, and lettuce. I brewed tea, squeezing in lemon and adding a sprig of mint for each cupful. We carted our feast to the covered entry at the front of the house. Rain drizzled. A cool breeze brushed against us.

"You know, Megan," Jake began, after swallowing the first bite of his sandwich, "there are times when I'm ready to return to the farm, although I must admit it's not because I miss the demands of being a shepherd, as you so aptly put it."

"Really? Tell me more," I said, surprised by his revelation.

"It's strange. Having you here with me is wonderful, but I've begun to notice a difference. I've thought a great deal about it."

"Now you're scaring me," I said, unable to understand his meaning. "I hope my muddling hasn't rubbed off on you."

He looked over at me, totally serious. "I don't know that it's muddling. In fact, I know it's not. It's a realization about life, something I've never felt before. It's strange. And once again, you're at the bottom of it."

"I'm not sure I like how that sounds," I said and then hastily added, "but tell me what you're feeling."

"I think we're missing something here," he said, taking another bite.

"Maybe it's the country influence," I suggested.

"Maybe. No, that's exactly what it is. It's Marlowe's country life." He grinned at me.

"You mean you miss the 'craggy mountains' and 'feeding the flocks'?" I encouraged.

"I'm almost embarrassed to admit it, but I miss everything about its simplicity, the solitude, the walks we took in the fields, our private dances, our talks, your poetic performances." He reached out and tweaked my nose.

"But you're back where you belong."

"Am I? I wonder. I wonder if I ever belonged here."

"Of course you belong here. You have so much to offer. The students need you. The college needs you."

"They got along without me perfectly well in my absence."

"But they're better off with you back."

"The question is, am I? Are we?"

"This is a question only you can answer," I said, repeating the very words he had recently said to me, and knowing within my heart that I, too, ached for whatever it was we shared in those rustic surroundings.

As we sat chewing the last bits of our sandwiches, I wondered if we had been more content at the farm because our love had been so new. One thing was certain: Each moment in the city placed a chokehold on my freedom.

We ate in silence, absorbed in our private dilemmas. Time would tell if either one of us could equalize the desires of the heart with the bidding of the mind. Could we or would we subdue one for the other? Yet the mere idea of returning to the country set in motion a fervor that had slowly been drained from me during the few weeks in the city.

That night, we chose to share a quiet evening reading in the library, setting aside any major decisions for the moment, yet providing time to sort through the questions in our minds.

I knew our feelings for each other were mutual, yet we came from two different worlds, and the only time we had been perfectly at peace with our lives together was in the highlands. Would that be enough for either one of us? To give up my independent quest would be a disappointment, whether we opted for the city or the country. For him to relinquish his hold on his position at the college might leave him unfulfilled and restless.

As I listened to the Old Caledonian grandfather clock strike its St. Michael chimes for ten o'clock, I glanced up to see Jake's eyes on me. I knew questions were on his mind, but instead of disturbing the peace with our misgivings, he wordlessly beckoned me.

I rose from my chair and crossed the room to where he had sat comfortably lounging since we'd entered the room two hours previously. He slid his tattered bookmark onto the pages open before him and closed the volume, placing it on the lamp table at his side. His fingers interlaced and dropped to his lap. He didn't move except to lock his gaze with mine. I stood quietly in front of him for some moments, aware of the doubt writhing between us.

"Jake," I whispered.

He looked up at me, his green eyes glistening from the reflection of the lights. "Yes?" he asked quietly.

"Jake, I don't know if I can do this."

He kept his gaze, but a trace of disappointment etched his smile.

"It's okay." He reached up and took my hand, gently pulling me down on his lap. "We'll figure it out in time."

I wrapped my arms around his neck and once again buried my head into his shoulder with no attempt to hide the tears.

"I'm so sorry, Jake. I'm really so sorry."

For a few minutes, I sat huddled in his arms, exhausted with thought. Then I kissed him good night and climbed the stairs to my room, shutting the door behind me.

I could feel myself sliding into sleep when the memory of Laura's picture above the bed materialized before my closed eyes. Her agonized gaze bore into me as her thin, lifeless body writhed, her arms and legs becoming snakelike. I woke with a start; crying and trembling, I sat up. The house was quiet. I lay back down and slept.

Chapter 20

Shannon and her entourage arrived in time for lunch the next day. They drove up with blaring horn and piled out of their tiny car like madcap clowns, reviving my dismal state. Mark wasn't with her. He had suddenly changed his mind, deciding to return home. I knew Jake was as relieved as I was.

Shannon brought along with her a cousin Ian, a friend of his named Keith, and two young women, Lindsey and Dona. As they began gathering on the porch, Shannon and I fought our way through the huddle of bags and bodies, grabbing each other and screaming our delight. The others stood around fumbling with possessions and feigning unnecessary adjustments to their belongings while patiently waiting for our titillation to subside.

When we finally calmed ourselves and she made the necessary introductions, I could see Jake standing at the door, observing the scene that had left him strangely behind. I quickly moved to his side and stood quietly but nervously, while Shannon gathered her band to meet their host. I couldn't help but notice the contrast between Jake and the young people who stood before him. Although each one was a picture of youthful health, they couldn't inch close to the figure Jake cut. And I wondered if he saw me as part of this lively bunch.

Jake opened the door wide and stepped back, welcoming the collection before him. He squeezed my hand as we walked in behind them and then quickly gathered up the girls' suitcases and led them up the stairs and into suitable rooms. All the while, they oohed and ahhed, expressing their admiration for their surroundings.

Shannon was to share my room, so I quickly ushered her up the stairs and into its privacy, where we dropped her belongings on the floor and stood facing each other.

"Gad, I've missed you," she said.

"Me, too."

"Oh, really?" she replied in disbelief, sitting on the edge of the bed and looking around her.

"Well, I've missed you somewhat," I teased, forcing a smile from her lips.

"We have so much to catch up on, don't we?"

"Yes," I said, pulling her up from the bed's comfort, "but much later. For now, we must remember our manners." I chided in mock civility, "The others are waiting."

We made our rounds to the other rooms to make certain everyone had all they needed and then the two of us hurried down the stairs and into the kitchen, where Jake was preparing lunch.

"We've come to save the day," Shannon sang in her Mighty Mouse voice as we entered the room and saw the kitchen island already boasting a hearty clam chowder and slices of dark-textured bread.

"Then slice the fruit and cheese," he said, motioning to the kiwi, oranges, and melon, and the block of Cheshire lying on the sideboard. Shannon took the paring knife offered and began sectioning the fruit while I arranged plates, utensils, napkins, and glasses.

Within minutes, Ian and Keith bounded into the kitchen, followed closely by Lindsey and Dona. Jake and I poured the requested drinks and then we all headed out into the garden, where we eased into familiarity.

Jake and Ian obliged each other with questions about family while Shannon and the others filled me in on the group's summer escapades. They all assured me I had missed out on a lot of action and urged me to join them in their final days of vacation.

"I really don't think there's room for me," I said, trying desperately to sound disappointed.

Keith wrapped an arm around me, saying, "Fear not. We'll make room for you even if we have to throw Ian out."

They all laughed.

"Megan, you'd be taking my place," Lindsey interjected. "I have to get back to work. But I have to warn you. You don't know what you'd be getting yourself into. They're mad. All absolutely raving mad."

"Then it's settled," said Keith, winking at me and raising his glass to the crowd. There was a "Hear! Hear!" and suddenly I felt a trap had been set.

I looked around for Jake, but he was nowhere to be seen. I wasn't sure when he'd escaped the frenzy. I led the others back into the house and found Jake gathering more ice and drinks for the group.

They ate heartily while Jake and I looked on, unable to entice our appetites. The remainder of the day, I stayed close to his side, mostly in silence, enjoying the banter of the crowd, but avoiding Keith's seeking eyes.

That evening, Shannon convinced us to join them in a trip into the city, and with Shannon and me at Jake's side in the front of his Range Rover, we packed the remaining four into the back.

We had dinner at a restaurant catering to jazz and Japanese cuisine and then moved on to a disco where the moves of the group proved to Jake and me that they really were "absolutely raving mad." Worn out from that, they suggested we move on to a karaoke bar where everyone had a turn at the mike. By early morning, we had cleared the room of all other spectators and decided we had had enough.

When we returned to the house, I offered Shannon "first dibs" on the shower, which she gladly took, and then I wandered back down the stairs where I found Jake locking up the house. I checked the kitchen for last-minute cleanup while he made his rounds, and then I followed him into the library, where he habitually ended his day.

"It was a good evening, wasn't it?" he said as he walked across the room to return a book to the shelf.

"Yes. I'm exhausted. It's been fun being with Shannon again. She's such a live wire. I can't even tell you how many times she has yanked me out of the doldrums."

"Have you been in the doldrums?"

"No," I answered emphatically, but I knew it was true. "No, absolutely not. That's not what I meant and you know it."

He looked at me and nodded. "But it has been something like that, hasn't it?"

I shrugged. "Well, maybe a little. I think we've both been on edge."

Jake turned from the shelf to face me. "Are you up to an early morning chat?"

"Of course," I said, even though what I really wanted was sleep. But I really didn't want to disappoint him.

"Let's go outside."

We walked out onto the patio and sat quietly, his arms wrapped around me as I leaned into his chest. He would have to do the talking, as I was too weary even to think of anything meaningful to say.

I closed my eyes and felt myself giving in to the cool night air and the sleep seeping into my exhaustion.

"Megan," I heard my name. "Did you hear me?"

"Oh, I'm sorry. I think I nodded off. Did you say something?"

He hugged me tightly and made a "humph" sound. "Yes, but I think I've been talking to thin air. Come on. I think we should turn in."

As we climbed the stairs, Jake asked, "Are you sleeping with me or Shannon tonight?"

I felt embarrassed. "I ... I ... think I'll sleep with Shan—I mean stay in my room. I just want to avoid any questions from anyone right now."

"Good night, then," he said. "I'll see you in the morning."

"We'll talk then," I said as I kissed him on the cheek and quickly entered the room where I shed my clothes, slipped on an old T-shirt, and crawled into the king-sized bed where Shannon was already breathing deeply.

Jake was right. Everything we've been told stays with us. Even I felt impelled to keep up appearances when need be.

Chapter 21

When I woke the next morning, it was after ten, and Shannon had already left the room. After showering, I dressed and went downstairs, where I was surprised to see her sitting alone at the kitchen counter drinking coffee.

"Good morning, sleepyhead," she said as I reached for a cup.

"Hey, how long have you been up?"

"About an hour."

"Have you seen Jake?"

"Yeah, he was up when I came down. We talked a few minutes and then he left."

"Did he say where he was going?" I asked, surprised he would leave without saying anything to me.

"He just said he had some business to take care of and would be back this afternoon. He left these for you," she said, indicating an envelope with a set of keys weighing it down.

I picked up the keys and saw they belonged to the Range Rover.

"But why would he give these to me?"

"Well, I guess he thought we might need them. I thought you were going. Aren't you?"

"I don't know if … no, I don't think so," I said as I looked at my name scrawled across the envelope and began to feel panic rise in my chest. "No, I'm not. I'm staying here. I'm staying with Jake … that is if he still wants me."

"I know there's no doubt about that," she stated emphatically.

"How would you know? What did he tell you?" I asked, wishing I hadn't sounded so desperate.

"He didn't tell me anything, Megan, except what I told you already. Besides, he didn't have to tell me anything. It's quite obvious Jake loves you. Surely you can see that." She shook her head, "Where in the world does your doubt come from, girlfriend?"

I turned away from Shannon so she couldn't see the tears welling up in my eyes, then walked out of the kitchen and into the library. I shut the door and tore open the envelope.

Dearest Megan,

Last night as we sat in the garden, I talked for some time about my feelings for you before I realized you were sleeping. I couldn't help but think that, perhaps, fate intervened in some way, forcing me to make some decisions I should have made long ago.

Shannon assured me this morning she would bring you back safely next week (she's a good friend, you know), so I want you to take the Range Rover. I really wouldn't want you to be crammed into a merry-andrew sort of situation.

When you return, we will get our heads and hearts together. Until then, know I'll be here waiting.

Yours,

Jake

Grabbing the arm of the couch, I slid onto the cool sumptuous leather. *My God, why have I been such a fool?* The thought of being without him jarred my senses. It made no difference where we lived—at the farm or in Laura's mansion. All I knew was I had to be with him.

As I lay there trying to figure out what he meant, I remembered a Chinese proverb my grandmother told me once when she found me poking at a cocoon nestled on a leaf of her mulberry tree. "With time and patience the mulberry leaf becomes silk," she said. I didn't know if that was true, but I had hopes the same would be true about me. Jake had been patient, allowing me time and distance. Why had it been so hard for me?

Shannon peeked into the room a few minutes later. "Megan."

121

I forced myself into an upright position as she came into the room.

"Are you all right?" she asked as she sat by my side. "What's wrong?"

"I'm fine now, but I think I just crossed the Rubicon," I said and began to fill her in on the events of the past few weeks.

We were still talking at noon when the others streamed out of their rooms and into the kitchen to rummage through the refrigerator and cabinets. Shannon and I joined them, cooking an enormous breakfast, more to celebrate my decision than to appease their hunger.

By mid-afternoon, they had crammed their luggage and themselves into the small car and drove out happily, all waving like the madcappers that had arrived the day before. I yelled my last good-bye and then headed back into the house.

As I passed the door to Jake's study, something stopped me in my tracks. I turned around and opened the door leading into the dark-paneled room. I looked around. Nothing out of place. All immaculate order. The way he was.

Without thought, I walked over to his desk and pulled on the drawer where I'd seen him place a notebook nights before. Locked. *Surely he doesn't carry the key around in his pocket all the time.* I searched the other drawers, all unlocked. No key.

I headed up the stairs to his room, thinking I might find the slacks he wore that night. *Maybe the key's still in the pocket.* I spotted them on a shelf, folded neatly, probably ready to take to the cleaners. I picked them up and stuck my hand into each pocket. Empty. I searched the room but came up empty-handed. As I stood in the middle of the room, I suddenly felt ashamed. *What am I doing?*

Rushing from his room and into my own, I slammed the door behind me and leaned into it, wondering what had come over me. Why would I think something in that drawer concerned me? I felt like a snoop.

Hours later, the house remained dark and quiet. Jake hadn't yet returned. Perhaps in repentance, I stepped into the shower and scrubbed every inch of my body, then shampooed, creamed, pedicured, and manicured myself into a state of perfection that I somehow hoped redeemed myself from my earlier actions.

I had just slipped into a white linen dress when I heard a sound.

"Jake's home," I thought.

I slipped on my shoes, fluffed my hair, and walked out my door and down the hall to his room. The door was shut. I knocked. No answer. I waited a moment and then turned the doorknob and looked in.

Darkness spilled from his room, but a line of light seeped from the bottom edge of his bathroom door. I heard water splashing in the shower. I curled up on his bed and waited. In a few minutes, I could hear his razor whirring. Then a drawer slammed.

He opened the door, scattering the darkness into the corners of the room. I sat up.

He stood in the doorway, his silhouette framed by the light behind him. A plush, khaki-colored towel wrapped his waist. *Déjà vu.* This time I didn't giggle, and I would not settle for a fantasy. My shoes fell from my feet as they dangled over the side of his bed.

"Megan, you're here. I didn't know," he said. "I thought you would be with Shannon and the others."

Without saying a word, I unbuttoned my blouse and unzipped my skirt. Each piece fell to the floor where I stood. I walked up to him, raised my arms, and pulled my delicately laced slip over my head and let it slide to my feet. My bra and panties followed its path.

As Jake pulled me to him, I slipped my hand into the folds of his towel to pull it loose from his hips. As it gathered at his feet on the floor, I whispered in his ear, "I think I finally learned my missing piece ... is you."

He picked me up and carried me to his bed, where he eased me into its comfort and whispered, "I love you," everywhere, as if becoming acquainted with my nakedness again. My every nerve rose to meet him.

"Jake," I mouthed. The rest was lost somewhere inside of me.

When I woke in the morning, I reached over to his side of the bed, expecting to find him close and warm. I ran my hand over the empty space and looked up.

"Jake." No answer.

Drowsily, I pulled myself free of the covers, reached for the slip still lying in folds on the floor, and pulled it over my head.

As I headed down the stairs toward the kitchen, I noticed the study door open. I peeped in. Sitting at his desk, he leaned over a thick notebook of some kind as he wrote furiously. I sneaked into the room and tiptoed up behind him. As I reached up to place my hands over his eyes and play the silly "guess-who" game, the words *Will she be my next victim?* leaped from the page.

My breath caught. In an instant, he dropped the book into the open drawer next to him, and then slammed and locked it. He stood, dropped the key into his pocket, and turned to me with fire in his eyes.

"What are you doing here?" he demanded with a harshness I had never heard cross his lips. Then just as quickly, he closed his eyes, grimaced, and reached out to pull me to him.

"I … I just wanted to—"

"It's okay. I'm sorry. You just startled me. I didn't hear you come in. Forgive me for barking at you."

I couldn't say anything. I didn't know what to think.

"What were you writing?" I asked.

"Nothing important, just something I've been working on for a long time."

"What?"

"Megan, you know I write all the time. Why are you so concerned?"

I buried my head in his chest. I didn't know if I should tell him what I'd read. I felt foolish … and scared.

He loosened his grip on me. I walked to a window and stared out into the manicured lawn.

He came up behind me, and as if sensing my thoughts, he took my hand and squeezed it gently. "Megan, if you must know, I'm writing a novel. I've been writing it for several years."

"A novel? Why haven't you told me?"

"I haven't told anyone. You just don't want to go around telling everyone you're writing a novel."

"I'm not everyone."

"No, I guess you're not. I'm sorry. I should have told you."

"Yes, you should have. So when do I get to read it?"

"Not any time soon. But now, I'm taking you out for breakfast. I know a wonderful place. You'll love it."

He walked me back up the stairs, opened the door to my room, and gently urged me into its safety. "Get dressed," he said and then turned toward the stairs. I entered eagerly, shutting the door behind me.

During breakfast, Jake told me he had put the house up for sale the previous day. We would return to the farm. There, we could both focus on our writing. I couldn't believe it—back to the magic and away from the stark sumptuousness that seemed to suck the life from me bit by bit each day. I convinced him to let me take the truck the next morning and return to the farm on my own. He would follow in a few days, bringing the Range Rover.

Later that afternoon, he returned to the university to clear his office. I repacked my belongings, toted them down the stairs, and set them next to the front door. As I headed back up for a few more items, I stopped at the door to the library. The words I had seen still nagged at me. I looked at the desk. I knew he'd locked the drawer.

I rushed up the stairs and into his room. *The key. Surely he didn't take it with him this morning.* On a shelf in his closet, a second pair of slacks lay folded. I picked them up, and as I reached for the pocket, the key fell to the floor. I quickly refolded the pants, placing them as they were, grabbed the key, and raced down the stairs. I peered through the sidelight to make certain he had not returned, then entered the library and knelt in front of the drawer. The key slipped easily into the lock. I turned it and the drawer slid open.

A ledger, long and thin, lay upended against one side of the drawer. I pulled it out and thumbed its pages—nothing but figures of income, assets, and holdings, meaningless to me. I placed it on the floor and lifted the large notebook I had seen on Jake's desk that morning. It had to be the one. I had seen him toss it into the drawer.

As my eyes scanned the front cover, large, red letters caught my eye. A sickening wave of nausea swept over me. I felt faint. I closed my eyes, and then opened them to see my name staring back at me. MEGAN. *What is this? What the hell is this? A novel? Of me?*

Steadying myself, I set the book at my feet and fanned a few pages. A beautifully written handwriting filled the white sheets with a perfected script. A flawless penmanship.

I didn't have much time. I couldn't read it now. He'd return any minute. I couldn't take it with me because he'd pack it before leaving for the farm. I had to figure out a way. I sat with it on my lap, running my hand over my name. *What can I do?*

In the next moment, I placed the notebook on the floor and began searching the room. The desk, nothing. The shelves, nothing. *The closet.* I opened the door. *Voilá.* Stacks of paper, the three-hole kind that filled the notebook. I grabbed a ream, stripped it of packaging, and then removed the center bulk of Jake's book, replacing the space with blank paper. With any luck, the remaining top and back pages would be enough to fool Jake for a while, at least until I could read and return it.

I replaced the notebook filled with blank paper in the drawer, and then shut and locked it. I picked up the stack I had removed and ran up the stairs to my room. I tucked it into the bottom of my backpack and set it behind a chair, hidden from view.

Within minutes, I heard him call my name. I took a deep breath, smoothed my hair, and hurried into the hallway where I saw him walking up the stairs as he looked at me. "Hey, I see you're packed and ready for your trip."

"Yes, I think I got it all," I said, suddenly remembering the key I still gripped in my palm. As he stepped on the stair below me, I eased my hand into my jean pocket and deposited the key, then reached up and fingered a strand of hair dangling on his forehead, the same curl I noticed the day we met.

"Did you finish at the university?" I asked, desperate to cover my nervousness.

"Yes. Yes, I think they're glad to be rid of me, what with my moving in and out." He took a deep breath, exhaled heavily, and took me in his arms. "But now I have you."

He scooped me up, carried me back up the stairs and into his bedroom, and playfully tossed me on his bed. He came down on top of me, pinning me under his weight as he kissed my face and neck. "I love you, Megan. Oh, God, how I love you."

As he pulled off my jeans, I thought of the key and wondered what he'd do if he knew. My heart raced, both from this thought and his touch. Both had me on edge.

Long after our lovemaking, I lay staring at the ceiling until I heard the strong, even sounds of his breath, drawing in, then sighing out rhythmically, no movement other than the rise and fall of his chest. I rolled out of bed and onto the floor, crawling to my jeans. Slipping my hand into the pocket, I found it empty. *No way.* I tried the other one. Nothing. *It must have fallen out.* I ran my hand over the carpet as I turned in circles. *Damn.*

I heard Jake stir. I peered over the edge of the bed, without the faintest idea how I would explain crawling around on the floor naked if his eyes met mine—not quite the same as running around naked in the rain.

With his eyes closed and his mouth slightly open, his hands began to explore the bed next to him. I stood and slipped under the sheet. He nuzzled his face into my breasts. My breath caught.

"Where were you?"

"Just went to the bathroom."

"Hmm."

Moments later, he slept again and I lay locked in his arms. I couldn't sleep. I couldn't do anything but worry about getting the key back into his pants.

When he woke about an hour later, I pretended to sleep. He gently pulled away from me, rose from the bed, and walked to his closet. I could see him fumbling with the slacks folded on the shelf, first one pair and then the other. He was searching for the key. He dropped each pair one at a time on the floor and stood motionless. His head turned in my direction as he gazed into the darkness of the bedroom. Moments later, he dressed and walked to the door where he hesitated, then turned and walked back to the bedside. I could feel his eyes on me. *He suspects.* I knew it. He then leaned over, kissed me on the forehead, and walked out the door.

I jumped out of bed and went to the door, cracked it, and watched him descend the stairs. I returned to the bed and fell to my knees, tossing the clothes out of my way. Still nothing. In frustration I searched through my jean pockets again, stood, and shook them upside down. Nothing magical happened.

Deciding to dress, I looked around for my panties. Not on the floor. Probably under the covers. I flipped back the blanket and sheet. They lay tucked at the foot of the bed, along with the key. I grabbed them both, rushed to the closet, and stared at the slacks on the floor.

Jake called my name. I knew he stood at the foot of the stairs. I placed the key on the floor next to the wall. He'd think it just fell out of his pocket, just like it had fallen from mine.

I ran into the bedroom, wrapped a blanket around me, and walked to the top of the stairs, pulling my hair back from my face. As I looked down at him, I wondered how I had gotten into this mess.

We ate breakfast before the packers arrived. After that, Jake stayed busy giving direction, so I went up to my bedroom and sat on the floor by my backpack. *What'll I do? Dare I read it now?*

I had just pulled out the stack when I heard movement on the stairs. I jumped up from the floor, ran into the bathroom, and locked the door.

A moment later, I could hear him enter the room. "Megan."

Frantic, I shoved the papers in a cabinet, took a breath, and opened the door.

"There you are." He looked at the backpack lying on the floor. "Cleaning it out?"

"Uh, yes, just trying to get organized."

He walked over and picked it up, setting in on the chair. "I thought you would like to take a few things from the kitchen with you tomorrow. A basket of cheese and fruit, maybe. I wouldn't want you to go hungry."

I turned to head back into the bathroom with hopes of escaping any contact with him, but he intercepted me and ran his hands up my arms. I suddenly understood. His touch ignited me. I couldn't resist him. He kissed and I kissed back, desiring more with each second.

Several hours later, I woke. The bed lay empty beside me. I wondered what would become of me if I stayed in his presence. I thought about the words I had read over his shoulder. Were they meant for me? Did

I really know what happened to Laura? Why couldn't I resist him? Or was it just my imagination?

My mind searched for an answer. *What if he's a spirit or a demon lover, like in some romance novels? Is that possible? Maybe that would explain why so many strange things have happened to me. Maybe he was responsible.* I panicked.

I retrieved the stack of papers from the bathroom, stuffed them once more into my backpack, and walked to the head of the stairs just in time to see Jake walk out the front door with the movers. I ran down the steps and out the back door and into the garage before I remembered I didn't get the keys. After tossing my backpack into the truck, I returned to the house and found the keys in a drawer by the back door, exactly where I knew he'd keep them. A meticulous man.

I walked around the corner of the house and onto the driveway and watched as the movers loaded furniture from the living room. Jake had stepped back inside the house. It was now or never. I ran to the garage, started the truck, and drove down the long driveway and into the street.

Chapter 22

Within an hour, I was well out of sight of the city. I pulled the truck onto the side of the road and stopped. My hands trembled. I felt sick. *What would he do when he discovered I was gone? Why did I take the book in the first place or, for that matter, why had I fled? I should have confronted him.* It was another of those "pea in a mattress" situations. Something just wasn't right. And I didn't like the words I had seen on that page.

I could go to Inverness where I knew Shannon would be returning in a few days. Dare I go to the farm? I didn't do either. I headed to the cairn.

Hours later, I pulled into the familiar parking lot, unable even to reason why I was there. Maybe the isolation drew me. Maybe because Jake wouldn't look for me there. I headed for the trees. I plopped on the soft turf and pulled the pages from the bag.

My heart raced. As I turned each page, I became more stunned by the moment. *Am I dreaming? Am I crazy?*

I fanned the pages on my lap. *Impossible. How can this be?* But it was. They were all blank. I looked back in my bag. Empty.

I reviewed my actions that morning. I knew I had replaced his notebook with blank paper. I took the guts of the notebook. I knew I did. At least, I thought I did. *Could I have screwed up?*

I pulled myself up and began walking to the truck. As I stepped out from under the trees, I heard a stirring behind me. I turned to see a swirling of leaves where I had been sitting, yet the branches of the trees never wavered. I shivered, climbed into the truck, and headed for the farm.

Darkness surrounded me as I entered through the back door. I hadn't expected to be so late and wouldn't be able to find the power switch in the dark, but Jake kept candles and matches in a kitchen drawer. I rummaged blindly until I found them. I lit a candle and looked around. At that moment, I couldn't imagine why I had been so eager to return by myself.

I hefted my backpack over my shoulder and picked my way up the stairs, anxious to close the door behind me and climb into the familiar bed. Removing my shoes and jeans, I climbed in and huddled under the covers. As my eyes adjusted to the dark, I could see the light of the moon as it reflected on the white walls surrounding me. I sat up and turned to the picture on the wall.

"Good night, Laura." I lay down.

"Good night, Megan," she whispered. Or was it just an echo in my mind?

Chapter 23

When I woke in the morning, Jake sat in a chair by my side, his face heavy with exhaustion. I didn't know what to expect.

"Good morning," he said.

"Hi," I whispered.

He leaned over, his forehead against the edge of the bed. Like a magnet, my fingers reached for the curl kinking above the others.

He looked up, pressing his lips together. "Are you all right?" he asked, his fingers playing in my hair.

"I don't know. I guess. I feel better now that you're here." His hand moved down to the bend in my arm, caressing it gently.

"I don't blame you. I should have told you more."

"More about what?"

"About Laura. I just didn't want to frighten you."

"I don't understand."

"It's my fault. I ... obviously I'm not writing a novel. It's all just a personal journal of my thoughts about you and Laura ... the two of you. She was so much like you."

"But there was nothing—"

"Shh. Don't worry," he said as his hand moved under the covers and massaged my stomach.

My breath quickened, "How were we alike?"

"She felt things, just like you."

"Jake, I don't understand."

"Shh. Shh. Don't try to. Don't worry. Just know I love you."

"But that day in the library. I read the words you wrote. I thought that maybe ... oh, this seems silly."

"What? Tell me." He sat on the bed and moved back the covers.

"I had to find out if ... if you were some sort of evil—"

"You thought I was your demon lover?" His eyes sparkled as his fingers trailed downward, seeking me deeply.

His lips opened and his tongue played on mine while he began pulling at my clothes and removing his. Raising his head, he made a howling noise, then leaned down, his lips wet and fervid on my neck.

I pushed him away, laughing, but chilled to the bone. In an instant, he moved into the bed with the same smile I had seen on his face that first day.

In the weeks that followed, I realized I'd quit muddling. The attraction between us was too much to resist. I gave in. To Jake. To myself. To my own desire. My head and heart finally struck what I called a *balance*, and I knew, without a doubt, I wanted to be with Jake. Permanently. So I hung around long enough to see Jake in his clan's highland kilt—at our December wedding.

A few weeks later, I received a thousand-piece puzzle of Scotland's highland from Mark. With it was a note that caused a momentary aching in my chest.

> Megan,
>
> You always said you felt something was missing. I guess you found what it was. I'm happy about that. I wish you the best. May each piece of this puzzle serve as a reminder of the marvels of life—all we have to do is search—something I have taken up since you left, Megan. Although I'll always wonder what might have been for us, I have you to thank for forcing me to look deeper within.
>
> > Your good friend,
> > Mark

I really had loved Mark—I guess you could say I *grew* to love him—but I realize now my mind controlled how I felt about him. He was what I *thought* was supposed to happen. For some reason, at that time in my life, I wasn't in touch with my heart.

In the evenings of the winter months that followed, Jake would build a fire, and we'd huddle together on the couch and talk about our dreams—writing, traveling, remodeling the house, and having children. Sometimes we'd stand in front of the window, sipping our wine and gazing out on old man winter's handiwork—the bare stalks that bore the Iceberg rose he gave to me that first day in the garden, the dry-stacked fences festooned in miniature moguls where I'd done a balancing act during the summer, and the hills, looking more like giant igloos, no longer boasting their checkerboard patterns as they hid camouflaged under the blanket of newly fallen snow.

Everything seemed so perfect.

Part II

Chapter 24

My undoing was lying right next to me. I'd been through the temptation phase, and I did fairly well for a time, but after a while, the enticement was too much for me, and I'd given in. To Jake. To myself. To my own desire. Jake with golden-brown curls, a little more golden than brown. But temptation hadn't been my only problem. There was more to it than that.

I watched as his chest rose and fell as if whispering to me, then slid across the cool space between us, warming it. I cuddled into his curve and ran my finger across his cool skin and along the length of his nose and lips and throat and chest.

His hand grabbed mine, stilling it instantly. He pulled it to his lips. "Good morning, luv," his said, his throat raspy.

"Good morning, luv," I echoed, the sound muffled in his flesh.

"Did you sleep well?"

"Like a baby."

He stretched long and hard, and then turned to face me, lifting his weight upon his elbow. As he nuzzled into my hair, his lips nipped at my ear, firing off a heat wave that targeted deep within me. "What would you like to do today?" he asked.

"Silly question," I whispered. "At the moment I just want to do *you*." And I shoved him to his back and eased up onto his warm and well-armed body.

Minutes later we lay huddled in each other's arms.

"I need to get out," I whispered.

He rolled to his back, spread his arms in mockery, and said, "Well, I'll ask the question again. What would you like to do today?" I poked him playfully in the side and sat up, wrapped my arms around a pillow, and hugged it to me. "I don't know. I just want to get out of the house and do whatever. Drive. Walk. Think."

"About what?"

"Whatever comes to mind."

He pulled me and my pillow against him, his face nestling into my neck, "I know just the place."

"Somewhere I've never been, I hope."

"It will be."

"Where?"

"Just trust me."

"Is it another secret?" Surprises were his forte.

"Until we get there. You game?" He lifted his head to look at me; a few strands of my hair trailed through his mouth as his eyebrows formed an arch with his question.

"Yes, oh yes." The words sprang from my lips with childlike enthusiasm. "I need to get out in the open and clear my head so I can think." I hadn't left the farm since winter boxed us in three months ago, not even for supplies. Jake called them in for delivery. But the sun was shining today.

Jake left and I dressed and then pulled my backpack down from the shelf in the closet, clutching it tightly. I hadn't used it since the night I ran away, the night I stood behind Jake as he wrote those horrifying words in perfectly formed script. I had stolen the key to his desk, stashed his manuscript into my backpack, and left him and Laura's mansion. Months ago.

My intention was to drive back to the farm, the only place I would feel safe. When I finally stopped hours later, I realized it wasn't the farm where I parked, but at the ancient burial ground where I had danced and sang and ... and lost myself.

I had climbed out of the truck and, within minutes, was sitting on the soft earth leafing through his manuscript, searching for ...

As I stood in the darkness of the closet, clutching my backpack, I struggled to remember. *God, what was I looking for? Think, Megan.*

I closed my eyes in an effort to concentrate. Neatly formed words began to materialize, as if being scratched out by some unknown hand. *Will ... she ... be ... my ... next ... victim?* I knew those were the exact words I had seen. Yet as I sat with the pages spread before me that evening in the cairn, I saw nothing, just blank, white sheets, nothing more. At the time, I wondered if I were crazy.

Dammit, I know I took the manuscript he had been writing. I'd run out of the house in a panic, thinking I'd stumbled on a piece of him I didn't know existed, a piece that would change all the goodness between us. But it hadn't worked out that way.

I hadn't been to any of the islands off the coast of Scotland, and as we crossed the waters of what Jake called the 'warrior road,' a strange feeling came over me. At the time, I didn't understand what I was feeling, but in the weeks to come, I would realized I had entered a world beyond my understanding, one that would test me well beyond the lessons of my youth.

Standing on the ferry that morning, looking out over the splashing sea, Jake filled my ears with stories of Gaels, Picts, Britons, and Angles. Of warrior kings, tribes, and wars. At the time, I had no idea Scotland's past would threaten my very existence.

We spent the day at the Isle of Mull. Jake must have thought it funny to take me there. Actually, it worked. He took his books, and I walked along the rocky coast, admiring the cliffs and feeling at peace with the goats and their sidelong glances.

In my solitude, thoughts of home and the staunch refuge I'd left behind wearied me. How ironic. I'd sought independence and freedom, even dabbled in it a while as I prodded fortune, thinking fortuity had served me well. And now I felt almost imprisoned—my personal paradox. How odd to have one's freedom and lose it at the same time. Yet, I really wasn't sure if that was actually the case. There was Jake, and having him as my cellmate kept me from going stir crazy.

Later in the evening, we returned to the farm to find Shannon's throaty voice on the all-too-silent answering machine.

"Hey, you two, hate to disturb your seclusion, but I'm here, here in Scotland ... at Aunt Anne's. I've got news and want to share it with you face to face. I'll be there tomorrow, like it or not. Probably in the afternoon after lunch," she added.

My spirit soared. The very thought of her shook me right out of my melancholy. We had taught school together for seven years, and although she was younger than I, she possessed a will of iron, something

I seemed to be struggling with at the time. She was the one who had urged me to take charge of my life, to escape from what I called the "bright lights and campy music of a carousel." I wondered if her will could help me escape again.

Jake seemed pleased about Shannon's return. We hadn't seen her since she left for the States at the end of summer. We made a list of supplies for her visit. Jake called it in to the village grocer. He'd pick it up later.

We worked together picking up our stacks of books and manuscripts, scrubbing sinks and tubs and floors, and changing linens. By nightfall, we were worn out but prepared.

Jake built a fire, inserted a cassette of Scottish ballads, and poured a glass of wine for each of us. As the Mull of Kintyre wrapped its strains around the flames licking the edges of the fireplace, he crossed over to the window where I stood, handed me my glass, and gently tucked me into his side.

"Do you remember when we waltzed around the room that night?"

"I'll never forget. You gathered me in your arms, and as we waltzed, we were one. It was magical."

I remembered it well, feeling every ounce of my being streaming with his, every step, every turn. And even when the dance ended, we stood wrapped in each other's arms perfectly still, breathless, but wanting more ... more than a waltz.

Shooting him a questioning look, I asked, "And do *you* remember what you said to me that night?"

The corners of his mouth turned down, "Mm, what was that?"

"Well, if I recall correctly, 'Whits fur ye'll no gin by ye.'"

He laughed and shook his head, "I can't believe you remember that."

"How could I forget? I wrote it down in my journal and repeated it over and over, thinking there was something magical about it."

"Well, it worked didn't it?"

"I got you, if that's what you mean."

"The magic is in you, my luv," he said and pulled me closer, kissing me softly.

"Hmm." I breathed in and responded, "I'm not so sure about that. I think it's in you."

"How's that?"

He watched me in amusement as I set our glasses on a side table and playfully shoved him onto the sofa. As I eased into his lap, I whispered, "You're irresistible, quite simply irresistible." I nuzzled into his warmth, my lips finding his. Within moments, he lifted me, cradling me like the bride I was, and climbed the stairs to our room.

Chapter 25

When I woke in the morning, I stretched an arm across his side of the bed. Cold, as usual. I slipped from the covers and wrapped myself in the white terrycloth robe hanging on the bedpost; then, calling his name, I made my way down the stairs and into the empty kitchen. On the kitchen table, a note lay flat for me to see: "Gone to check on the lambs. May be gone a few hours. Will bring back an appetite, for lunch and you. Love, Jake"

I poured a cup of coffee from the pot he had brewed earlier that morning, and then sat at the table staring at his note. It had been nine months since we met. So much had changed. So much in me. I had won his love but had lost something within myself. It was as though something sinister had edged its way into my life. And it sounded wicked to even admit it. I couldn't understand what I felt. It was there, but it wasn't. Not something I thought, but something that slid into my psyche like smoke under a door. To shut it out was futile. What was it Nietzsche said? Evil is "good tortured by its own thirst"?

As a child, I had been warned about temptation. And if "thirst" tortured good, then my thirst for life was wreaking havoc. And right now, Jake was my life. Not that Jake was evil and not that our love was evil. There was something else.

Something had intervened in the months since we met, and I couldn't wait for Shannon to get here. I had to talk to her. Maybe I could dig out what stirred inside me. But it was so hard for me to think about ... all that.

At 1:15 in the afternoon, I slipped on my garden shoes. I was ready for a stroll into the warming weather. Jake hadn't returned. As I opened the back door and stepped across the patio, spring's precocious beauty surprised me. The white blooms of snowdrops peeped around the back corner of the house, and as I followed the path leading out into the narrow road behind the house, daffodils dotted the surrounding bleakness, waving their yellow petals like heralds of better times. *Migod. Why haven't I been out here before now?* Instead of elation at their sight, my chest began to heave. I fell to my knees and wrapped my arms around a large mass of the long green leaves encasing a single, golden flower. Tears fell in droplets; some disappeared deep into the foliage, others sprinkled the velvety petals of the offered portent, and another dropped into the orange cup of the flower's center like an offering to the gods. "Daffodils! Daffodils! O 'fluttering and dancing daffodils.' Oh, Wordsworth, if you could see me now as I cry over your daffodils." His poem ran through my head, and I laughed at myself and my tears and my silliness. A voice behind me broke into my frenzy:

> In vacant or in pensive mood,
> They flash upon that inward eye
> Which is the bliss of solitude;
> And then my heart with pleasure fills,
> And dances with the daffodils.

Jake helped me to my feet and engulfed me in his strength. "You all right, my luv?"

"Hmm, I am now," I said, wiping away my tears and looking up at him. "I guess I have the winter doldrums … from being shut in for too long." I reached down and plucked a flower. "Their beauty overwhelms me."

"Oh, my Megan, I should have brought some in to you."

"Yes, I think that would have been nice. I had no idea they were here. So hidden away. I'll have to plant them everywhere so they can signal winter's end from all directions."

"We'll do that together," he said as he took my hand and we turned toward the house.

"I'd like that."

"And so would Wordsworth." His cockeyed grin spread across his face. "Have you heard from Shannon?"

"Not yet, but I'm sure she'll be here soon."

"Can we eat? I've brought an appetite."

After lunch, we settled in the living room with our books, Jake with his Highland history and me with my stacks on Ireland. My Irish ancestry lured me, and with the isle so close to Scotland, I felt it made sense to seek its mystery of mythical gods and heroic kings. But I hadn't mentioned my desire to Jake.

"Did you know that more people of Irish descent live in the States than in Ireland?" I asked, breaking the silence.

He nodded as his lips curled downward at the corners. He lowered his book to his lap. "Yes, so many wars, disasters, famines. Leaving was their only hope." We sat silently for a moment before he asked, "Your mom's Irish, right?"

"On her daddy's side."

"What was her maiden name?"

"Nowlin. N-o-w-l-i-n," I spelled out to him. "The spelling has changed since early times. I think it was an O'Nuallain who indentured himself to an Englishman and left Ireland for the States. He wasn't but fifteen or sixteen years old. I guess he must have been a fairly decent sort. He married the man's daughter."

"Very decent indeed, I'd say."

"Maybe I should go to Ireland," I continued, unsure if I was making a statement or asking a question. "And just maybe I would find the gravestone of Hugh Donogh O'Nuallain while I was at it."

At that moment, we heard the blaring of a car horn. "No doubt that's Shannon," I said, slamming my book shut and heading toward the back door. I peered out into the driveway. Strands of her golden-red hair caught in the breeze and whirled around her face as she unloaded the car. She looked up. "Hey, girlfriend, did you miss me?"

I didn't bother to answer or put on a jacket or step my sock-covered feet into galoshes, just dashed into the afternoon rain and ran to her, wrapping her in my arms and squeezing so hard she yelled, "I give up."

Releasing her, I stepped back and we both laughed.

"You're glad to see me, huh?"

"You have no idea, Shannon, no idea."

Jake walked up behind us. "I'm glad to see you, too, but I'd rather see you in the house. Let me help you." He gave Shannon a quick kiss and picked up her luggage, and the three of us scampered eagerly into the house.

Jake carried her belongings up to the spare bedroom Shannon and I had shared the summer before. I hadn't changed a thing. It was still meticulously tended, but cheerless with its stark white walls, white bed linens, and lack of personal effects, except for one thing—Laura's self-portrait. It still hung above the bed, her nakedness making more sense to me each time I saw it, something I didn't understand.

Minutes later we settled into the living room, Shannon, ebullient after her drive from Inverness, standing with her back to the fire, Jake, graciously serving tea, and I huddled warmly in my accustomed chair, attentively listening to our guest's chatter.

After a spiel of news from home, she quieted, took a sip of Earl Grey, and said, "You'll never believe." She paused and turned to face the fire, picked up a poker and stoked the logs with her free hand, then wheeled around, the tea in her cup sloshing on the floor. "I quit my job!" she screamed.

I was stunned, not certain if she were telling the truth.

"I did. Really," she stated, almost as if she were pleading.

"But why would you do that?" I asked.

"How can you—you who quit *your* job—ask me that question?"

"Well, I didn't quit before the end of the year. I did have a plan, you know."

"What makes you think I don't?"

We just stared at each other. Embarrassed, I looked down, and Shannon turned her attention to Jake. He sat undisturbed, still sipping from his cup, eyes twinkling, presumably enjoying the stir around him.

"Well," she said, "I guess the truth is I don't have much of a plan. I thought I would let you two help me figure it out."

"But you left the classroom in March. How could you do that?" I asked, as she turned away to stoke the fire once again.

"That was definitely the hardest part. I hated leaving the kids, especially so close to the end of the year, but I really left them in good hands. Or I wouldn't have done it."

"I'll just have to trust you on that one, but you probably should have waited."

"Don't scold me," she said, a tinge of irritation in her voice. "The students have a well-qualified teacher with more experience than I do."

I grinned, rose from my chair, and draped my arm around her neck, "Well, then it's too bad you didn't quit sooner.

We spent the remainder of the afternoon in the act of catching up. That's when I learned, much to my chagrin, she had abandoned home, friends, and job in response to my own exodus. Little did she know that what at one time had been an attempt to dig myself out of a rut had become the dredging of my soul.

Chapter 26

After breakfast the next morning, Jake left with his brothers for their daily routine. I hadn't quite figured out what exactly that entailed, but I knew it kept him busy for most of the day. Shannon and I took a walk on the road behind the house. Amidst the dull and gloom blanketing the meadows, the daffodils behind the back wall continued to wave brightly as we strolled along their border.

Shannon was caught up in her own excitement, an excitement I couldn't share, not really, not like I would have at an earlier time. I wanted to talk, but didn't know how to start. Besides, I wasn't certain what I wanted to say. Especially now. She was following in my footsteps. Mine. Risking everything for a dream. Just as I had. So I didn't say anything. Just walked. She seemed to be content in the silence as we straddled slushy ruts and puddles.

As we came to the stacked-stone fence marking the end of Jake's meadow, she leaned her weight into it and, with her uncanny knack of sensing my innermost thoughts, peered questioningly at me. "So what's on your mind?"

Shivering, I stuffed my bare hands into my pockets, away from the cold. "I wish I knew." I joined her by the fence and gazed at the frosted grass on the meadow. Capering lambs in play broke the stillness as their dainty hooves bit into the earth. I stared across the fence. "I feel like nature's winter. Cold. Lifeless. Like my life's on pause."

Shannon was quiet for a moment, waiting for me to say more. When I didn't, she said, "On pause? How can that be?"

"I don't know. Maybe waiting for understanding ... for something to happen ... maybe to wake up from a dream."

"What do you mean? What's wrong? I thought this was what you wanted." She pulled me around to face her. "Megan, what's wrong? Tell me."

"Let's go in. I can't talk out here. It's too cold."

We walked back to the house in silence. She followed me up the stairs and into the guest bedroom, where she began unpacking. I sat on the edge of the bed watching as she placed neatly folded stacks of clothing into the open drawers.

"Okay, talk," she urged me.

Hesitantly, I began. "Everything was fine until I saw the book he was writing."

"Who was writing? Jake?"

I nodded, and then shut my eyes and lay across the bed, not wanting to go on. Would she believe me?

"Okay. Continue. I need a little more."

I sat back up and concentrated until I could visualize myself back in Jake's dead wife's mansion, coming down the stairs and looking for the man of my dreams.

I looked up at Shannon, "Everything was wonderful until one day about three months ago. We had made love. Then slept. When I woke, he wasn't lying next to me. I went downstairs looking for him. When I finally found him, he was in the study. The door was just barely open. I could see a light behind it. I looked in. He sat at his desk, leaning over a thick notebook of some kind. He was writing … furiously. I sneaked into the room and tiptoed up behind him. I reach up to place my hands over his eyes to surprise him. That's when I saw what he had written." I paused, waiting for her response.

"What had he written?"

"The words 'Will she be my next victim?'"

Shannon shut the drawer in front of her and sat down next to me. "Are you sure?"

"Sure, I'm sure."

"What happened then?"

"Suddenly, I couldn't breathe. I must've made a sound because he slammed the book and dropped it into the open drawer next to him. Then he locked the drawer, putting his key in his pocket. When he looked at me, he had fire in his eyes. He was angry and demanded to know what I was doing standing there. Then, just as suddenly, he had me in his arms, apologizing."

"Well, you just startled him, that's all."

"No, that's not all. There's more." I continued to tell her how I had found the key to the drawer where he had placed the book. "I took the manuscript and fled the mansion ... and him."

"Megan, that's crazy. Why would you do that? He was just writing, probably a novel. He is a writer, you know."

"That's what he said."

"Well, it makes sense. He's published a number of books."

"True. But there's something else."

She waited this time, without saying anything.

"Shannon, when I finally drove to a place where I could stop to look at the manuscript, there weren't any words on the pages."

One side of her mouth pulled back as her head jerked back and eyes widened. She didn't move.

"Really, there weren't. It was blank ... every page," I said.

"Then you got the wrong notebook. That's all."

"No, I didn't. I took the pages from a notebook inscribed with my name. I'm sure of that ... at least I think I am."

"You think you are? See. That's all it is."

I shook my head. "No, you're wrong."

She took a deep breath, stood, and walked across the room, looking out the window. Without turning back to me, she asked, "So, tell me, where did you go when you left him?"

"To the cairns first and then I came back here to the farm."

"To the cairns? Why? Why would you go there?"

"I don't know. I guess they drew me."

"*They* drew you? What's that supposed to mean? Some evil spirits beckoning you, tempting you? Megan, this is nuts."

"Then let's not talk about it anymore," I said, feeling hurt she didn't believe me, but angry at myself for thinking she would.

"No, I want to hear the whole crazy thing. Where's the manuscript?"

"I hid it."

"You hid a blank manuscript?"

"Yes," I said, nodding my head. "I hid a blank manuscript. Strange isn't it?"

Her voice softened, "Where?"

"Under the bed."

"Under what bed?"

"This one," I said as I rubbed my palm across the chenille spread.

I slid off the bed and kneeled at its side, reached under the dust ruffle, and pulled out a cardboard box, wiping the inevitable dust from its lid. I then shoved it onto the mattress in front of us and removed a two-inch stack of paper. I fanned the pages in front of her face.

"See, they're blank."

She sat back. "Well, that doesn't prove anything."

I couldn't think of a response that would contradict the obvious.

She took them from me and began thumbing through them. "What else? Is there anything else you haven't told me ... besides this?"

"You wouldn't believe it either."

"At this point, probably not. But try me."

I began to tell her how I left the cairns and drove to the farm, how it was as though something was directing me there. How I felt powerless. She interrupted, saying, "Yes, I know, like a spirit. Right?"

I tried to ignore her sarcasm, "Yes, something like that."

"Go on. I'm listening," she said as she placed the vacant manuscript back into the box.

"It was dark when I got here. I lit a candle and came up the stairs to this bedroom, anxious to close the door and climb into bed. I just lay here, staring and listening until my eyes adjusted to the dark. It was strange. After all that had happened ... the words he wrote ... the fire in his eyes ... the blank pages, I wasn't afraid any more. And that night, lying here, it was beautiful. The moonlight filled the room, and all I could think of was Jake and how much I loved him—after all I had been through, after what I'd seen. Then, for some strange reason, I sat up. I was right here. On this bed. I sat up and turned to that picture." I pointed to Laura's portrait on the wall above the bed.

Shannon looked up at it. "So?"

"I don't know why, but I ... I said good night to her."

"To the picture?" Her face contorted, lips pulling back and brows raising.

"Yes, to the picture. And then I lay down. And then I heard a whisper."

Shannon shifted her weight on the bed, biting her lips, the corners twitching. I knew she wasn't buying into my story, and I really couldn't blame her.

"She whispered good night to me, Shannon."

Her eyes rolled up. "Ohmigod, Megan, you don't expect me to believe that?"

I couldn't say anything. How could I expect her to believe such a thing? I just looked at her, not really seeing her or anything else. She eventually stilled. I knew she was trying hard to stay with me.

"Is there more?"

Before I could continue, I heard the back door open and close and knew Jake had returned. "Yes, but it'll have to wait. Jake's here. We'll talk later. And don't tell him anything about what I've said."

"No, I won't."

"Promise?" I pleaded.

"Absolutely. Scout's honor," she said, holding up her fingers in pledge.

As we walked down the stairs, I realized how absurd my story must sound to her. How utterly ... crazy.

But something was going on. Something I hadn't been able to put my finger on. I guess that's why I was so glad to have Shannon back in my life again ... someone besides Jake. Maybe, through her, I could figure out what was wrong inside me.

When Jake was near, I couldn't think of anything, or anyone, but him. I felt jinxed. From the first time he laid eyes on me, or I laid eyes on him, my will dissolved.

And what was really strange was I used to be so happy. I mean really happy. Childlike happy. Dancing in the rain happy. But as time went by, I felt like a weight was tied to me, pulling me down, except ... except when he was near. Then something gushed up, overwhelming my senses, leaving me toppled.

We entered the kitchen as Jake rummaged in the refrigerator, no doubt searching for something to eat. Wrapped around his waist was an old washed-out apron, the one with cavorting lambs tracing its edges. I walked up to him and took the cold dishes from his hands. "Hungry again?"

"Isn't it time to eat?" His eyes widened, his eyebrows lifted, and he grabbed me around the waist.

"Well, if eleven's not too early for you," I said, pulling away while holding the dishes high above my head.

"It's never too early for me—for anything." He grinned at both of us. Shannon laughed with more enthusiasm than sounded natural. I think it was more in relief—relief from our earlier conversation of blank pages and talking portraits—than in amusement.

We sat at the table and talked about the sheep and the weather until I could stand it no more. "Jake, Shannon and I want to go somewhere." The words popped out of my mouth, surprising all three of us. I looked over at Shannon. Her eyes flitted to mine, and then went to the ceiling. We hadn't talked about a trip, but I knew she'd catch on. We'd been friends a long time.

Jake gave a nod. "Well, certainly. You can do that. Where do you want to go?"

I gave Shannon a nod, saying, "You tell him."

She shrugged. "Umm, lots of places."

She wasn't helping much. She'd traveled all over Scotland last summer. I was sure she'd come up with something more tangible than that.

"We just want to get in the car and go," I said. "Just a few days. We'll be back before you know it." I reached across the table and laid my hand on his arm. "You don't mind, do you?"

"No, of course not. You deserve it after being cooped up in this place all winter. Besides, the weather's warming." He carried his dishes to the sink, kissed me on the cheek, and walked toward the door. "But there are many places to explore close by. You might consider day trips." He winked at me and added, "Then you'd be by my side at night."

Shannon laughed and placed her palms to her ears, saying, "I'm not hearing any of this."

Ignoring her, Jake blew me a kiss. "Make your plans and tell me about them tonight." The door closed behind him.

Shannon pushed her chair back and folded her arms across her chest. "You could have warned me."

"I'm sorry. The thought just came to me all of a sudden."

"Well, you could have told him where we were going. How was I supposed to know?"

"I just thought you'd come up with something."

"Well, I guess I came up with as much as you did." She smiled, relaxed her pose, and slapped the table. "And now we're finally going to see Scotland together … even if it is just *day trips*. And, my dear, you still have more to tell me about those spooks." She laughed, but it wasn't funny.

After cleaning the kitchen, we returned to her bedroom. I felt drained and collapsed on the bed. Shannon took one look at me and told me to sleep a while. We'd talk later.

Sleep came easily. As I dozed off, I could feel my breath ease and my body relax into a cloak of gray haze, as I seemed to rock back and forth. A white stallion moved below my straddling legs, a stallion I had ridden over and over in my dreams. My legs embraced his girth as it pressed inward and upward into my center. A muscular torso pressed against my breasts, sending surges of raw energy into my slumber.

Even in my sleep, I recognized his warmth. He had held me countless times. He turned his head to gaze at me, smiling, saying, "Hold on, Megan, hold on. Stay with me." My body swayed away from him, only to be drawn back by a gyrating force.

Suddenly a voice pulled me from the clutches of my fantasy, echoing again and again above me, an eerie but strangely sweet sound. I knew it was Laura.

With difficulty, I crawled from the covers and sat up, turning to look at her picture. "What? What do you want?"

"Megan."

"What, Laura? What? I'm here."

I stared boldly at her naked form. How many times had I heard her call my name? How many times had I ignored her, figuring she was a figment of my imagination? Maybe so, maybe she was. But right now she seemed all too real. Trembling, I climbed from the bed and walked to the window. I could see Jake walking from the barn, toward the house. I had to end this now.

I whirled around, my eyes riveted to the portrait on the wall. Suddenly I felt her nakedness begin to seep into me. I was drowning, drowning in a delusion brimming with flesh. The pale pinkness streamed down my body and onto the bed, soothing and calming me. I felt powerless, yet empowered. I looked back at the portrait. She was still there, looking at me. And then I began to understand. I'll never be able to explain how I knew. But one thing was certain. Her nakedness was meant to expose. Not exposure for the female sake, not for sex, not for shock, but to expose the truth … to me.

I climbed back on the bed, took the picture from the wall, and shoved it into the pillows in front of me. "What? What do you want?"

Her haunting eyes cleared, the blue of her irises widening as she leveled her gaze to mine. "Megan, listen closely," she said in an angelic voice. "You're in trouble. Jake's in trouble."

My heart skipped a beat and began to pound against my chest. I couldn't speak. I wanted to scream, throw the picture against the wall, and run to Jake. And then I could hear him calling my name from the kitchen—then from the bottom of the stairs.

Laura's words of warning echoed in my mind as Jake continued to call my name. I looked at Laura and frantically begged her to tell me what she meant, but when she spoke, her words were lost in the intermingling of Jake's and Shannon's voices as they moved up the wooden stairs.

"Don't say anything to him about what I said. We'll talk later."

"But I have to tell him," I said, shaking the picture as if to make her listen.

"You can't tell him. You can't. Believe me. If you love him, have faith in what I say … in yourself."

I heard Jake and Shannon talking as they made their way up the stairs. They would both think I had gone mad if I told them about flowing flesh and a talking picture, so I replaced the portrait and fled from the room, running headlong into them as they reached the landing.

"Whoa!" Jake's arms enveloped me and held me still. "Where're you going in such a rush?"

I held him tight, hoping he wouldn't notice the trembling that had taken hold of me. I didn't trust myself to speak, just lifted my head and kissed him on the mouth. Right there in front of Shannon. I could hear her giggle. I looked over his shoulder and into her face.

She flinched. "Megan, what's wrong?" she mouthed.

I shook my head at her and pursed my lips in a silent hush. "Nothing," I blurted. Then calmly, "I was sleeping and heard you two coming up the stairs, so I thought I would surprise you."

She took a deep breath, turned, and walked down the stairs with Jake and me following.

We ate at the local pub in the evening. Almost like old times. With Shannon sitting across from me and Jake at my side, I could almost chalk Laura's warning up to another bout of imaginary rendering. That is, almost. Not quite.

On the surface, we looked like three friends out for a night of dinner and good company. But we were more than that. They talked. I listened. They laughed. I listened. They often looked at me, it seemed, as if they wondered about my state of mind. Shannon had witnessed my ravings over a mysterious blank manuscript and a talking portrait, not to mention beckoning spirits. But Jake? Sometimes I wondered. He kept reaching for my hand, asking if I needed anything, sending me questioning glances. I wanted to tell him about Laura's warning. Instead, I sat sipping the ale I hadn't ordered but had been placed before me, silently struggling with the nagging questions and my sanity.

It was late when we returned home. I left Shannon and Jake warming themselves in front of the fireplace, deep in conversation about family members, both past and present. I climbed the stairs and closed and locked the door to the guest bedroom, lifted Laura's portrait from the wall, and sat down on the bed, ready for another tête-à-tête. As I stared at the narrow, blue slits representing her eyes, her lids fluttered.

"Sorry. Hope I didn't disturb you," I said, surprised by my nonchalance.

She didn't waste any time, "Where did we leave off?"

Strangely, she couldn't remember. Surely a portrait that had its own life wouldn't need a mere mortal to minister trivia.

"You had just told me Jake and I are in trouble. What do you mean? What kind of trouble?"

"Megan, when Jake was a little boy, a spell was cast on him."

"What do you mean?"

"A spell. I know it seems fantastic, but it's true."

"Why would someone or some*thing* cast a spell on a little boy?"

"I'm not sure. All I know is he fell into a cave somewhere out in the woods and a spell was cast on him."

"That's ridiculous." Yet in an instant, I realized the whole affair was ridiculous, so why shouldn't he have a spell on him?

"I know it sounds weird, but it's true. An ancient spirit decided he didn't belong in the cave and decided to punish him."

"An ancient spirit?"

"Yes."

A guffaw followed her answer. Then I realized it came from my mouth. I was acting like Shannon—me, the one who started the whole gruesome business. I decided to get on with the interview, so I asked, "By casting a spell on him?"

"Yes. I know it sounds like voodoo."

"It is voodoo. And I don't believe it."

"Listen to me. I don't know why it happened. But the entire time I was married to Jake, I could feel my life dwindling … especially when we made love."

I shut my eyes and tried not to think about it.

"But I couldn't resist him. Every time I was near him, I—"

"Okay. Okay." I knew exactly what she meant. "And, so, when you made love—"

"Yes, making love sapped my strength. I didn't understand it, but I could feel it, and I know it's happening to you." She paused, and then added, "Isn't it?"

Speechless, I turned away from her, wanting desperately to wake from this ghastly conversation. She was quiet. I looked back at her image, an image staring right through me. "So what do you want me to do?"

"Find out how to break the spell."

"And what kind of a concoction or witches brew do I stir up to do that?"

"Be serious. Listen, I know you go to the cairns. Go back. Try to contact the spirits. Talk to them. Get them to tell you where the cave is."

"What cave?"

"The one Jake fell in as a little boy. Maybe you can find it and learn how the spell can be broken."

"Why didn't you do that?"

"Well, I would have, had I known. I just didn't know." She shut her eyes and made a faint moaning sound. When she opened them again, she said, "How could I have known? I didn't find out about the spell or the cave until I was dead."

I covered my mouth in an effort to stifle a laugh bordering on hysteria.

She continued, "And you need to settle this thing before you're too sick and weak to do anything about it."

As I looked at her face, I could see she was weary. The lines under her eyes had gotten heavier, darker, mirroring my own weariness at hearing her words.

"I'll go tomorrow." The words just popped out of my mouth.

"Take Shannon with you. She'll give you strength."

"I wouldn't think of going without her," I said as I placed the picture back on the wall.

"And, remember, don't say anything to Jake. If you do, the spell can't be broken."

Taking a deep breath, I opened the door and rejoined Shannon and Jake, neither of them acknowledging my entrance into their cloister of story swapping. The flush of the fireplace splayed across the room as the potter's clay walls reverberated the warming embers.

I plunged into the overstuffed chair next to Jake and watched as Shannon's eyes flitted between my own and Jake's. As he winded down a saga of university life, Shannon burst forth, "Glad you could finally join us. We've been catching up. It's really sad that relatives don't even know what's going on in each other's lives." She leaned forward and adjusted the quilt covering her legs.

"Sometimes it's better that way," I said.

Jake rose from his chair, leaned down and kissed me on the top of the head, and headed toward the kitchen. "Anyone want something?"

"No," Shannon and I said in unison.

"I'm still up to the brim from dinner," Shannon continued, "and I couldn't eat another thing until morning."

As soon as Jake was out of earshot, I leaned forward. "I talked to her again. She said we should go to the cairn and try to find some cave where Jake fell in."

She looked at me as if I were nuts. "He fell in a cave?"

"Yes, when he was a little boy. And someone or something cast a spell on him."

"Let me get this straight. We go to the cairn to try to find out where a cave is. Someone or something is going to tell us where that is?"

"Yes," I said, not believing my own words. "At least that's the theory."

"Why don't we just ask Jake? That might be a bit easier, don't you think?"

"We can't because then the spell would be unbreakable. He can't know anything about it."

"Duh, Megan, we don't have to ask him about his falling in a cave … or a spell. Just ask him where he used to play as a child."

I stared at her, my mouth agape. No wonder I had her for a friend.

Jake walked in with a box of chocolates, offering the tartan-designed box first to Shannon and then to me.

"You're full of surprises," Shannon said between bites. "Where did these come from?"

"Ordered them yesterday. Thought you girls would like to indulge in some of Scotland's finest Drambuie truffles."

Shannon reached for the box again, "Well, I know I said I couldn't eat another bite, but I did. May I have another?"

"Ah, temptation," Jake said, setting the box on the coffee table in front of her. "What did Wilde write? 'I can resist everything except temptation'? Something like that."

"Well, I suppose that's true for me," Shannon said.

Wrangling the conversation toward childhood, I added, "Me, too. I remember as a child being tempted to do things I knew I shouldn't."

As he let his weight pull him back into his chair, Jake looked at me in disbelief. "Really? You a naughty child? What tempted you?"

In an effort to stall, I reached for another truffle and popped it into my mouth, chewing slowly. After a few seconds, my imagination took hold. "Oh, I don't know, ah, well, once when I was about six or seven, I went down the block where there was a vacant lot and hunted horny toads. I wasn't supposed to leave the yard."

"Horny toads? Horned toads tempted you? I can't even imagine. I can see you collecting flowers, but not toads," Jake said as he laughed at my fabrication.

"Well, what tempted you? Where did you like to go? I bet you did things that got you into trouble." I waited for him to reply, but he didn't. He just sat looking into the fire, probably thinking of the very incident I wanted him to reveal.

Shannon tried not to let her curiosity show in her voice as she waved her hand out into the air, vying for his attention. "Oh, Jake, are you there?"

"Oh, right. I suppose I was as full of vigor as the next chap, but you have to realize I was raised in Scotland. I was free to wander the hillsides, no restrictions. Everything was game."

"You didn't ever roam into the woods and get lost?" I asked. "Maybe a burial ground or something? I would think a young boy would be dying to explore the unknown."

He looked up at me. "Of course I explored, but nothing unusual happened. Nothing to tempt me. No, sorry to disappoint you. I'm afraid not."

I had expected more, but he seemed sincere. Maybe nothing unusual had happened, at least nothing that stayed with him.

My mind whirled with questions as I lay in bed that night. I thought about the first day I walked into the farmhouse, mesmerized by its antiquity, dazzled by its distance from home, from the ordinary. Walks in the meadows tranquilized me. Visits to the cairns opened up a world of spirituality I had never known existed. And his embrace, tender beyond the dreamer's touch, lingering even in his absence. Never had I felt so alive. Until lately. And, then, this … this hideous curse. Temptation had weaseled its way into my life just so it could snare me for its own hunger and thirst. Or was it my own?

Chapter 27

By the next morning, I had decided I wasn't going to end up a picture on his wall. I had been tempted. I had succumbed. But I wasn't about to let my desires ruin me. I could lie around wondering "what if" this and "what if" that, but the truth was, I'd been caught up into a netherworld that wasn't offering any escape, at least as far as I could see. And I certainly wasn't going to chance sitting around mothballed in lethargy.

After Jake went out to the barn, I cornered Shannon and told her we were definitely going to the cairn. I wanted to find out about the curse. It was ruining my life. Either that or I was crazy. And that idea scared me.

I had been leery of returning to the graveyard after last summer's experiences. I remembered too well how I'd fallen asleep on the soft turf under the trees and wakened on the hard surface of a boulder at the center of the burial ground, my body writhing pleasurably in response to some unseemly rake. I didn't want a repeat performance, but I had no choice but to make contact with "it" again. If there were spirits to be contacted, the cairn seemed the likely place. Maybe, just maybe, I'd handle the situation differently this time.

Shannon shut her eyes. I could see her taking in deep breaths. When she finally looked at me, the hard, straight line of her lips told me she wasn't thrilled with the prospect of wandering into ancient grounds. "So what makes you think *they* are going to communicate with *you?*"

"I don't know. I just don't know what else to do."

"Have they ever communicated with you?"

"Well, no." Then I thought about the poem that had scribbled itself in my notebook weeks ago. "Actually, they have in a way."

"What do you mean?"

"It was after my last visit to the cairn." I told her about my frenzied dancing, the voices, and the strange experience on the stone. "That day, after I woke up on the stone, I left the cairn and drove to a small café. I was scared and felt sick. I ordered something to drink and sat in a corner away from everyone. After a while, I pulled out my notebook and started writing. But it was like I wasn't writing at all. My pen just took over."

"Oh, Megan, I don't know about this. Maybe you should see a doctor." She was serious.

Without another word, I jumped from the chair and raced up the stairs and into my closet, pulling my backpack from the shelf. My notebook lay tucked inside. I flipped through the pages until I found it. There it was. Just as it had been written.

Clutching it and thankful the words were really there and I wasn't dreaming, I ran back down and sat next to her again.

"Look," I said, shoving it under her nose. "Read it."

She laid the notebook on the table and peered down into the page. She read:

> Devouring hush, dull thou the living brow,
> And bid the sweet consume each breath's decay;
> Yank the gasping sighs from th' lover now,
> And scorch the canker where it seethes today;
> Beware the mask of clouds that hides the crime,
> With hideous rack and bonds of blackest doom;
> The rose with thorns will prick before its time,
> With all its beauty spoiled and love entombed;
> But hear the noise that deafens all the dreams,
> To spread madness cloaked—seduction's friend;
> Make hast, O Sweet, abandon all that seems
> To awe with touch, a kiss, the bitter end.
> If weak and feeble minds delay to choose
> Then grieve for all the pain it dreads to lose.

"What do you think it means?" I asked.

"How am I supposed to know? You're the literature teacher."

I could see her eyes skimming the lines again. "It sounds like a warning. But why did you write this? It's like you're warning yourself."

"Shannon, I don't think I wrote it. Something else wrote it. I've never written something like this."

"Oh, but you have. You used to write sonnets with your classes every year."

"But not like this. Why would I write something so ghastly?"

"Because subconsciously you know. You know that something's not right."

"Then you believe me?"

"I really shouldn't believe a word you say, except that you wrote this. But that's all I believe." She tossed the notebook in front of me. "I should pack up and go home right now. But I won't. I'll go with you to the cairn. If I don't see or hear something to convince me that what you've told me is true, then I'm out of here."

"That's all I ask."

We dressed for the day and packed a few things for our trip. I went to the barn and talked with Jake. He didn't mind our leaving for the day, but was adamant about our returning by evening. As I kissed him good-bye, the rising feeling in my belly reminded me of the overpowering desire I had for him. Had it not been for the surrounding stench and the black, saucer-eyed gaze of the oblivious lambs, I could have stayed longer and subdued my aching. Instead, I turned and left him.

"Megan," his voice tugged at me, "be home by dark so I don't worry about you."

I turned and looked at him, once again dazed by the magnetism between us, by the lure of this Svengali, a man who had won me even before he said hello. I rushed back to his side, wrapped my arms around him, and buried my face into the warmth of his neck.

"I promise."

Shannon and I piled into Jake's old truck, and with her driving, we headed for the cairn. I'd been there before. Months before. It was the place I'd taken Jake's manuscript when I swiped it from his desk, where I'd sat on the ground and found its pages blank. But it was also the place where I lost myself. Why I say "lost," I'm not sure. Maybe I found myself. It was there I experienced a side of myself I hadn't known existed until that day. I'd laughed and danced amongst the trees—and heard voices. What was it they whispered? Something like "fill me, gorge me … with your love." I felt their wispy touch. They called my name over and over again. I felt liberated, exuberant. I whirled around the trees, encircling each trunk, holding on with one hand and swinging around it like a child spinning around a flagpole, my body gyrating in my jubilation, just as the trees had gyrated above me. I fancied something, maybe some spirit brushing against me, whirling around me, caressing me. I yearned to wrap myself in ghostly attire, to be one with whatever played around me, but my humanness resisted. And, gradually, I became aware of a repeated sound, not a voice, but a kind of stirring, almost a whisper brushing around me. I lay down on the leaf-strewn ground to stare up into the swirling canopy. I listened intently but could make out nothing more than the rustling branches as they lulled me unmenacingly.

I thought about how lucky I was. Who did I know who had experienced what I had experienced? No one. Something special had taken place. I didn't know what it was, but I knew I kind of liked it.

And then the second time I visited the cairn, I wanted more of the same, but that time I came away disturbed and shaken. And wrote "Devouring Hush." And began to suspect something was wrong. Maybe with me. I didn't know. And something told me my desire for Jake was something other than worldly.

It had been summer then, but as Shannon and I drove into the parking lot, I could see something different about the shadows, the angle of the sun, the redness emanating from its craggy texture.

As usual, the parking lot leading into the grounds lay deserted. We sat quietly for a few minutes. She placed her hands firmly on the wheel and leaned her head against it, as if mustering courage.

"It's going to be all right, Shannon. All I ask is that you stay with me. That way we can both be sure about what's happening." I couldn't believe I was the one consoling her.

"Right." She opened her door and stepped out without another word, but waited for me to grab the backpack and lead the way through the stile, an entryway allowing only one person at a time to pass. She managed a laugh and said, "I can't imagine why this contraption is here. I certainly don't see throngs waiting for a chance at entry."

"I've been here three times and I've never had company." Then under my breath, I added, "At least not the living, breathing kind."

Morning sunlight flung shadows of sinewy darkness across the ground, casting silhouettes of tangling branches, like a loose matting of threads from a timeworn doily. As we stepped gingerly across the ground, I looked down at the aggregation of stones paving our way. I wondered whose footsteps we followed.

I pointed to a kerb cairn about thirty feet in front of us. "That's a grave. Or it used to be."

"Used to be? What does that mean?"

"Well, they think it used to be a grave, but they've never found any remains."

"So what happened to them?"

"No one knows. Either moved or grave robbers. Either way, they were obviously important at one time. Notice the boulders set around the cairn, clearly marking the area."

"Okay, we're here, now what?" The edge on her voice warned me. She wasn't going to linger here listening to my feeble explanations.

"Follow me," I said as I walked to the entrance of a chambered cairn. Instinctively my fingers reached out to drag along the edges of the stones in the passageway leading into the cairn's center. I pointed above to the open sky. "Can you imagine being in here when it still had a covering?"

"I doubt I would be doing any imagining, or anything else for that matter. I'd just be dead." Shannon walked out of the circle of stones and looked around her. "Really, Megan, this is quite interesting, but I really don't see how it answers any questions. Not that I really believe there's anything to all this."

We walked out to a boulder in the center of the cairn. "This is it. This is the core of the graveyard."

I circled the massive rock's bulk, reached into my backpack, pulled out my camera, and began taking pictures. I then replaced the camera and inched toward the massive stone, spreading my arms, pressing cheek, breast, stomach, and thighs firmly against the abrasive surface. Shannon stood behind me, no doubt guarding her thoughts.

I tried to close my mind against her ... against all humanness. I rose onto my toes, stretching upward, straining for something unearthly, some light, airy gossamer of a sign… a hint… a way to untangle the mess I had made of my life.

Nothing happened. When I couldn't stand there any longer, I sank to the ground and curled up into a fetal position. Something in me had shrunk from the world I had been begging to enter. All I could do was cry and wonder how much of my life was real. But all I got from my shenanigans were puffy eyes and questions from Shannon.

She sat patiently next to me. She placed a hand on my shoulder. Her touch pulled at my reserve. "You okay?"

"Yeah, just miserable."

"Did you feel anything?"

"Yeah, I did," I said, rubbing a scrape on my cheek. "And I have blood to prove it."

She stood, extended her hand, and pulled me to my feet. "Well, that's something. At least I know you're real." She hesitated and then asked, "What else?"

"I just need some time. Maybe if you wander around on your own, I can do better by myself."

"Then how am I going to know when something happens?"

"I'll know. Just give me some space."

She walked off mumbling something about "coming by yourself," but I knew she wanted to be there with me. She just had her doubts. And I couldn't blame her.

As she moved away from me, her hair lifted in the breeze, swirling out from her head. She ran her fingers through her hair, pulling it down in front of her shoulders, holding on to the red-gold mass as though somehow it would escape her grasp … as if it might be snatched away. I knew they were with her. She didn't.

When she disappeared into the trees, I turned back to the stone, closed my eyes, and again inched into its harsh corrugated surface. I lowered my arms to my sides and relaxed. I sought deliverance unto its ancient power. I drew in my breath and slowly released it. *Come. Come. Come to me.* I felt myself sink into its center.

Warmth buried in next to me as I woke. I nestled down into the heathery fragrance, breathing it in deeply, and then recognized the dark closing in on me. I sat up and inched my hands over the ground, then began to creep on all fours, hesitating as my hands reached out over smooth, hard stone.

My heart beat hard against my chest as my mind recaptured the moments before I woke. Something cautioned me against calling out. Fear would surely fracture the privilege I had been allowed.

Within minutes, I heard a faint sound. I sat motionless, straining, listening. Something like a murmur sounded far off, almost like humming multiple voices, each murmuring its own tune, entwining, soft, eerie tongues.

I sat within the quiescent intensity, unable to stir, my body and mind suspended, waiting for something to happen. Maybe the spirits I'd been seeking had found me. Then gradually, their tune dissipated and I lay back down. I must have slept because when I woke, a figure of a wiry, old man sat by my side. He was bent over as if dozing, his long white hair falling forward, covering his face.

Warily, I sat up. As if aware of my movements, he lifted his head. Ghastly pale, his face came even with mine. One hand came up to my cheek, and then curled around my chin. His touch, though tender, set off a spiraling shudder that all but lifted me from the ground. My nails clawed into the earth below me. He leaned forward until we were nose-close. His skin was smooth, his features fine, almost pretty. My eyes widened as I peered into his. It was as if he were reaching down into me, down into my soul, beyond my façade, my thoughts, my desires, wrenching all away from me. I felt myself empty into him.

When he finally spoke, I felt my head jerk back as if I had been released from shackles. His words floated from his mouth like a siren's song, lulling my life's breath. I felt woozy and couldn't concentrate on their meaning.

"Megan, I am here for you. You want to know about Jake."

Jake's name met my consciousness and pulled me out of my stupor.

"Listen carefully. Laura has told you the truth. A spell has been cast. I can't help you to break the spell, but I can tell you where he was that fateful day. Can you hear me?"

My head buzzed with the clamor filling the dark around me. I heard what sounded like the crushing thud of waterfalls, the humming of discordant voices, and the strikingly harmonious appeal of a male version of Persephone's companions, and echoes of all.

Unable to speak, I forced myself to nod.

He continued, "When Jake was a young lad, he fell into an ancient Celtic cave … a burial cave. He wandered through the passageways, splashing in the stream of water that ran its course on the rocks below his feet, unaware of the phantasmal world surrounding him. Never would he have found his way out had we not intervened by luring him with sounds that moved him like a magnet toward an opening."

His breath entered my nostrils and I struggled to remain still. He continued, "After that first day, he returned often. He learned his way around the cave and seemed, by instinct, to explore its mysteries, but avoid peril. We watched and became used to his presence and, ultimately, protected him."

I found my voice and asked, "Then why the curse? Who or what did that?"

"Be patient and you will know all." He looked over his shoulder as if seeing something, shook his head, then continued, "The last day he appeared, he explored a rock shelter where he had never been before. It was there I saw him pick up a beryl stone. It was large and shone bright and clear. He dropped it into his pocket and ran from the cave."

"What does the stone have to do with the curse? Who would care?"

"It was not just a stone. It was a beryl stone."

The sinewy form stirred at my side, silent, his eyes still boring into mine.

"I don't understand."

"It was an emerald, highly prized by a powerful Celtic king. It had fallen from the master's shield to the floor of the rotunda and been swept by time toward the opening of the cave. This is where the boy found it."

"Why didn't you stop him?"

"Hmm. I have asked myself that from time to time. But the beryl had been here for centuries, and it seemed a little thing to sacrifice for the pleasure he brought us. You see, he had become a diversion among those of us who remain here."

"What do you mean, diversion?"

"An amusement."

"Then why did he end up with a curse?"

"It is forbidden to remove such objects from holy ancient grounds. And as fate would have it, he was found out."

The wraith rose and motioned me to follow him. At first I hesitated, but then realized if I didn't follow him, I would be sitting in the dark again as the light surrounding us began to move with him. As he stepped away from me, I was swallowed by a returning gloom. Wasting no time, I hurried off after him.

We hadn't taken more than a few steps when I glimpsed a strange sort of drawing on the rock walls. Crude elongated animals wrapped themselves in swirls of confusion. Eyes peered from etched patterns of various shapes. I stumbled and he cautioned me to watch my step. As I looked down at my feet, skeletal remains lay in haphazard fashion, as if knocked around by other stumblers in the dark.

I wanted to grab on to my guide, but something about the way he moved warned me that latching on to him might summon something more grisly than the safety I sought.

Within minutes, the light dimmed around us, and ahead I could see a ray of sun as it filtered down into an opening to the cave, large enough for my escape.

"This is the place the boy found the stone," he said as he turned to me and bent to the ground beneath him. "Here, in this crack, the beryl stone had fallen and hidden itself."

"And you just let him take it," I whispered, not questioning him, just not believing that any spirit, ancient or otherwise, would allow a mortal to trespass on ancient ceremonial ground and remove an artifact, especially one so precious. That is, assuming it was true.

"Yes. It's true." He gave me a knowing look. "Now he carries a curse, just as I do."

"You? Why?"

"For allowing him to pocket the stone, I will wander the caves of my forefathers for all time. Never to rest." He paused, then looked back over his shoulder to where I stood paralyzed in fear. "I know you have been to the cairns before." His gaze slid over me and I felt a soft wind stir around my face and lift the ends of my hair.

"But if you were down here, how do you know?"

"You remember the first day you were here? You danced and sang with the others." He stood to face me, his eyes burrowing into mine. As hard as I tried, I couldn't tear myself from the hypnotic hold he had on me. I stared at him in horror and disbelief.

"And the day you slept on the ground?"

Suddenly, his form seemed to spin, almost disappearing before it settled back on the ground. A sickening feeling washed over me. What was he saying? Had he been there the day I had fallen asleep under the trees and awakened with my spine and head pressed mercilessly against a hard surface, my legs and arms spread wide, my face streaked with tears and perspiration, and … I shoved the thought out of my mind.

Taking a deep breath, I asked, "And you said Laura told you I was coming?"

"Yes, but there are many lines of communication amongst the dead. And because you have won the favor of the others," he paused and added, "as well as with me, word has been passed down that only you have the power to break the spell that has been cast on Jake."

I looked at him in disbelief, then pulled myself up as if girding for a storm. "Tell me what I have to do."

"I can only tell you where to go."

For a moment, I was afraid he was going to tell me I was on my way to hell.

He smiled. "No. You will not go there."

As I listened to his instructions, my eyes closed, and, within moments, I was lying on the ground again with Shannon at my side.

I heard a whimper and looked up at her. She had placed my head on her lap as she stoked my hair.

"Shh, it's okay. Don't cry."

I looked up into her face, then sat up and threw my arms around her. After that, I didn't waste any time. "Okay, you're real. Now let's get out of here."

I fled out of fear of the shadows lurking among the swaying trees and of the vortex of madness encircling my head. I wanted to distance myself from it and whatever else was to come.

We both ran toward the exit, and though I had never before beaten Shannon in a foot race, I climbed into the truck and slammed and locked the door before her hand reached out to pull hers open.

She leaned into the cab. "Whew, what got hold of you? You'd think the devil himself were after you."

I wanted to scream at her. To tell her to get her butt in the truck and drive like hell. Instead, I took a deep breath and answered, "He was."

Chapter 28

On the way back to the farm, we rode in silence. Shannon tried to question me, but I told her I didn't want to talk. I had to think. To get the facts sorted out in my screwy head. I had the urge to write everything down in case it just flew out of my mind.

When we pulled in the drive, the lights were on. Jake was waiting up for us, but I wasn't ready to face him. I told Shannon to go on into the house … that I needed to be alone.

"What'll I tell him?"

I sat in the passenger seat next to her, unable to move. "Just tell him I went for a walk."

"I don't mean that. I mean what if he asks what we did?"

"Well, what did we do?"

I could hear her sigh and cluck her tongue. I knew she was frustrated with me. "We went to the cairn."

"And?"

I could feel the intensity in her words, "I know that I walked around the cairn while you lay on the ground crying. You want me to tell him that?"

"Just leave out the crying part. Say I fell asleep."

"Megan, tell me what's going on." Her hand reached out into the darkness, searching for my own. "Tell me what happened."

Taking her hand, I squeezed it gently. "Shannon, I don't expect you to believe me. I know I wouldn't believe what I just went through if I hadn't been there."

She didn't move. I knew she dreaded my answer as much as she wanted to hear it.

"There are some things I haven't told you. Things that happened at the cairn last summer. And I can't tell you now. Jake is bound to know we're here. He'll be wondering why we haven't come in."

"Just tell me what happened tonight."

It seemed senseless, but I said, "I talked with a spirit."

She jerked her hand out of my grasp. "Not again. Another séance?" She flung the door open and stood looking at me in disbelief. "I'll just tell him you fell asleep. I'll see you in the morning." With that, she slammed the door and walked away.

Watching her walk toward the house, I felt the "girl thing" rise up into my throat, fill up my eyes, and run down my cheeks. I wiped my sleeve across my face, climbed out of the truck, and walked out onto the meadow.

I could hear bagpipes filtering from the ancient windows, their reeds wafting gently to meet me. After listening a few moments, my heart stilled, and Burns's lyrics forced me to join in song. I whispered the words,

> Flow gently, sweet Afton,
> among thy green braes,
> Flow gently, I'll sing thee
> a song in thy praise;
> My Mary's asleep
> by thy murmuring stream,
> Flow gently, sweet Afton,
> disturb not her dream.

I sang his words over and over until the melody ended and the night was still. I looked through the window and could see Jake in his chair, his head bent forward. He wasn't sleeping. He was reading. I could see him look up from time to time as if listening. Then his head would nod down again to rejoin the page.

And Mary's still sleeping. Her dream's not disturbed. For over two hundred years. And mine? Not even two months. Maybe it was just weeks before it was disturbed. Kept pulling. Unraveling. Until only a scrap of it remained.

And that one piece sat in that chair, and I felt myself clinging for dear life. Yet something in me was afraid... of him... or of something I couldn't explain.

I need to go in. I've nothing to tell him ... that I can tell him. Just sit with him. He won't pry. He's not the kind.

I slipped off my shoes at the door and padded into the living room and up to his chair, tossing my jacket on the couch. I leaned over and removed the book from his lap and sank into him.

"You're cold," he muttered as he gathered me in.

"Hmm," I let out my breath and shoved my arms under his and around his chest, nuzzling into his warmth. "You miss me?"

"Truthfully?"

"Uh-huh."

"Then, yes. I missed you."

"Good."

"Shannon said you went for a walk."

I didn't want to talk about it. Just nodded my head. "Where is she?"

"Went up to bed. Do you want a drink?"

"No." I knew I'd start jabbering too much. I needed time and sleep.

His hands slipped inside the back edge of my shirt and moved along my sides, his fingers kneading deep into my flesh as his lips played lightly over my mouth. Tilting me backward, he eased my shirt over my head, then released my bra strap from my shoulder. His hand cupped my breast as his tongue traced a path to its center, rounding eagerly over its quest. I arched against him, relishing the tug of his lips.

Within moments, we slipped from the chair onto the rug in front of the fire, wrestling with our clothes. His hands stroked the inside of my knees, pushing them out, pulling them up. He buried his face into my belly, his strength bending over, pulling me close. Then he released me into the floor and stretched over me, hovering as his whispers brushed against my face. "Megan, you drive me crazy."

As he eased down to me, a flash of light stole into my consciousness, and I saw the white-haired spirit from the cairn whirl in front of me. I moaned as much in horror as in my frenzy. I wanted to scream for Jake to stop, but he moved against me with an intensity that drove me into my own delirium, and within moments, the phantasm faded and my own pleasure denied its appalling reality.

Minutes later, we lay warmed in the chill around us, the reflection of the flames from the fireplace dancing in his eyes, lighting the gold in his hair as it dangled boyishly across his forehead.

"Oh, my Megan, so beautiful, so good," he said as he gazed down at me.

I looked up at him and smiled weakly. I wanted to ask him how I could be good when I talked to spirits in graveyards—and even the one on his wall—when I saw phantoms swirl when we made love... when the ground opened below me... when I danced and sang and laughed with poltergeists and spooks... and even when words disappeared before my eyes and others inked their way across my page... by themselves. How could I be good?

Instead, I remained silent, smiled my "good" smile, picked up the small quilt lying over the arm of his chair, wrapped it around my waist, and urged him to bed. As we came up the stairs, we peered into the Shannon's darkened sanctuary. No movement or sound. We tiptoed into our room and shut the door, puzzled at our lapse of consideration for her presence.

As we slipped under the covers of the bed, the quilt I had wrapped around me tangled between my legs. I pulled it free and snuggled against it. Its musty fragrance filled my nostrils, causing a fit of sneezing. I'd have to wash it.

Chapter 29

Early the next morning, Shannon and I sat at the kitchen table discussing our previous day's adventure. "Morvreckleven Abbey," I said. "I know it's strange, but that's what he said."

"Morofwhichit?" Shannon's face screwed up.

"Morvreckleven Abbey," I repeated.

"Oh, Megan, you made that up. How in the world could you remember something like that?"

"He told me I wouldn't forget. And I didn't," I said, sitting back in my chair.

She curled her fingers into the handle of her coffee mug, raised it to her mouth, and sipped noisily. I could tell she was doing it on purpose. A way of mocking me. "Well, I have this much to say for you. You're persistent."

"I thought you were with me on this."

"I wouldn't miss it for the world, but you better come up with more than that Morvreckwhatchamacallit castle.'"

"Morvreckleven Abbey," I spit out. "Morvreckleven Abbey."

"Okay, Morvreckleven Abbey. I think I've got it. Now where is it? Maybe we could go there tomorrow. Get an early start."

I knew her eagerness was a façade, but I answered her anyway. "I don't think so."

"Because?"

"Because I don't know where it is. Or if it even exists."

She didn't even try to stifle her laugh. "Well, that fits right in with everything else," she stated flatly, shaking her head and looking away from me.

"Shannon, just bear with me. Either I'll figure this out or I'll just figure I'm… crazy.

She turned and walked to me, wrapping her arms around me and pulling me close. "Megan, I don't think you're crazy, maybe a little confused, but not crazy. I know you too well."

I pushed away from her. "That spirit thing… said I'd figure it out. He said it would come to me." I didn't add I'd seen the white-haired man again when I was lying in Jake's arms the night before. That *could* easily be my imagination.

Shannon's next words were hesitant, "Did he—it—say *how* it would come to you?"

"No, but I've thought about it and think that, just maybe, Laura will know something."

"When are you going to try to talk with her again?"

"Well, since Jake's going to be gone most of the day, I thought the two of us could try to talk to her together. We'd have plenty of time. And, if you hear her, then you just might change your attitude."

"That might do it." She picked up her cup, asking, "Do you want some more coffee?"

"No, I've already had enough stimulation." I pushed my chair back and walked to the door leading into the hall. "I'll go on up. Wait a few minutes, and then come on."

I turned and made my way to the stairs, dreading each step.

The bed lay mussed, the covers bunched into multicolored mounds of plaid, the pillows harboring pockets where Shannon's head had left little nests of slumber. I stepped out of my slippers, crawled up onto the disarray, and, kneeling at the headboard, lifted the frame holding Laura's yet-unstirring form.

I propped the portrait against the bedpost at the foot of the bed, sat cross-legged, and stared at her. Her hair fell heavily across her shoulders, lackluster, but dark and thick like her lashes. The ashen skin encircling her eyes gave way to a creamy complexion, spoiled immediately by the hollow of her cheeks.

This is the woman who once possessed my lover's attention—touched him, kissed him, made love to him. I reached out, my fingers stroking her painted breasts and wondered if his touch could make her—

"Megan, what are you doing?" Her words were sharp, penetrating my musing.

175

I practically jumped out of my skin. "Oh, Laura, I was just thinking about—"

"Never mind. It's not important." Her eyelids flitted like the wings of a moth. Rays of morning light broke away from morning clouds and streamed through the window upon her loveliness. "Did you go to the cairn?"

"Yes."

"And what did you learn?"

"I met a man, or something like a man. I thought at first he was old. His hair was white and long, but when he spoke and I looked more closely at him, he didn't seem old or young. It was strange."

"His name is Welzen. His spirit belongs to the cairns. So what did he tell you?"

"He said Jake came to the cairn when he was a boy. That he somehow got into the cave, and they, the spirits, had to show him the way out."

"But did he say anything about a spell?"

"Yes, he said Jake found a stone, what he called a beryl stone, and that he took it. He just put it into his pocket and left the cave."

"Oh, poor Jake, he didn't know that to remove so much as a grain of sand from sacred ground is taboo."

"And the spirit—Welzen—didn't stop him or see to it that he put it back. He just let Jake leave the cave. He said the spirits liked him, got kind of used to him."

"Did he say who cast the spell?"

"Yes. Some Celtic king. The stone had fallen from his shield and lay on the cave floor for hundreds of years."

"Thousands," Laura mouthed, the sound barely reaching my disbelieving ears.

"Thousands?"

"Yes, possibly... probably thousands. So what did Welzen tell you to do?"

I leaned against the headboard and shut my eyes. I didn't want to pursue this conversation until she agreed to talk to both Shannon and me. "Before we go any further, I want you to let Shannon come in so she can—"

"I know, so she can see that you're not crazy."

"Yes."

176

"That can't be, Megan. We can't risk it. If she were to tell anyone, there might not be any chance of saving Jake and you."

"But I need to know." I sat up, grabbing the sides of the frame, ready to smash it on the bedpost, when I heard tires crunching on the drive. I crawled from the bed and glanced out the window and saw Jake's truck, Old Molly, moving slowly up the drive. "What's he doing here?"

At the same time, Shannon called up the stairs, "Megan, Jake's here. He just drove up."

I replace the portrait, not even bothering to tell her I had already told Shannon about the stone and about Welzen and Morvreckleven Abbey. And I didn't bother to say good-bye to the *memento mori* that had taken shape in my world. I just ran down the stairs, through the hall and kitchen, and opened the door.

Jake looked surprised and laughed. "My goodness. Where are you going in such a hurry?"

"Nowhere. Just came to see you." I backed up to let him enter. "And what are you doing here? I thought you were going to be gone all day."

"We were, but Sally's nephew showed up late last night, and they decided he could take my place today."

Shannon walked into the kitchen, and as she filled her cup of coffee, she said, "Omigosh, I haven't seen Colin since we were both—I don't know—five or six, I guess."

"Well, he's going to be here a while. I told them to come over tonight. We'll cook those chops we ordered the other day," he said, glancing my way.

I was ecstatic and grabbed Jake, giving him a hug. "That's wonderful. Company at last." It had been a long time since we'd had guests. "The last time we had guests was when Shannon and her friends visited us in Edinburgh."

Shannon grimaced, saying, "Grief, don't remind me. We were such a rowdy group. It's a wonder you didn't throw us out."

"Hmm, I certainly was ready to throw out that young fellow that kept eyeing Megan," Jake said as he reached in the cabinet for a mug.

"You mean Keith?" I shook my head and added, "You didn't have anything to fear and you know it." Yet I knew Jake had struggled with a few pangs of jealousy, mainly because of the "young fellow's" youth.

Shannon broke in, "Okay, let's plan the menu. I think we ought to have a cake."

"I'll second that, but I'll leave it to the two of you," Jake said.

We stayed busy the remainder of the morning. Thoughts of the spell and Welzen and Morvreckleven Abbey flared at intervals, especially when Jake would grow quiet in the midst of the commotion. Once, he walked to the small window above the sink and stood unmoving, ignoring our prattle. I wondered if he thought of Laura, of her knack for gardening, bringing beauty into the world. I suppose I had a few pangs of jealousy myself.

Jake surprised me that evening when he brought out the china he kept hidden away in a chest in the dining room, swirl-rimmed pieces edged with pink and yellow roses on a white background, the same china I had seen the first day I met him. Sally, his brother's wife, had led us into the kitchen where the large, well-worn table was spread with antique cups and saucers ready for tea or coffee. Tiny egg and cucumber sandwiches, shortbread, and biscuits topped with sweetened clotted cream and strawberries offered up a feast for eyes and appetites. We had filled our plates, and then moved to the dining room where we gathered around the carved cherry table at which we were to dine tonight.

"The table's beautiful, Jake. It feels so grand, almost like ..." I couldn't continue. I didn't want to bring up Laura's mansion.

"Like what?" he said, grinning at me.

"Like a fairy tale and I'm a princess and you're a prince." I felt silly, childish, but I couldn't tell him the truth.

He looked down at me and wrapped me in his arms, saying, "You are my princess, and if you can think of me as your prince, then indeed I am. Now, my dear, your prince wants to sit by the fire to await our guests. Will you join me?" He extended his arm.

We walked arm in arm into the living room where warmth filled every corner. Shannon had settled on the couch with a cup of tea as she stared into the fire. I eased down next to her. She didn't seem aware we had invaded her space.

"Penny for your thoughts," Jake said to Shannon after he settled into his favorite chair across from us.

17

Startled, she looked up and then laughed. "Oh, sorry. I was just thinking about our trip to the cairn. I just hadn't realized how ... how much history was so close."

I could tell she hadn't meant to mention the cairn, at least not to Jake, but he just smiled at her and nodded, saying, "Megan will have to take you to some of her other haunts. She's taken a number of trips on her own since last summer. You two could go out again tomorrow if you like."

I didn't have any intention of going anywhere tomorrow. Shannon and I had too much to discuss, and I needed to talk to Laura again. And, fortunately, at that moment, the back door opened.

Hints of spice and sweet intermingled with the cool night air that evening as our guests trooped through the door. The kitchen table brimmed with fresh bread and butter, an assortment of cheeses, and a large three-layer chocolate cream cake topped in fresh, ripe strawberries. On the stove, yams, carrots, peas, and onions simmered while whiffs of roasted lamb intermingled with all. Introductions were made, and Jake poured wine. We led them to the warmth of the hearth.

I was embarrassed as I faced Jake's brother Hugh. I hadn't seen him since Jake and I were married three months earlier. He and his wife Sally had been our witnesses. Since then, I only had glimpses of Hugh from a distance as he and Jake worked together. And I hadn't even seen Sally since then.

Hugh was older than Jake, maybe ten or so years. I wasn't sure. Colin seemed to be my age. Hugh and Sally were proud of him and went on about his being a computer engineer and working in Cardiff. Obviously embarrassed, Colin managed to break in, saying he had decided on a visit because he had been sailing in the area for several days. He was testing his new boat, and when he docked so close to the old home place, he decided to rent a car and surprise his aunt and uncle.

As he stood next to Shannon, I could see the glint in his eyes. He liked her. Wherever she moved around the room as she talked to others, his gaze went with her, and it wasn't long before he had her cornered, away from the rest of us.

Shannon was the confident type, not one to be taken in by a smooth talker, and as he attempted to position his well-tuned body in front of her, she moved to his side, leaving him talking to the wall. He adjusted quickly, but I could tell he was put off by her evasive tactic. Even so, the two of them spent most of the evening deep in conversation, and as the evening ended, Colin offered to take us out on his boat. We set a date for the next week, the second week in April.

Later, as Jake and I lay in bed, I asked him why it had been so long since I had seen Hugh and Sally.

He said, "That bothers you?"

"Well, sort of. I've been here a very long time."

"You're right. I should have had them over sooner."

"They haven't even asked us over."

"Ah, Megan, you have to understand. They're quiet people. They don't interfere in others' lives. Besides, we've never been close. We work the farm. That's all."

"I just thought that maybe they resented me."

"Do they give you that impression?"

"No, but—"

"Then don't fret over it. All that matters is we're happy." He pulled the covers over our heads and began kissing my neck.

"Jake, tell me about your grandmother."

His kisses ceased and his head came up out of our cloister. "Now?"

"Yes, you've never told me much about her. What was she like?"

He took a deep breath and turned onto his back. "She was unbelievable."

"In what way?"

"In all ways."

"Give me an example."

"Ah, she could cook like no one else in the world. At least, I always thought so. To eat at her table was to feast. She didn't have just one meat, but two. And so many vegetables I couldn't fit them all on my plate. And desserts, two and three at a time. Now when I think of it, I can't imagine how she was able to do it. My grandfather didn't help her in the kitchen."

"Didn't you and Hugh live with her for a time?"

"Not the both of us. Just me. How'd you know that?"

"Sally mentioned it tonight."

He nodded. "Yes, my parents were going through a tough time. I begged them to let me stay with her rather than my aunt. She agreed and so I was off. She lived a little further north."

"Closer to the cairn?"

"Yes, much closer. So close I walked there nearly every day."

I was excited about what I was hearing. I had wondered how he had gotten to the cairn when his parents lived so far away. He had always been reluctant to talk about his childhood, so I knew better than to ask too many questions. He'd just clam up. I was hesitant to ask him, but I had to. "What did you do there? I guess you explored the cairns and the cave. You—"

"There was no cave," he cut in. "And why so many questions?"

"I don't know. I just want to know more about you and your family. The other night when I got into bed, I had the quilt your grandmother made you wrapped around me, and I could smell it. It had a—oh I don't know—a kind of fusty smell that clings to old things."

"And you thought of my grandmother?" He laughed.

"No, actually I thought of my own grandmother. Then I thought of yours. Because I had your quilt around me."

"I guess it would smell a bit. I doubt it was washed too often. Just a good shake from time to time."

"When did she make it?"

"While I was living with her. Now, my dear, let's get some sleep," Jake said as he rolled back onto his side and nudged me into him.

We were quiet for a few minutes. I wanted to question him about the cave and the stone, but figured he'd cut me off like he just had, so I asked, "Did you ever get into trouble with her?"

"Huh?" His voice was groggy.

"Trouble. You know. Did you ever come home late, or do anything else that upset her?"

"Of course, I did. I was a boy." He rolled over onto his back, then onto his side, away from me. "You ask too many questions. Go to sleep."

Obviously, detective work wasn't my forte. I couldn't just come out and ask him about the stone. The only other thing to do was look for it. Even if I found it, then what? And maybe it wasn't even here. Maybe he had thrown it away. Or maybe I could just find another one that looked like it and… do what? I'd have to talk with Shannon. Maybe she could think of something.

Chapter 30

As usual, Jake's side of the bed was empty in the morning. He'd left way before my head came off the pillow. I walked into Shannon's room. The covers gathered around her, outlining her slender form. A pillow pulled over her head only half disguised her creamy complexion. Tangles of red hair poured from the guise.

I crawled over the bed and slid under the covers next to her.

Her head shot up. "Oh, it's you."

"Who were you expecting? Maybe Colin," I teased.

"Yeah, right, I thought he'd just slip right in here this morning, especially after he passed up his chance last night."

"Oh, really?"

"No, but never mind. This conversation isn't even happening. We're not going there. Besides, he's a relative."

"Well, as I understand it, he's not a blood relative. He's Aunt Sally's brother's son."

She looked over at me and grinned, "You've given it more thought than I have. Maybe you're the one interested."

"Ha, when I have Jake? Why would I need a green, young thing like Colin? No, not at all. I just couldn't sleep last night. And I noticed how the two of you slipped off before dinner."

"We didn't *slip* off. We just moved away from all the family talk." She turned on her side to face me. "And what else were you thinking about last night? Did you talk to her?" she asked as she motioned to the picture hanging above us. "And by the way, I really would appreciate it if you would put *her* in another room, maybe in a closet downstairs. She gives me the willies."

"You're safe. She's not going to hurt you."

"And how do you know that?"

"Well, has any harm come to me?"

"It depends on what you think of as harm."

We were silent a moment, and then she continued, "Did you ask her about my being here when you talk to her?"

"Yes."

"And?"

"She didn't like the idea. She said we'd be risking too much."

Shannon sat up in bed. "What the hell? Risking what?" She stared up into Laura's picture and then turned away, leaning back. "I guess you didn't tell her you've filled me in on a lot of it."

"Shh, she'll hear you."

Shannon broke into a fit of laughter I soon joined. Thank goodness we were lying on the bed at the time, because I know we would've fallen on the floor and rolled in our nonsensical raucous hysteria if we hadn't.

As our frenzy eased, I realized that if Laura wasn't a figment of my imagination, then she'd be summoning the both of us soon. Or maybe she'd just scold me next time I talked to her. I didn't have to wait long. Neither did Shannon.

Laura's voice drifted from above, "Megan. Shannon. I need to talk to both of you."

Before I could move, Shannon shrieked, jumped from the bed, and ran out of the room, slamming the door behind her.

I figured Shannon would believe me now. I looked up at Laura, saying, "She'll be all right. I'll go get her."

When I opened the door, Shannon was standing with her back to the wall.

"Migod, Megan, she really does talk."

"I tried to tell you," I said, leading her back into the room that had, until a few minutes ago, encased a gale of laughter.

We stood at the foot of the bed, both of us looking up at a rather lively form of death as she opened her eyes and looked directly at Shannon. "I'm sorry you have been brought into this, Shannon, but now that you have, you must promise to keep what you know to yourself. Otherwise, you may lose a friend as well as a cousin."

I looked over at Shannon. She stood motionless, her gaze transfixed upon the nude form before us. "No problem. I won't breathe a word." And then, under her breath, "Besides, no one would believe me."

The form in the picture stirred, her arms folding in front of her. "Megan, we didn't finish our talk."

"I know. I'm sorry. I guess I just got upset. This whole thing is a bit overwhelming. And I wasn't exactly thrilled I'd have to go it alone."

"Maybe it's for the best that Shannon joins you. But I trust that your friend can control her emotions a bit more than she demonstrated a few minutes ago."

Shannon didn't say a word, so I elbowed her and gave her a look, like she better say something.

She flinched, grimaced at me, and then turned back to Laura. "I'm fine. I'll be fine."

"Good. I'm sure you will. Now, Megan, did Welzen tell you anything else about what happened?"

"It's all rather hazy. I don't remember much. Just the words Morvreckleven Abbey and another name, something like Magad or Mugabad—"

"Was it Muoghda?"

"It could have been. Actually, that sounds right," I said, nodding up at her.

"It's a name that is known, so it could very well be."

"But how do I find him?"

"Didn't Welzen tell you to go to Morvreckleven Abbey?"

"I don't really remember his telling me anything after he showed me where Jake found the stone. I vaguely remember being very tired, and the next thing I knew, I was lying on the ground at the cairn."

"She was crying," Shannon piped.

"Yes, well, I suppose she would be after such an experience," Laura said, sounding unamazed at Shannon's revelation.

I could feel myself bristle at her words. I guess she thought I was a big baby. I wanted to ask her what she meant, but her eyes locked with mine, and she continued, "Now, Megan, you woke up. And then what?"

Shannon interjected, "I heard her crying. I'd been wandering around. And, quite honestly, I was worried. She'd disappeared. Then, I heard her crying and found her under the trees."

I joined in, "And then we came back here."

"She wouldn't tell me anything," Shannon added.

"I just didn't feel up to it," I added. "But I thought about it on the drive back to the farm. That's when the names came to me. Well, Morvreckleven Abbey. I vaguely remember Welzen's telling me I would remember."

Laura suddenly squirmed, saying, "Get me down off this wall. I'm getting tired of staring down at the top of your heads."

We scrambled on the bed, lifted the frame, and set her against the bedpost. Shannon and I took our positions at the headboard.

"That's better. Now, has Jake said anything about the stone?"

I shook my head, "No. Never any mention of that, but I did learn he lived with his grandmother for a while. And she lived near the Celtic graveyard, the same one where Shannon and I went the other day. At least it could be the same one."

"Did he say anything about the cave?" Laura asked.

"Just that there wasn't one."

"Hmm, he's bound to remember. Just doesn't want to talk about it for some reason. We must have more."

Shannon nudged me, "Have you told her about the manuscript and 'Devouring Hush'?"

"No, what does it matter?"

Laura's voice was stern. "Everything matters. Tell me. What manuscript?"

I told her the whole thing. How I'd taken Jake's manuscript and run away, thinking that Jake might have plans to get rid of me. How the words he had written simply disappeared on the page. And how he'd said for me "not to worry about it."

Laura nodded. "Tell me about the manuscript."

"I saw him writing one night when I walked up behind him. When he saw me, he closed the manuscript and put it in his desk drawer and locked it up. Later, when I found the key, I took it."

"And did you see another one in the drawer?"

"Yes, one with your name on it. But I didn't take it. I assume he still has it."

"I know about the manuscript that had my name on it. I saw it, but never had a chance to get my hands on it."

"It would have been a waste of time. The words just disappear," I told her.

"Only sometimes," Laura said, looking as if she were slipping into a sleep. Then suddenly her head jerked up, and she added, "Of course I didn't know that then, so if I'd tried, I probably would have been looking at blank pages too."

"What do you mean only sometimes? Do they reappear?"

She nodded, "A strange phenomenon—"

Shannon broke in, "Like your poem, Megan."

"But it doesn't disappear. You read it."

"Well, maybe I'm not the wrong person. Maybe—"

Laura interrupted, "Tell me about the poem."

But I had left the room already, heading to the closet and my backpack. I returned with the notebook in hand, "See, it's still here. No disappearing act." I put it in front of Laura so she could read it.

When she finished, she looked up and said, "Hmm, well, it's not the best I've read. But not bad." I knew the teacher was coming out in her. She and Jake had both taught at the university.

"Well, I don't think I wrote it. It just wrote itself," I said, feeling rather defensive.

"There's a definite warning here. Assuming something or someone else did write it, it would be worth a try for you to make an attempt to do some more writing."

"What do you mean? I write all the time, but *I* do it, not something else."

Laura shook her head at me and looked over at Shannon, "So, Shannon, what do you think?"

"I think it would be worth a try. Maybe she should go back to the cairn and try to stir up whatever it was she messed with last time."

"Ohmigod, I don't want to go back there. What if Welzen pulls me under again? I really don't want to tangle with him again."

Ignoring my protest, Laura nodded, "I think it's a good idea. You might find something out about the Abbey and Muoghda."

"But I really don't think—"

Laura broke in, "Do you have a better suggestion?"

"Yes, yes, I do. You're the dead one—the spirit. Why don't you go? Why do I have to do it all?"

She looked straight at me and didn't bat an eye. "Because you're the only one who can break the spell. And you must. Now, put me back. I'm exhausted. I'll talk to you again when you have more information."

I turned to Shannon, reached out, and shoved her gently, nothing serious, just to let her know I wasn't pleased with her suggestion. "Thanks a lot."

"What?"

"You know darn well *what*."

And I stormed out of the room and down the stairs.

Chapter 31

Early the next morning, Shannon and I were heading north again. The morning was clear, and as I leaned against the window glass, the warmth from the sun eased the commotion in my head. I'd been awake most of the night trying to drum up excuses to wangle my way out of yet another trip to the cairn. I came up with none.

I wanted to talk to Jake and tell him everything. Part of me believed that if we just went away and never returned, everything would be all right. I couldn't help but wonder if such a thought was denial, especially since Shannon had entered into my unlikely supernatural realm. She had talked to Laura. So I guess there wasn't a smidgen of a possibility I'd dreamed the whole thing up. Or maybe I really was crazy. Part of me thought lunacy would have been an easier predicament to deal with than noisy portraits, primitive spells, and spirits, especially Welzen. I'd tried not to think about my encounter with him at the cairn. And then there was his untimely appearance in the midst of Jake's and my lovemaking. I hadn't allowed myself to dwell on those episodes, much less admit they might have actually happened. I wanted to believe they were a figment of my imagination or even a dream, but not the kind I'd want to come true. And there was the issue of my life. If what Laura said was true, then my days were numbered.

I looked over at Shannon. She gripped the wheel with both hands, staring straight ahead. She hadn't said a word since we left. Guess she now had her own fears to deal with.

"You okay?" I asked. I couldn't help but be concerned with her, especially since I had dragged her into this mess.

"As good as I think I'm going to get. What about you? Did you sleep last night?"

"No. You?"

"Maybe a little. On and off." She sighed heavily, and then asked, "Are you mad at me?"

"Should I be?"

"Well, I was the one to suggest you go back to the cairn."

"I guess I might be if you weren't here beside me. Besides, I'm sure Laura would have insisted one way or another."

We rode the rest of the way in silence, either too tired or too frightened to put our thoughts into words. From time to time, a rut in the road would jounce us from our seats, and we'd each utter an oath in surprise, but I knew the *damn*s and *shit*s were more of a release of fear of what lay up the road, rather than on the road.

When we pulled into the parking lot, I got out of the truck and went around to her side. As she rolled down the window, I reached inside and grabbed her hand. "Wish me luck."

"Are you sure you don't want me to go with you?" she asked.

"It's better this way. At least, I think it is."

"Yell out if you need me. I'll keep the window down so I can hear."

"Okay."

I entered the graveyard, and, as if heeding an inner urge, I bypassed the megaliths and walked beneath a grove of gnarled oaks. I remembered being awestricken by them on previous visits. I pulled my notebook from my backpack and sat on the litter of leaves encircling the boles. The air was still. I sat looking at the blank page before me, not knowing what to expect, if anything.

I shut my eyes, wanting to forget why I had come today. I wished Jake sat next to me. I'd certainly feel safer. And he could rub my shoulders. They were tense. My head hurt and I was tired—tired of chasing dreams and ghosts. I started writing:

I'm here waiting for some unseen thing to take ahold of my thoughts and help me find a way to break the spell that holds Jake and me in captivity. I wonder what's in store for us if I'm unable to figure this out. I must find the Celtic king and convince him to release Jake from the curse. I'm so scared. What if I don't find him? Then what? I'll die some horrible death and, Jake, oh, Jake, you'll go on, but you'll be unable to find happiness in love, watching as some unknown force destroys everyone you love—

Suddenly, the burled trunks and knotty boughs above me groaned as their canopies waved in slow motion in the still morning air. Decayed debris around me lifted from the ground, spinning in miniature twisters around my head.

They were here. I forced myself to continue writing.

Give me a clue!!! Where can I find the king that cast the spell on Jake? How do I get to him? And what if I find him? Oh, please, spirits, whatever you are—

Without warning, my pen skipped down the page, taking my hand with it and began:

O' woeful voice that clamors from the light
I warn of mists and hermit's matin hours
Of living dead that rot for time untold
That if to seek may risk a brave one's fate
O heed, my sweet, of distant lands enshrined in time
To cross o'er water'd lanes no laud may give
To columns damp and bleak and ivy strewn
Where sea-breakers wash against the spine
Eroding tribute to drum towers barbican
There, looms a lofty hall the west does face
With ancient barrel-vaulted floor below
And at its side a face of stone doth groan
Where faulty door hides shield and tomb and king
Who chides the living flesh, ere he goes.

Within seconds of seeing the last word ink across the page, my hand relaxed and the pen stilled. My heart raced, but not much faster than I did as I grabbed my bag and headed for the parking lot. I could see Shannon in the distance as she jumped from the truck and came toward me.

"What is it? What happened?" Her face was scrunched, eyes narrowed.

"Just get in the truck. Let's get out of here!" I hollered, waving my notebook in the air. All I would allow my mind to think was that the mission was over. Words had been written. Who or what did the writing, I didn't care. What did they mean? I didn't have a clue.

We sped out of the drive, the old truck's engine straining as we pulled onto the narrow road leading away from the cairn. I couldn't contain myself. "I got something. I got something. It's amazing. I was sitting there just writing down the thoughts in my head, and suddenly the pen took over and wrote another sonnet. I can't believe it. I just can't believe how the words seemed to have a life of their own."

I sat staring at the flared handwriting so different from my own. Shannon begged me to read it aloud.

"No, not now. We should go somewhere safe. Away from all of this," I said, staring out the window as the dreary landscape sped in the opposite direction.

"Where do you want me to go?" she asked.

I felt giddy and looked over at her and laughed maniacally. "Who cares? Anywhere. Just away from here. But I don't want to go back to the farm just now."

"Where's the café where you stopped before?"

"I don't know if we should go there."

"Why not? Weren't you there when the other poem came to you?"

"Yes, but how can that be safe? *It* was there, too."

"What was there?"

"Well, the thing that wrote the other poem."

"Megan, listen to yourself. Doesn't that sound a bit nuts? If any of the… the spirits are going to harm you, they would have already. Don't you think?"

"I don't know. Maybe. I guess so."

"Besides, I would imagine they can be anywhere they want to be."

"I suppose." I began to see her reasoning.

"Then let's go to the café. Where is it?"

"Just follow the road home. It's on the way."

Breakfast was still being served when we arrived. Neither of us felt like eating. We ordered coffee and pored over the poem.

After a time, Shannon shook her head, blowing air through her closed lips. "I don't know."

"What do you mean?"

"Well, what does it really tell us?"

"That we're going to have to go over the water. I get that much."

"Megan, we're surrounded by water. Which direction would you suggest we go? Besides, in this part of the world, remains of old buildings are everywhere."

"I haven't the slightest. But it's over the water. That's clear. It's not on the mainland. Somewhere that has an old castle or fortress. It speaks of towers and columns."

"Could be the abbey. Morvreckleven," she mused. "It warns of 'mists and hermit's matin hours.' I guess a monk or an abbot could be considered a hermit... tooling around."

I couldn't help but laugh. "Tooling around? What does that mean? What would he be doing tooling around?"

"I just mean *wandering* around the place. Don't get so picky."

"Okay, you're right. It could be the abbey," I said, tearing out a blank page from the notebook and placing it next to the poem. "Okay, so we know we're looking for an abbey, specifically one called Morvreckleven." I wrote the name slowly, struggling with its supposed spelling. "It's over the water, so just maybe it's on an island." I looked up at Shannon. "This place could be closer than we think. Just before you came, Jake took me to the Isle of Mull. He mentioned others."

"The question is which one."

I continued adding to my list. "There are towers, a lofty hall, and a faulty door."

"And behind it must be that king. What's his name?" she asked.

"Muoghda." *King Muoghda*, I wrote.

Shannon groaned, "And don't forget he 'chides the living flesh.'" The corners of her mouth told me she was struggling with her rational side as a groan began to metamorphose into laughter.

Sitting back in my chair, I stared at her. "You don't believe any of this, do you?"

"Well, you must admit, it's rather bizarre, certainly not a run-of-the-mill situation. Even if it is for real, I'm not sure we should pursue it any further. Not that it's just so unreal—but it could be dangerous." She took a deep breath and fell silent.

"Do you believe I wrote this poem?"

"I don't know what I believe right now."

I watched her as she stirred the cold remnants of her coffee. I knew what she was feeling. And she didn't have the benefit of the doubt that the poem was really the work of some force other than me.

I reached out and touched her gently on the arm, saying, "I know. But *I* don't have any choice, and I understand if you don't want to be a part of it anymore."

A faint huff came from her nose. "Well, I can't let you tackle this alone. I'm just having an adjustment problem, I guess." After sliding her coffee cup back, she glanced up at me. "Do you really believe there's a curse? I know some really weird things have happened to you, but just because Laura died, it doesn't mean you're going to. Besides, she was really sick. The doctors said so."

"I know. And I think about that. I often wonder if I shouldn't just ignore it all. Just try to get Jake to move to the States with me and then maybe it would just go away. But then I think about all that's happened and what keeps happening, and I know I can't pretend that none of it's real."

Shannon's reminder that I might suffer Laura's fate touched nerves that set me trembling inside. I felt my chest constrict as my heart skipped a beat. My breath caught and I leaned back and closed my eyes.

"Megan, I know it's hard and you don't want to think about it, but have you really felt any different since you met Jake?"

My head came up. "Yes, yes, I have. He has awakened something in me that I've never felt before. I can't explain it. All I have to do is look at him and an unbelievable flurry of desire and energy stirs within me."

"Ohmigod, you're beginning to make me jealous." She cleared her throat, screwed her lips at me, and said, "But what I really meant is do you feel different physically, other than sexually? You're not feeling ill, are you?"

"I'm fine... as far as I know. I felt fine until we left the farm and moved to Edinburgh so Jake could go back to the university. I was bored and got tired of wandering around in Laura's mansion. I wasn't writing. I felt listless. He was gone much of the day. All I wanted was to come back here."

"But you're feeling all right?" she insisted.

"Absolutely. Nothing unusual."

She smiled at me, saying, "Good. It seems country life is more to your liking."

"Yeah, I was glad when he decided to come back."

"What made him change his mind about teaching?"

"I don't know. He just came home one day saying he was selling the house, and we were moving back to the farm. Said it would be best for us."

"Maybe he sensed your unhappiness about being there."

"Maybe. And it has been better—except this winter. We didn't go anywhere."

"There're going to be a lot of winters."

"I know. That's why I just have to travel and write the rest of the year."

"But he doesn't want you to leave overnight. That doesn't give you much leeway. Unless he comes with you."

"No, unless I break the spell. I just know that has something to do with it."

"How?"

"I don't know. But I feel there's something more powerful than his love for me. Something beyond what I understand."

The thought of ancient spirits finagling their way into my life was surreal. But when I thought about it, I hadn't exactly avoided them.

It was nearly noon when we returned to the farm. A message from Colin blinked from the answering machine. He said he wanted to come over to discuss our boating adventure, but what he really wanted was to see Shannon. Of that I was sure.

Chapter 32

Later that night, Shannon opened the back door to Colin. He stood before her with his cocky grin and a mixed bouquet of snowdrops, daffodils, and bluebells. He was decked out in Donegal-tweed slacks, a crisp button-down shirt, and spit-shined loafers. The scent of the freshly cut flowers swept into the room as he stepped inside. With a flourish, he wrapped his arms around her and planted a fervid kiss on her unsuspecting lips. Her eyes opened wide in shock. As he released her from his arms, he whispered something into her ear. Jake and I stood within six feet of the two of them. Colin hadn't noticed. Jake winked at me and continued putting away the dishes, and I wrung out the soggy dishcloth, pretending to be unaware of our visitor's display.

Although she hadn't said a word, I knew Shannon had been swept away by the sight of him. I knew because I heard her giggle. And Shannon didn't giggle very often, except when she was really tickled. It must have been one of those times.

As I wiped the kitchen table, she buried her face in the fragrance of the bouquet, probably trying to steady herself. Though his back was to Jake and me, the clanking of the dishes and my movement must have caught his attention. His hands swept down her arms and he took a step back as he offered an overly enthusiastic hello. He was embarrassed, but in spite of himself, he was charming.

"Hey, we were beginning to think you weren't coming tonight," I said, pretending I hadn't witnessed his flamboyant entrance. Strange, how things change. Moments earlier, Shannon had said she kind of hoped he wouldn't show up. From the flush on her face, it appeared she had changed her mind.

Colin walked around the table, hugged me, and shook hands with Jake. He then handed me a warm loaf of apple bread he had somehow managed to juggle amid his cyclonic entrance. He said Sally sent it with her love.

After Jake put the last dinner dish inside the cabinet, he made coffee. I sliced the bread, and the four of us settled in the living room with our cups and plates full. Colin made himself at home on one end of the couch as Shannon curled up on the other. Jake settled in his usual place by the fire, and I joined him in the chair to his left.

For a few moments, we were all silent in a tasting and sipping frenzy. Jake and I usually reveled in our quietude and could sit for hours reading and staring into the fire, but Shannon was rarely at loss for words. After a few minutes, Colin cleared his throat, seemingly aware his arrival had created an awkward situation. At least it was awkward for Shannon. She hardly knew the young man, and he was dazzling her with flowers and passionate kisses, and all within twenty-four hours of setting eyes on her.

I looked over at Shannon. She had tucked the bouquet into the crook of her arm and was now sitting quietly fingering the delicate petals of a white snowdrop, her eyes inspecting it closely. Jake sat across from Colin with a grin on his face. Clearly, he was enjoying each second of tension ticking by.

Colin had come over to discuss the boat trip, but clearly, he had ulterior motives. To get the preliminaries over with, I said, "We're really excited about the trip. We appreciate you asking us."

"My pleasure. We'll have a good time. I've had the *Deirdre* for a short time, but I've been sailing with a good friend of mine for years. In fact, he sailed with me on this trip. He's staying with friends right now. We'll meet up with him this weekend.

He set his cup on the table. "So can you be ready early Saturday morning?" His gaze wandered from each of us.

Shannon offered a sweet humming sound and a nod.

I could have puked. "Sure. What time?" I asked, wanting to kick Jake for allowing himself the privilege of absolute silence.

"Is five too early?"

"Sounds fine. What can we bring? I could pack a basket," I offered.

197

"No, I'll take care of that. We'll be out for a couple of days, maybe three; that is, if it's okay with you. I figured we might as well take the time to really enjoy ourselves. The boat's fairly well stocked now. I'll just need to get a few things."

"Well, we'll be happy to bring whatever you need. How about wine? I think Jake has a closetful." I gave Jake my most evil of stares, hoping he'd join the conversation.

Colin looked over at Jake as he nodded his head in agreement, offering a simple "Absolutely. No problem."

Colin smiled self-consciously, glancing at Shannon, who sat unmoving, still nosing the flowers. "Well, that's settled," he said, slapping his knees with open hands. "I guess I'll go."

"No, you stay right there," I ordered. "Jake and I are going upstairs. We've had a busy day and I'm ready to hit the sack. You two visit awhile."

Colin started to rise. "Oh, stay seated. Jake can help me. I'm sure Shannon has a lot of questions about Saturday," I said as I began gathering up the cups and plates. Shannon looked up as I passed her, placing the bouquet to her face and sticking out her tongue.

Jake finally set himself in motion, and as I walked out of the room, he reached out to pat Colin on the back. "So good of you to come over. Looking forward to the weekend."

We cleaned and put away the dishes in silence. By then, I was ticked at both Jake and Shannon.

As I walked up the stairs and into the bedroom, I fought the urge to slam the door behind me, just to let Jake know how frustrated I felt. But he was right behind me, making it virtually impossible to do. I wouldn't have done it anyway. It was just the idea. He closed the door gently, slipped up behind me, and wrapped me up in his arms.

"Don't be angry. I just found the whole scene insanely delightful." He pulled me closer.

I turned around to face him. "And if I hadn't rescued us from your and Shannon's foolishness, we'd still be sitting and staring at each other."

"Maybe, but, ah, the amusement." He looked down at me. "Now, you said you were ready to hit the sack. Is that like hitting the hay? Or falling under the spell of Morpheus?"

His words reminded me of the task before me. I slipped out of his arms, walked to the chest of drawers, pulled out a pair of clean pajamas, the red ones with black and white coffee cups splayed in all directions, and began undressing. "Do you believe in spells?"

"Absolutely." He sat on the bed and pulled off his shoes, placing them side by side under the bed.

As I pulled my shirt over my head, my words became muffled. "Have you ever had one cast on you?"

His shoulders hunched over as he began unbuttoning his shirt. "Yes." He looked up at me with his wide, wonderful grin.

"Really? When?" I was foolish enough to think he thought I was serious.

"That day in the garden." He stood and unbuckled his belt. His pants slid down around his feet.

I laughed at the sight of him. So big. So strong. So handsome. So vulnerable. I had to resist the urge to shove him on the bed as he stood there trapped by his pants. Instead, I sloughed my jeans. "The day we met?"

"Yes, that morning in the garden." He stepped over his slacks, hooked a toe into them, and flipped them into the air where he caught them, then tossed them into the hamper. "You were like ice."

"And you were enchanted by that?" I asked as I slipped out of my bra and reached for my pajama top.

In boxers and socks, he strode across the room. My eyes were glued to his torso. Though pale from always being clad to protect from the Highland's harsh climate, his form was a fusion of rippling muscle and sinew. Each step he took resonated deep within me. Slowly, pleasurably, every inch of me turned into liquid.

My pajamas slipped from my hand, dropping to the floor.

"No, by *this*," he said, as he kissed my lips and traced the curve of my hips with his hands.

I had wanted to continue our conversation about spells, but suddenly he caught me up in his arms and transported me into a world riveted with his charms.

When I woke the next morning, Jake lay at my side, his fingers toying with a lock of my hair, his eyes perusing my face. As soon as he saw I was awake, he smiled and said, "The spell still lingers, even after all this time."

"What do you mean, all this time? It hasn't even been a year since we met."

He cupped my chin into the palm of his hand, "I just don't want it ever to be broken." He shut his eyes and pulled me against him. "Ever."

I lay unmoving, loving the feel of his warmth and wondering if he understood the full extent of his words.

Chapter 33

Saturday morning, a few minutes before five, we stood huddled in the kitchen, coffee cups in hand. Shannon sat on her duffle bag with a cup cradled between her palms. She blew across the top of the steaming liquid.

"It's too damn early to be up," she complained.

I gave the bag beneath her a gentle kick. "Well, you could have spoken up the other night when he was here. He asked, you know. Both you and Jake just sat there stone still."

Shannon moaned, "That was awful. I can't believe I was such an imbecile."

"You were moonstruck. And he *was* dashing." I gave her a playful shove. "He just waltzed in here and swept you off your feet. I can understand you somewhat. On the other hand, Jake here," I said as I leaned into him, "well, there's no excuse for him."

Jake kissed me on the top of my head, then took my cup from my hand, "He's here. Time to move."

Shannon rose from her resting place. "It's about time." She picked up her bag, rinsed out her cup, and we all walked out the back door. It wasn't displeasure at the hour that chafed her senses. It was Colin's absence.

Jake had already pulled the Range Rover into the drive. He had offered to take it since we couldn't all fit into the truck comfortably. I'd told Shannon she could sit on Colin's lap. She balked at the idea, but she wasn't fooling me. I saw her eyebrows arch in consideration.

Shannon and I slipped into the backseat, Jake eased behind the wheel, and Colin took his place in the passenger seat.

As we drove toward the coast, I buried myself in my journal, rereading all the notes recapping my experiences in the cairn. When I came to the entry about Welzen, my heart skipped a few beats and seemed to lodge in my throat. I knew it was fear, fear of the unexpected, fear of knowing I had no control once I ventured into the nether region. I yearned to tell Jake the whole story, to escape, to flee from Scotland and its magic. But I couldn't. If the spell were real, then bringing him into it would be disaster for both of us.

Having Shannon by my side was a blessing. Just knowing she believed I wasn't crazy gave me resolve. Finding Muoghda was critical. Welzen said I'd have to talk to him, since he was the one who placed the curse on Jake. The idea of a grown man, a Celtic king, no less, putting a curse on a little boy made me fume. I'd give him a piece of my mind; that is, if I ever found him. But if he was vindictive enough to place a spell on a young boy just because of a lousy stone, he probably wouldn't tolerate any interference from me, a mere mortal.

The *Deirdre* cut through calm waters by afternoon. Shannon and I sunned on deck, and Colin, his friend Kevin, and Jake manned the boat. All afternoon and into the evening, we sailed along the shoreline, crossing over the warrior road expanse only to circle an island from time to time.

Before dark, we moored at a marina on the mainland and gathered below for a festive evening of wine, shrimp, and fresh vegetables. Everyone seemed to talk at once and, at times, all meaning was lost amid the laughter. After the long day, the food, and the wine, I hadn't a clue as to what was being said. I just laughed and nodded when appropriate and thought of all Welzen had told me. Of Muoghda. Of Morvreckleven Abbey. Of the beryl stone that had caused such havoc in my life.

After sating our appetites, we wrapped up in blankets and sat on deck to view the stars and a full moon. Colin sat next to Shannon as he aimed an imaginary bow and arrow at a gull flying overhead, following its path into the gauzy expanse of the water's edge. They talked in whispers.

I sat nestled within Jake's open legs, leaning against his chest. Kevin had perched on the side of the boat across from Jake and me, a rope in his hands. I looked up at him. "Colin says you've been sailing for a number of years."

"For twelve years on my own. Before that, my dad used to take me out. So I guess you can say I've been sailing for about twenty years."

"I guess you know the area well."

"Fairly well."

"Do you ever stop at any of the islands?"

"Yeah." He was silent for a few seconds, then pointing across the horizon, he said, "Look out there. That one is deserted. I moored there last year for a few days. Nothing much there except silence and beauty."

"Are there any with castles or abbeys?"

"What's left of them." He looked over at me and smiled. "You like to explore, do you? I think we can find a few rustic sorts of dilapidated history for you."

I didn't want to be too obvious, but I couldn't take a chance of missing an opportunity that might get me one step closer in my search. I persisted, "Are there any near here?"

"Well, there's one that isn't far. I take it you'd like to see it."

"Oh, yes. I would. I'd love it."

Jake knew my love of adventure and how I longed to continue my travel writing, so I wasn't surprised when he added, "Megan is a writer. She explores the unusual and then tantalizes the world with her discoveries."

"I don't know about *tantalizing* them. I just enjoy seeking out rare pieces of enchantment and then sharing my awe with anyone who's interested."

Even in the dark, I could see Kevin's eyes widen in interest. "Okay, Megan, I'm your man. I can take you to dozens of islands along the mainland that should offer enough frozen history to keep you busy for a lifetime."

I had to bridle my impulses. My instinct was to throw my arms around him. To kiss his face over and over again, saying thank you, thank you, thank you, but I knew it would appear a bit extreme, although it would be totally appropriate since he had made an offer that might just save my life and free Jake from a love-ravishing spell.

Instead, I said, "Thank you, Kevin. You have no idea what that means to me." I looked up at Jake. "Isn't that wonderful? Now I can start writing again."

His legs and arms tightened around me. "It's good. It's good," he said as his chin nuzzled into my hair. "It's time you get back to your work."

"Yes, it is, isn't it?" I agreed as I squeezed his arms.

Deirdre lifted gently in time with the waves as they drifted toward the dock, rocking us gently, sedating our senses, allaying my fears for the time being.

Kevin was the first to leave topside and go below. Then Jake and I abandoned the new lovers as they lay hidden beneath a blanket sheltering them from the nip of the night's air.

Chapter 34

The fresh scent of apples filled my nostrils as I woke the next morning. When I opened my eyes, Jake was leaning over me, a piece of the fruit extending from his mouth to mine.

"Open," he ordered.

I opened my mouth and bit. The crispy tidbit released its sweet liquid, awakening my senses. "Hmm, good. More, more," I begged.

"Only if you get up. You've missed the sunrise, but there might be a tad left if you hurry." He pulled me up next to him. "Looks like you got your beauty sleep," he whispered as he kissed my face. "But enough of this. Get up, my luv, you're missing out." He stood and walked toward the door, looking back at me. "I'll meet you on deck."

I pulled on my jeans and sweatshirt, slipped on a pair of canvas shoes, and ran my fingers through my hair. "Enough primping," I told myself. Passing through the galley, I grabbed a handful of apple slices and made my way topside as I munched.

The angle of the early morning sun blinded me as I came up the stairs. As I turned away from the glare, an abundance of lush, green pastureland, edged by a series of rocky promontories and inlets, passed before me.

From above, I heard a voice call out, "This is for you, Megan."

I turned to face the words that had been yelled above the rush of the wind. "You wanted islands," Kevin yelled from the helm, Jake by his side. "You've got them. Take your pick." His long, blond hair moved in the wind, blowing away from his weathered face, revealing a strong jaw much like Jake's.

I smiled, waving and yelling, "Thank you! It's beautiful!" Overhead, dark-colored birds darted around a cliff. "What kind of birds are those?"

"Choughs," Jake replied. "You know, crows."

"I came all the way out here to see crows?" I laughed as I walked up to join them, grabbing Jake around the waist, hugging him.

Kevin looked at me and smiled, saying, "No, you came to find castles and abbeys, ruins of tombs, remnants of Celtic kings, of rotting warriors. And in about an hour, I'm going to turn you loose, so you better be ready. You'll have enough to write about to keep you busy for months."

"Ohmigod. Thank you," I squealed as I stepped in front of Jake and planted a kiss on Kevin's cheek. "Thank you so much. Now I better get down below and prepare. And get Shannon up so she can join me."

"You might want to leave them alone for now," Jake said. I could hear a hint of amusement in his voice. "They haven't come up yet. Their door has yet to be cracked."

"Well, I'll get my stuff." I turned and climbed back down the stairs and into the cabin, thinking it was about time. I'd known Shannon for years, and she'd never been smitten by anyone. Yeah, it was about time.

I packed my gear—camera, notebook, binoculars—and threw in a hat and rain jacket, just in case. As I passed Shannon's door, I could hear the springs on the cot groaning rhythmically, almost simultaneously with the muffled moans of my friend and her lover. This time I didn't hear any giggles, except the one escaping my own mouth. I guessed she had better things to do than traipse around the island with me.

Going topside, I plopped down on the side of the boat to watch our entry into a beautiful cove with a deserted, rocky beach. I could just imagine an ancient Celtic village tucked somewhere beyond its desolate shore, a place where warriors like Muoghda stormed the land. I could imagine his killing warriors of opposing tribes with his bare hands, destroying everything crossing his path or getting into his way— men, women, children, and animals—an evil but necessary method of becoming king in ancient times. And he probably added curses to the chaos—curses on women who shunned him, curses on men who threatened him, even curses on children who had the misfortune of crossing his path. And I was looking for him?

I shook myself out of my daydream as I heard footsteps come on deck. Shannon was radiant. Her tousled hair flew in the wind like beams of morning sun. Her cheeks were flushed, her lips scarlet and bruised in the morning light. Colin, jeans low on his narrow, sinewy waist, strode shirtless and barefoot behind her. They grinned in unison as their feet pattered on the deck.

"Hey, good morning, you two," I said, hoping there wasn't any egg on my face. But I could feel my cheeks burn. I looked away. Shannon didn't seem to notice as she perched next to me, extending her long bare legs out in front of her. She had on shorts while I huddled in my jacket.

"We overslept," she stated blandly.

"Yeah, we noticed," I said, giving her a knowing smile.

"I bet you did," she said, looking up at Colin. He tucked his fingers into his jean pockets and grinned. She shut her eyes and leaned back. When she opened them again, Colin had stepped from her view. Instead of his rippled body, she took in the lush fields rolling into the distance. "Oh, my. Where are we?" she asked, as though she'd just been dropped into wonderland.

"Kevin brought us here," I said, staring into the island's mystery.

"I know who brought us, girlfriend. What I want to know is where *are* we?"

"Kevin said we're off the southern shore of the mainland and that there are ruins all along the coast. I'm going ashore to see what I can find. Why don't you get changed and go with me?"

"Okey-dokey," she said as she stood and tiptoed across the cool deck. Just before she reached the stairs, she turned and sauntered seductively toward Colin. Her hands rubbed at her arms. "I'm cold. I'm going to change. Then I'm going ashore with Megan."

Colin nodded, pulled her hand to his lips, kissed her fingers, and said, "See ya."

She turned toward the stairs, and he moved toward the helm, his long, black hair a maelstrom of movement above his head. As he took the wheel from Kevin, he looked my way. Our eyes locked for a moment. I looked away, trying to focus on the island and Muoghda and Morvreckleven Abbey.

Shannon and I left the men fishing from the side of the boat. Jake had finally joined Kevin and Colin in stripping to the waist, revealing the pale skin of his torso, a contrast to the two younger men, who were tanned from their many days on the water. But Jake's physique proffered something the younger two didn't. Comfort. As I looked at him, I realized why I loved lying in his arms. Yes, I loved him, but it was more than that. His broad chest muscles curved downward at the center, just the right place for my head or lips. A nestling place. His hips were wide enough to hold my own, sturdy enough to tender succor. The corded muscles in his legs, well, they gave my own a sensual resting place, a place where each flex of his became a kneading of my own.

We climbed into a small rubber raft, paddled until we hit bottom, and then waded through the shallow water onto the sand. I followed Shannon up onto dry ground. We found a log, sat, and slipped on our socks and shoes. Then with our backpacks slung over our shoulders, we headed inland.

We walked about ten minutes before we came to the crest of a hill rising out of the water. Before us was a field of flowers and shrubs. We stopped to gaze across the multicolored glade before us.

"Oh, my, it's beautiful," Shannon sighed, hesitated a moment, and then trudged on.

I pulled my camera from my bag and began snapping pictures, all the while oohing and aahing and knowing I'd have to get a flower book so I could put a name with each of nature's scented wonders.

"These look like anemones," I said to no one. Shannon had moved on. "And I know these are snow drops." I leaned down to smell their honey scent and plucked a white beauty to tuck behind my ear.

Shannon disappeared from my sight. I walked on, stopping only when I found a new variety of blossom. And then I'd stop, consider the angle, the light, the shadows, and click away some more.

I followed the path Shannon created as she tramped through the tall grass, and before long I could see her waving at me from under a small stand of trees. They looked like sycamores, but I wasn't certain.

"Hurry, I think I've found something," she called. She watched as I stashed the camera back into my backpack. "Come on. Hurry up." She turned and disappeared into the shade.

I found her roaming through the ruins of a small structure. "It's probably just a house. Certainly not a castle or abbey," she said as I joined her.

I looked around at the crumbling walls. "No, it's certainly not. Besides, Kevin told me we'd have to walk up the edge of the island. That way," I said pointing to a distant cliff.

"Then I guess we better get started."

This time she waited for me, and we walked side by side. I kept waiting for her to say something about Colin, but she didn't—so unlike her. She usually shared everything. And I was feeling nosey, but what was I going to say? *Sleep okay last night? Are you having fun? I heard you making love. Could you keep it down?*

"You're awful quiet," she said. "Cat got your tongue?"

I looked at her. She was grinning and loving every minute she kept me in suspense. So like her. So much like Jake. "Well, are you going to tell me or not?"

"Tell you what?" she taunted. "Whether he's any good in bed or not?"

"No, but yes, now that you mention it. Is he?"

"He's great!" she screamed at the top of her lungs. "He's *magnifique!*" She pursed her lips and blew a kiss off her fingertips.

"And so you like him," I stated emphatically.

"Oh, yeah."

"I mean really like him. Better than you've ever liked anyone."

"Better than anyone, anytime, anywhere," she belted as she ran out in front of me. "Race you to the top." She took off, leaving me behind.

There was no way I could catch her, but there was no way I would straggle behind either. We'd had races before. She usually won, but that didn't keep me from playing the silly game.

In the distance, I could see the ruins of a castle, maybe the one Kevin had mentioned. I doubted it held any clues for me, but it was certainly material for an article.

As I neared the top of the cliff, I could see Shannon hanging out of a tower window, waving madly. "Help, help, I'm being held captive by a Celtic king, and he wields a really heavy iron mace, so be careful."

"You're an idiot," I yelled back, then entered a crumbling doorway.

We examined the ruins with excitement, searching for secret stairways, trapdoors, and even hermits. But there were none to be found. I sketched and took notes and pictures as Shannon led me from one remnant of a room to the next, pointing out, as she said, the finer details of Celtic life.

By the time we returned to the boat, the guys were gathered around a small table on deck where they had placed sandwich makings. Although disappointed I'd made no progress in my search for Muoghda, I was satisfied with the discovery of more ancient grounds but wondered how in the world I would keep track of nameless islands. My notes were of little use.

Chapter 35

For the next two days, we seemed to sail in circles. To stay oriented, I carried my notebook and attempted to draw a rough sketch of our path, taking notes and pictures of everything I saw, including puffins, shags, sea otters, and plant life. Although I scoured every island where we anchored, I had yet to find any clue or feel any vibe of a possible connection to the mystery I needed to unravel.

Sometimes, we docked on the livelier of islands to eat in local stone-built inns, but most of the time, we spent on board in awe of Scotland's Outer Hebrides and the glorious weather that followed us.

On our last day, we sailed early in the morning. Colin said he had one last surprise before heading back to port. As the sun began to lift off the horizon, we rounded the precipitous cliff of a small island. Facing us was a splendid opening with a gorgonlike mouth that bawled menacingly as the waves gently heaved. We sailed into what Colin called a basaltic cave.

As soon as the boat anchored, I jumped ship and set out well ahead of the others. I wanted to gain some distance between us to create private space for beckoning any stirring spirits. Progress was slow as I groped my way on the narrow ridge along the emerald water wending its way below the cave. I could hear Jake calling my name as they moved behind me. And I could hear Shannon assuring him that I would be all right. I wasn't so sure.

After some time, I came to two openings. I decided to enter the smaller of the two, hoping Jake and the others would choose the less constrained. No voices followed my progress, and within minutes, I was alone. Although the light within was quite dim, I could still see well enough to inch along the pink marblelike wall that gradually faded into the darkness ahead.

After groping my way for some time, I stopped and sat under the arching roof and attempted to sort through a mixture of sounds whirling from all directions. I could hear what sounded like lapping waves, a strange guttural humming, a hideous hissing, and a distant roaring, all converging on my senses like a well-planned cacophonous oceanic opus. After a time, the sounds intensified, becoming almost maniacal, or so it seemed to me. I huddled against the cold ledge, thinking the setting seemed just right to call forth some sort of phantasm, so I began to let myself be drawn into its frenzy.

In no time, I could feel myself slipping away. I floated. My body bobbed and wagged back and forth. I could hear a hum, a hum that wound through me, lifting me into a void.

And then I felt a cold wave of air pass over me, followed by a brush of warmth against my face, its touch flitting from cheek to cheek, eye to eye, and lip to lip—Eros-like kisses awakening a desire I knew well.

Suddenly I knew. My eyes flew open. Welzen was at my side.

"Not you!" I screamed at him as I sat upright and scrambled in the opposite direction.

"Whom did you expect?" he asked, unperturbed by my reaction. "The king of Scotland?"

"Well, actually, yes. At least, I was hoping for one."

"Which one might that be? Or need I ask?" His grin sent a shiver up my spine as he brushed back the pale hair hanging loosely around his shoulders. He sat eyeing me for a few moments before he said, "Come. Walk with me."

He extended his hand, but I feared his touch. Without pause, he turned and led me from the dankness of the cave into sunshine. I followed close behind until we reached the safety of the light. Underfoot, soft turf cushioned my steps as I tiptoed, stepping carefully to avoid crushing the tufts of buttercup blooms lining our path. Overhead, sea eagles hovered, as if waiting for some reward from the ground creatures pacing below them.

As we made our way up a hill, I could see the top of a stone cross rise out of the ground, and I wondered if this would be where Welzen would actually offer more information for my search. When we reached the cross, he stopped beneath it and turned to look at me. "Your king has been here."

"What do you mean?"

"He was here over a thousand years ago. He fought here. He died here."

"Here? On this island?"

"Yes. This is where he died."

"Is he buried here?"

"No. Not here."

I knew I couldn't be so lucky. "Then where?"

"Not far from here. But you will have to go there alone. No one else is to go with you."

"Not anyone?"

He turned away, and then started walking again. I followed but kept my distance until we came to the edge of a cliff overlooking the sea. The wind whipped his beard, hair, and tunic into a frenzy of white madness.

For a moment, I thought his papery-thin form would be swept over the precipice. I reached out to pull him away from danger, but his glance stopped me.

He pointed out into the emerald expanse to an island in the distance. "There. There's where you must go. Your king will be there."

"He's buried there?"

"Yes. In the abbey. Where I told you."

With that, he turned and began walking away from me.

"But what's the name of the island?" I yelled to his back. "I can't go there now. I have others with me. I'll have to come back later. How will I know where to come?"

He stopped and turned. "Do not wait too long."

Then he left me—just turned and walked away. I stood staring at his back, hoping he would stop and offer more. I watched until his form faded into the distance. *Where did he go?* Panic began to rise in my throat. I wanted to cry for help—for what I didn't know. There certainly wasn't anyone to hear. Then I saw the top of the cross and began walking toward it. From there, I followed the flush of buttercups lining the path to the cave.

Once back inside, I had only to follow it out to the opening, where I eventually saw the *Deirdre* rocking silently, the waves making a hushing sound against the tranquilizing blue, green, and pink rock lining the entrance. The sun was higher, and the magic of the morning distorted.

I climbed onboard with no thought of looking for the others. Finding the warmest spot on deck, I sat and waited, mulling over my conversation with Welzen. *I'd have to go alone. But he was there. The Celtic King was there.*

It wasn't long until I could hear the echo of voices as the rest of the crew retraced their steps and climbed on board. No one said a word although Shannon threw me a questioning look. Kevin tapped me on the head as he passed, and, if I wasn't mistaken, Jake growled. They all went below for a few minutes before they straggled back on deck one by one, settling in various positions as they relieved their weariness—everyone, that is, except Jake. He didn't resurface.

Shannon sat next to me. "Is he angry at me?" I asked her.

"I don't know if it's anger. I think he was beside himself with worry about you." She took a drink from her water bottle. "Where were you anyway? Jake and Kevin spent the entire time trekking through the cave looking for you. I was afraid they were going to end up vanishing the way you did."

"I wanted to be alone." I was sorry for what I'd put them through, especially Jake, but I knew I didn't have a choice.

"Well, you should have let us know before you took off like that."

"You're right. I should have. And I will from now on."

Colin stood and stretched, looking at Kevin. "You ready to head out?"

"Yeah," said Kevin, "Guess it's that time. You girls ready?"

"No," answered Shannon as she stood and pulled me to my feet. And to me she said, "You better go down and talk to him, girl. You owe him that."

I found Jake in the galley where he had been slicing bread, cheese, and a smoked ham. He glanced at me as I came down the stairs.

"You okay?" he asked as he reached for two red tomatoes.

"I'm fine. What about you?"

He didn't say anything, just nodded his head. He wouldn't cause a commotion. He was like that. He knew I'd get around to my side of the story sooner or later.

"I'm sorry, Jake. I wanted to be alone. You know how I am. I get more out of my surroundings when I'm not hemmed in by others."

He placed the knife he was using on the cabinet, scooped the tomatoes up with a spatula, and slid them onto a paper plate, placing it on the table. He then turned toward me, grabbed my arm, and pulled me close to him.

"I hope I'm not one of those who hem you in," he said in a low voice, a voice edged with passion. He looked down at me, not a trace of the usual good-natured grin on his lips. "I love you." He kissed me lightly. "I know it sounds silly, but I just don't want anything happening to you." He took a deep breath. I huddled against his warm chest. "What if you'd needed help and no one was there?" He hugged me closer. "I can't let anything happen to you."

"Nothing's going to happen to me," I whispered. And that's what he didn't understand. Unless I found some answers to the mystery surrounding him, his fears might come true.

We ate lunch and then prepared for the trip home. I joined Colin as he steered us away from the vaulted entrance of the cave, asking him if he would mind circling the island before we left. I told him I wanted to get some pictures from a distance. What I really wanted was a chance to get my bearings, as well as to learn what I could from Colin about the island's exact location. He showed me his map, and when I began sketching it, he said he'd give it to me when the trip was over.

As we moved alongside the basaltic columns and precipitous rocks forming the caves, the island Welzen had pointed out to me came into view. Using my zoom as I took pictures, I was able to detect what appeared to be a large building on the west side of the island. Maybe it was Morvreckleven. I asked Colin if he had heard the name before. He hadn't.

Chapter 36

The following week I spent with Jake, doing the kind of things we did when we first met, taking walks in the meadow, driving the countryside, picnicking on hillsides, and even making love under the stars. What I was really doing was procrastinating.

The roses had started blooming again, and, instead of a white rose, like the one he had placed behind my ear the first night we met, he cut dozens of scented red beauties. I'd be sitting in the garden reading or bathing, or even napping, and he'd come with an armful of flowers and lay them at my feet or scrunch a rose in his hand and drop the petals into the bathwater. It was a time of scrumptious indulgence.

One day, I rummaged through a stack of books piled at the back of the hall closet. I yearned to read Marlowe, Keats, and Shelley once again. I had fallen into a pensive mood and my senses were too sated to do much else. I didn't have the energy to write. As I pulled a small volume from the base of the stack, the others slipped to the floor. Restacking them, I noticed a small chest at the back right corner of the closet. It was a rustic, homemade little box, a bit lopsided, as if crafted by a child. I picked it up and fingered the small lock dangling from the rusted latch. The wood was rough and unevenly cut, and in the lower right corner, the words *For Gram, from Jake* were crudely etched. A warmth flooded over me. Jake must have made it for his grandmother. I set it back on the floor wondering what wonderful secrets it must hold about his young life.

Later I asked Jake about it. He said it was nothing special, just something he had made for his grandmother when he was a child. Before she died, she asked him to keep it to remember her by. As he talked about it, I sensed an embarrassment, maybe because he had left it at the bottom of the closet.

A few days later, I saw the box on the nightstand next to his side of the bed. He had placed a handmade doily underneath, probably some of his grandmother's handiwork. Jake didn't mention his childhood creation to me again, nor I to him, but I sensed there was more to that box than sentiment, something I didn't discover for a number of weeks.

Shannon's presence had been scarce since we returned from the boat trip. She and Colin had been making some explorations of their own. We saw her mornings only. She'd leave by noon, or, rather, the two of them would. Of course, they'd ask us to go with them, hiking or whatever, but we always declined.

Rarely did I hear her when she came in. I slept soundly, better than I had in months.

When Jake wasn't around, I thought of nothing but Welzen, what he had told me, and the trip I needed to make. I felt almost frantic, but when my head hit the pillow at night, I was out. Jake had noticed. He didn't disturb me once I went to sleep, something I tried to achieve before he had a chance to join me in bed.

One night, as I stopped to kiss him before climbing the stairs, he pulled me down into his lap, cradling me like a child.

"What's wrong, Megan? You seem so distant lately."

I snuggled into him, smelling the musky scent of his skin, "Nothing's wrong. I'm just very tired lately."

"Hmm, I've noticed. Don't feel up to a late-night chat, huh?" He rubbed his chin stubble against my cheek.

"I'm sorry. I'm just drained." I nestled deeper into him. "I don't know why I feel so tired all the time." I could feel his body tense under me.

"You're not ill, are you?" He pulled away from me, peering into my face.

"Oh, no, just worn ... probably from the trip. I just need some rest. I'll be okay."

"Promise me you'll let me send for the doctor if you haven't improved in the next few days."

"I promise," I whispered. I lay snuggled against him until I could feel myself drifting off, and when I woke, I could see Jake standing at my bedside with a tray in hand.

"Rise and shine, my lady," he said as he waited for me to come out of my sleep.

I sat up. "What time is it?"

"Almost noon. I thought I'd let you sleep until you woke on your own, but it's been almost fifteen hours. I thought you might starve before you woke up."

"Fifteen hours. I don't even remember coming up to bed." I looked up at him as he placed the tray of eggs, bacon, and toast across my lap. "You must have carried me."

"You were out. I couldn't very well sit there holding you all night," he said as he adjusted my tray.

"Oh, Jake, I'm sorry."

He knelt next to me. "No reason to be. I just want you to get well."

"I'm not sick, Jake; I'm just tired."

"Well, I called the doctor and he'll be here at two o'clock." He reached into my plate and picked up a crisp piece of bacon. "Now eat," he said as he poked an end into my mouth, then stood and walked toward the door. "I'm going to clean up my mess in the kitchen. When I come back, your plate better be clean."

"Yes, master," I said obediently, crunching away.

I wasn't keen on the idea of submitting to an examination, but, at the same time, even I was concerned with the way I was feeling. What I needed to do was get up from the bed and return to that island before it was too late. I had to find Morvreckleven Abbey and King Muoghda.

By the time I finished eating, I was determined. I'd talk with Laura again and figure out the best way to meet with a dead king. Yet the very thought of it sent chills up my spine. I also wanted to talk to Shannon. Even if I had to go alone, I wanted moral support.

I finished breakfast, showered, and straightened the bed before climbing back in. As I snuggled down, ready to nap again, I heard the back door slam and Shannon's lilting voice.

"Hey, anyone home?"

Jake didn't respond, so I assumed he had gone out to the barn to check on some pregnant ewes or some such task. I yelled out, "I'm up here."

Within seconds, she stood by the side of my bed. "What in the world are you doing in bed?" she asked, looking so full of life I wanted to hide in shame. Her cheeks were flushed, her lips rosy and smiling.

It took her only a second or two to take me in, and then she was sitting by my side, reaching out to me, her hand brushing against my forehead.

"Tell me you're not sick," she pleaded.

"I'm not sick—just tired." I looked out from the covers tucked under my chin. I could only imagine how pathetic I looked. I'd washed my hair, but had only meagerly combed at it before slipping on a clean gown and crawling back into bed.

"You are. You're sick. Ohmigod, the curse. We've got to do something."

"I know what I have to do. I just haven't felt like doing it. And I'm scared." I could feel tears well up. I wiped at them with the sheet.

She leaned down and hugged me. "Oh, Megan, I'm so sorry I haven't been here. I don't know what I was thinking."

I forced myself to laugh. "I know exactly what you were thinking."

"Yeah, well, he's gone back to the city."

"I'm sorry," I said, trying my best to sound sincere.

"No, it's for the best. He was killing me."

No sooner were the words out of her mouth than she was apologizing again and asking what she could do for me. I told her I wanted to take a nap before the doctor came. She asked where Jake was. I told her to check the barn. She slipped out of the room and shut the door, and I slipped into unconsciousness.

Chapter 37

My eyes opened to the stir around me. Jake, Shannon, and the doctor were hovering around my bed. After taking my vitals, Dr. McPherson asked the others to leave, and he set about poking and probing and asking questions. Nothing I had to say was cause for concern, and I knew he wouldn't find anything.

When he finished his examination, he left with instruction to get plenty of rest, but by then, I had laid out a plan in my head. I bid him good-bye, scrambled from the bed, dressed, and headed down the stairs just as Jake shut the door behind him.

"Good news," I said as I entered the kitchen. "I'm well. All it took was the good doctor's visit." I spread my arms out wide to show them I really was up and dressed.

Jake looked relieved, but I could see Shannon wasn't fooled. "Yeah, well, you're going to take it easy. I'm taking over around here until I'm satisfied you're really well."

"Sounds like a good plan," Jake joined in. He enveloped me in his arms. "What can I get you?"

"Not a thing. I'm fine."

"Well, if Shannon will keep you company, I have work to do."

"I'd love a walk," I said, looking at Shannon.

"Just what the doctor ordered," she replied.

Jake opened the door, and the three of us stepped out into the afternoon sunshine.

"So what's the plan?" Shannon asked as we stepped out onto the road leading away from the barn.

"I'm not really sure. I guess we need to figure out how to get back to that island."

"Which island?"

"I haven't told you, have I?"

She stopped walking and grabbed my arm. "Told me what?"

"Don't look at me like that. You're the one who's been preoccupied for the last week." Stonefaced, I stared at her, trying to make her feel guiltier than she had a need to be.

"Well, my source of stimulus has sailed away. So tell me."

We continued walking as I filled her in on my most recent experience with Welzen—how he had pointed out the island where I would find Muoghda's burial site.

When we returned to the house, I took out the map Colin had given me at the end of our trip around the islands. I had circled both the island we had explored and the one Welzen had pointed out to me. Then we pored over the poem my pen had so hastily written after my last visit to the cairn. I jotted down *columns... ivy-strewn... sea-breakers wash against spine... eroding towers... hall facing west... barrel-vaulted floor... face of stone doth groan... door hides king.*

"That's it. That's all I get from it, but it shouldn't be too hard to find once we get on the island," I said.

"Assuming we can even locate it again." She was silent for a moment, and then added wistfully, "You should have let me know sooner. I could have gotten Colin to take us back on his boat. I'm sure he would have."

"Well, it's best we don't drag him into this. Besides, there are ferry services. We'll just have to find out which one to take. For now, let's try to talk to Laura again. I need to tell her what I've learned."

Before I could even turn around, Shannon sprinted toward the house, challenging me to a race. I just stared after her, awed by her vitality. Within seconds, she slowed and began walking backward, staring at me. Suddenly she stopped and waited until I caught up with her. "Sorry. I forgot you're not feeling well," she offered. I placed my arm around her waist and we walked back to the house and up the stairs.

After removing the portrait from the wall and settling ourselves onto the bed, we stared expectantly into Laura's space.

"Why do you think she painted a self-portrait?" Shannon asked as her right index finger trailed delicately down the edge of the frame.

"Maybe she was making a statement. Maybe she wanted to let people know how she felt."

"You mean *naked*," Shannon jested, trying to stifle a giggle that sprang up as spontaneously as her response.

"You know, I think you're right. I think she meant to reveal herself—her vulnerability. She knew something strange was happening to her. It was more than the fact that she was dying... maybe w*hy* she was dying."

Shannon cocked her head, leaned down, and peered closely. "There's a certain helplessness about her posture." She sat upright. "Guess we'll never know... unless you ask her."

"Ask her what?" Laura asked, batting her lashes at us.

"Christ!" Shannon shrieked. "Don't do that. You scared me to death." She slapped her hand over her mouth and kind of wilted into herself.

I felt a slight qualm at discussing her portrait, especially after my earlier experience with her melting flesh. I quickly changed the subject. "I've seen Welzen again."

"Tell me about it," Laura said. Her eyes looked straight into mine. She really knew how to invade my space.

"Colin took us boating. On one of the islands where we stopped, I went exploring on my own and ran into Welzen."

"You didn't just run into him, believe me. He knew you were there and made a point of *running* into *you*," Laura said.

"At any rate," I continued, "he led me out of the cave and along the fringes of the island where he pointed out another island where he said I'd find the king's burial place."

"Then why haven't you gone there?"

Her question made me bristle. "Oh, it's easy for you to say—"

"Nothing's easy for me, Megan," Laura interrupted. "I just know that if you wait around, it's going to be too late to do anything. Don't you understand that? You don't have any choice. It's either go to the island or—" She didn't finish. She didn't have to. I knew what she meant.

"I'm sorry. I'm just tired," I said, embarrassed by my agitation.

Shannon placed her hand on my shoulder. "Jake sent for the doctor."

Laura's voice softened. "Have you seen him?"

"Yes."

"What did he say?"

"He said I'm fine. Just need to take it easy for a while."

"You don't have time for that," Laura shot back. "I want you to go to the island tomorrow. You must find out how to break the curse. Now put me back. Come see me when you get back."

Without hesitation, Shannon reached out, grabbed the frame by its sides, and hung it on the wall. She climbed off the bed, grabbed me by the hand, and pulled me out of my anesthetized state and down the stairs.

At the kitchen table with cups of tea, we began to make our plans. "We'll go tomorrow," Shannon said. "I'll find Jake and ask him if we can borrow the truck. Hopefully, he doesn't need it." Leaving her steaming cup on the table, she instructed me to rest and then slammed out the door. All I could think was *thank heaven for Shannon.* Without her, I wouldn't just crawl back into bed, I'd stay there.

Chapter 38

Titillating sensations woke me the next morning. Jake's breath was warm against my cheek. His lips played at my ear. My breath caught. I turned to meet his lips with mine, and, in an instant, he rolled onto me, his arousal welcome into my own. His movement was fluid, almost graceful. I moved with him eagerly though I realized each of his thrusts pushed me farther into my own termination. An inscrutable fascination clung to me like thorns under my skin. No pulling away. Nothing else mattered … except Jake.

Later, he playfully kissed my toes and slowly nibbled his way back to my mouth. As he settled his weight carefully against me, he said, "You are my life's blood. I couldn't live without you."

Dazed, not only from our lovemaking, but by his words, I buried my face into his chest. I wanted to tell him what was happening. That I really was his life's blood. That he was killing me. Or that a curse was killing me. But I couldn't tell him. I was incapable of resisting him, and with each lovemaking session, life was draining from me.

He pushed up on his elbows. "I really wish you wouldn't go out today. You know, the doctor did tell you to rest."

"I'll be fine. I promise I won't do anything strenuous. Just ride around. Walk a little. It'll do me good. I've been inside far too long. Now, you better let me up. I can hear Shannon moving around. We want to get an early start."

Jake gave me a peck on the cheek then flipped over and rolled off the bed. As he walked to the closet, my eyes stayed glued to his buttocks. His glutes moved up and down in cadence with his steps. I covered my head with the blanket.

After he went downstairs, I dressed and packed a small bag according to Shannon's instructions. "We just might spend a few nights away from here," she'd said. "You need to stay away from Jake as much as possible." She was right, I knew. As long as I was in his presence, I was captive to his will. And yet he was so innocent... so unknowing.

With Shannon at the wheel, we headed for the coast, enjoying the scenic drive through the highlands. When we arrived at the ferry landing, there were no crowds, and, in no time, we drove onboard into our allotted space. We were finally on our way.

"Man, I'm glad to be back out here, even if it is to chase a ghost," Shannon said as she stood looking out into the sparkling blue water. "It's so beautiful. I've never seen anything like it."

I took a deep breath of the cool, fresh air, "Yes, it is beautiful. And, in spite of it all, I'm glad we're here, even if I'm—" My voice trailed off. Shannon put her arm around my waist, and we stood silently for the remainder of the trip.

A stir of quaint village life met us as we drove along the pier on the southeastern side of the island, the island Welzen had pointed out to me. Small fishing boats moved in disarray along the wharf, children darted carelessly in and out of pedestrians, and local women, carrying small bundles, busied themselves with daily life.

After studying a local map, we began our trek to our first destination, a centuries-old monastery that lay crumbling on a rocky shore. Within a short time, we came to a fork in the road. A sign, directing to the left, offered a shady grove of trees.

Shannon slowed to a stop. "Let's stop for a few minutes and explore."

"Might as well. It's still early." I knew it was my inclination for procrastination prompting my reply. Maybe Shannon wasn't all that anxious to reach our destination either. At least, Welzen wouldn't be here. Or would he? I shuddered.

A cool breeze followed us as we wandered into a grove of trees. At our feet, a carpet of bluebells, sprung from the feathery blades of greenery, cushioned our steps. The startlingly brilliant blue petals drooped toward the earth, seeming to eavesdrop on some unseen disturbance.

225

"Aren't they lovely?" I said, taking out my camera. "Lie on the ground. Let me get a head shot of you among them."

"Ah, my big break. At last I've found my calling," she said as she eased down into the lush carpet at her feet.

Shannon posed for the next few minutes in seriousness, but gradually fell into silliness, capering like a nymph. At times, I lost sight of her as she darted around bushes, only to poke her head out from time to time, laughing impishly. Then she'd transform into her angelic form and pose again. Finally, exhausted from our wandering, I gave up trailing her and sat down on my backpack, waiting for her to return from her romp.

After a few minutes, I began calling her name. No answer. Not even an echo. I called again. All I could hear was the sound of leaves rustling in the wind. I got up, hefted my backpack, and walked in the direction she had gone. Eventually, I came to a clump of bushes that blocked the way. I yelled again. Surely she hadn't ventured into the snarls of thorny branches. I set my pack down and began jogging to the left, following the line of brush. Within a few minutes, my breath was coming in short gasps. I stopped and sat on the ground. *My god, where is she? Why is she doing this?* Deciding I'd go back to the truck and wait for her, I got up and made my way back to the point where I had dropped my backpack. I picked it up, looked around, and called again.

"Shannon, answer me," I yelled. And then I heard a cry, a thin, quivering sound rising from within the brush. I yelled again, and when a frail voice sounded, I recognized it as Shannon's. Something was wrong. I pulled a windbreaker from my backpack and put it on, hoping it would provide protection from the thorny clutches of the bramble. "Shannon, I'm coming," I yelled as I stepped in her direction.

As I forced my way through the thicket, I continued to call her name. Her pitiful responses spurred me forward, giving me both direction and impetus. The tangle of bramble slowed my movement as the thorns pricked at my hands, so I pulled the jacket's sleeve down until the elastic hooked over my fingers. This gave me some relief, although breaking away from the thorns' hold on my jacket kept me busy.

I hadn't taken fifteen steps when a gaping hole in the ground opened before me. I called her name again. Her answer rose from the ground like a shadow from the darkness. I opened my backpack and grabbed a small flashlight I hadn't used for months. I snapped it on. It worked. Taking a deep breath and sitting on the ground, I inched my way along the rocky precipice. At times, I'd lose my footing and small rocks would scatter out of my sight, down into the void below.

After a few minutes, I sat still and let the flashlight shine against the walls around me. They were close and solid. Farther below, the tunnel was littered with loose rock and debris. I couldn't see its end or any sign of Shannon. I called out again. No answer. For an instant, I wanted to turn around and make my way out, but I was sure I had heard her cries rise out of the earth. She had to be here, so I continued worming my way down into the dark.

I scooted along for several minutes when my feet suddenly met air and I began to slide on the small rocks toward the opening. Before I could cry out, I felt myself hurtling through biting cold air. I slammed on my back. My head jerked and I saw stars.

When my head cleared, I realized my backpack had broken my fall. I turned over on my side and slowly sat up. Miraculously, I was fine, just a bit sore and short of breath. My flashlight had slipped from my hand with the fall, but, within seconds, I saw a stream of light reflected against a rock wall. Scared to stand, I began to crawl, reaching out in front of me, grabbing hold of solid earth with each movement. I didn't want to meet air again. I hadn't gone but a few feet when I touched something very soft and human. Shannon.

"Shannon, it's me, it's Megan. Are you okay?" She didn't answer, but I could hear her whimpering breath. I ran my hands along her body, looking for broken bones. She seemed intact. I crawled the few feet to my flashlight and then back to her side.

Blood was matted on her forehead. Her cheeks were bruised. I sat stroking her hair and talking to her for some minutes before she looked up at me.

"Oh, Megan, I'm so glad to see you." She tried to sit up but winced and rolled back to the ground.

"Don't move until we figure out how badly you're hurt. I know you've hit your head. We need to keep you awake. No more going to sleep. Hear me?"

"I'll try," she said with little enthusiasm and none of the spirit usually lacing her words. "My shoulder hurts. I think I landed on it when I fell."

"Move your other arm. How is it?"

"Fine, I think."

"Your legs?"

She moved them slowly. "Fine, but I feel sore all over."

"I'm sure you are, but if we can get you up, we need to try to find a way out of here before this flashlight gives out."

"I'm all for that," she said, forcing a smile.

Working with her good shoulder, I helped her sit up, and then tied her injured arm to her side with a spare shirt from my backpack. "Just to keep you from moving it," I said as I tightened the knot.

We then began limping our way further into the tunnel.

After several minutes, I stopped. "Do you hear that?" I asked.

"Yeah, it sounds like water."

"We're near the coast, so there must be an opening ahead."

We quickened our pace and in a short time could see light flickering on the walls around us. "We're going to get out, Shannon. It's going to be okay."

Our progress was slow, but we made our way out of the cave and back to the truck, weary and relieved.

Within a short time, I pulled up in front of a quaint bed and breakfast. The proprietor helped me tuck Shannon in bed and then called the doctor. He arrived promptly, and after examining her, told us she would be fine, just a strained shoulder and some bruises, and she needed to rest a few days. As he walked out the door, he turned, saying, "My dear, I suggest ye stay away from caves. Ye're a lucky lass to come away unharmed." He put on his hat, tipped it, and walked out the door.

Shannon looked at me as if I were responsible for getting her into this mess, which I was. "You heard him. Stay away from caves if ye know what's good for ye." We both laughed but knew there was more truth in the words than even the good doctor knew.

For the remainder of the day, Shannon rested. Her shoulder ached, and she had a bit of a headache. I stayed at her side even though I was anxious to scout out the abbey.

The next morning I was up and dressed by the time Shannon awoke. She had slept well in the night, so I figured she'd be all right, although she'd suffer from a sore shoulder for some time.

She opened her eyes as I sat by the bed putting on my shoes. "Where do you think you're going?" she asked, slowly sitting up.

"I'm going out… by myself. I've got to find that abbey today. I called Jake last night, and he expects us home by tomorrow. He wanted us to leave today, but I told him you weren't feeling well—that we needed another day. I didn't tell him what really happened."

"Well, I'm going with you," she said, and then winced as she leaned on her arm.

"No way. You're staying right here. You need to let your shoulder mend, and you can't do it traipsing around with me. I can do it on my own. It's better that way, anyway. Laura said so."

"I don't care what she said. You can't do this alone." She tossed the covers with her good arm, and then groaned again, her brow knitted in pain. "I just wish I could use this arm."

"And just how much help will you be?" I eased her back onto the pillow. "Besides, I can do this by myself. I must." I was trying my best to sound brave, but the last thing I wanted to do was chase the angry dead by myself.

"Promise me you'll be careful," she said, grabbing my hand and squeezing it.

"Promise. No heroics." Picking up my backpack, I walked to the door. "By the way, you never explained why you went into that thicket. What was that all about?"

"Just curious. Then when I saw the opening, I thought it might have something to offer."

"Like what?"

"Like some sort of clue. Like where they might've buried your king." Shannon laughed. We both knew how crazy it sounded.

I shook my head at her and smiled. "Now, you rest. Breakfast will be brought to you. I'll be back before you know it."

"Be careful," she said with a note of concern in her voice.

"Say a prayer for me."

Chapter 39

I made my way to the abbey without being sidetracked this time. The map's directions were clear, and there on the north coast of the island, the ancient ruins rose before me. I caught my first glimpse of a crumbling tower as I rounded a winding curve that traced the emerald coastline.

I pulled onto the shoulder. There was no trace of a road leading in. I'd have to walk. As I switched off the engine, a jolt of fear stuck in my throat. My heart began to pound. I felt weak, scared, scared of my footprints tracing a path to this supposedly deserted place and not coming back. Perhaps Shannon was right. I couldn't do this by myself. But if I didn't, I'd be staring death in the face. And I'd already felt its sting in the last few weeks.

My hand trembled as I grasped the door handle and willed myself out of the truck, stepping out onto the rough terrain, slinging my backpack over my shoulder. Though the morning was cool, the air around me felt thick and humid, probably a result of my nervousness.

I trudged through the cotton-tufted grass bobbing at my feet. At first, the walk was difficult, but as I closed in on the abbey, the land lay relatively smooth, pocked from time to time with shallow holes and a scattering of black Herculean boulders rising from the ground like warders against attack.

I moved slowly, uncertain of what I'd find—if anything. One thing was certain. If I didn't go through with this, I might walk away, but not for long. I stopped and pulled my notebook from my pack, scanning the lines of the sonnet that spoke of "the distant land enshrined in time."

I walked around to the west side of the structure to see the ivy-strewn columns, leaning heavily toward the sea. Between them, a weatherbeaten door lay prostrate and rotting before the entrance. With caution, I stepped across it and entered the abbey.

The floor, splotched with inky, gaping holes, creaked beneath my wary steps. I picked my way around the edges of what appeared to be the main hall. Then, instead of entering one of the many passageways beckoning along my path, I stood in the sunlight pouring from a window, hugging my jacket to me. The air was mild, yet a chill swept over me. I hunched my shoulders and shrank as far into myself as possible. I didn't want to move. Even though I was afraid of finding some dreadful thing, I was even more frightened I wouldn't find anything. Then what? What would I do? Where would I look for the godforsaken king who had cursed Jake—and me?

The entire situation was absurd. And if it wasn't so tragic, it would be rather comic. How could I have talked to ghosts, been visited by ghosts? And the talking portrait. Was I dreaming? Was Shannon in this dream with me? And the vanishing words and the poems that wrote themselves. What next? What the heck was next?

I closed my eyes and tried to pull away from my thoughts and out of my panic, and then walked to an open window and leaned out into the space below. As I looked down, restless breakers washed against the wall below. Instantly, I knew they were the "sea-breakers washing against the spine."

"Well, it's time to gird my loins," I said to no one, wanting to laugh but not having the stomach to do something so frivolous.

I decided I didn't want to risk climbing any stairs. They were rickety and avoiding accidents was high on my list of priorities. Besides, my assumption was that a Celtic king would be down in a crypt or something of the sort. Within minutes, I located steep stairs carved from the earth, winding down within a wall. I began my descent.

When I reached the bottom step, a door barred my way. I leaned my weight into it. It groaned, making an almost human sound. Without hesitation, I spun around and took a few panic-stricken strides up the stairs, and then collapsed against their edges, silently laughing at myself. I couldn't believe I'd run from an ancient, groaning door. Scared as I was, it wasn't the time to run. Not now, not when I might be so close. I wanted to be brave and laugh out loud, but alerting anything lurking on the other side of the door didn't seem wise. Instead, I clamped my mouth shut and bit my lip. Taking a deep breath, I forced myself to stand and walk back down the steps. I stood there, trying to think of any excuse to turn the other way.

With an effort, I placed an open hand against the splintered surface of my monster door and gave a halfhearted push. It budged a few inches. I pushed again and, surprisingly, it swung open. Inside, the air was dank. The dismal light from the stairway offered a dim window into the sinister gloom surrounding me. I stood motionless, hoping my eyes would adjust. Within seconds, I remembered the flashlight and pulled it from my bag.

The room was small, with earthen walls and floor. Even with my puny light, I could see it was empty. No crypt. No king. For a moment, I felt relief. I could just leave the godforsaken hole. But then what? The thought galvanized me into motion. I walked around the room, moving my hands up and down the walls, searching for a hidden door, one hiding the secret that would hopefully free me from a certain death, and free Jake of a curse potent as poison. Even so, if Welzen hadn't assured me the king was there, I would have turned around on the spot.

Finding nothing, I walked toward the stairs. To my astonishment, I suddenly flew across the room, striking my head against the hardened wall. As my senses cleared and my racing heart began to slow, I realized my shoe had caught on something. I crawled a few feet, retrieving my flashlight, then continued crawling, swiping one hand across the earth in front of me until I struck something hard. Within seconds, I uncovered a type of door rising out of the earth, then disappearing a few feet away.

I flashed a narrow stream of light across its surface. A face peered out at me. I screamed and fell back on my haunches. If it hadn't been so dark, I'd have gotten up and run. After a few seconds, I realized it wasn't anything more than a face carved into stone, not some evil-tempered fiend. Maybe this was the barrel-vaulted door mentioned in the poem. I leaned forward, slipped my hand under a corner edge, and heaved; like an anguished warrior, weary from war-torn strife, it groaned bitterly as I pulled with all my might.

The few strands of light accompanying me down the narrow stairs suddenly vanished into the abyss at my feet, and, at the same time, my flashlight began to flicker. I ran the struggling beam of light along the edges of the door, looking for a way down. At one side was a decrepit wooden ladder. Not wanting to waste time, I sat on the edge of the doorframe and eased onto the rickety rungs. A strange sense of déjà vu swept over me as the slats under my feet began to make crackling sounds. The sinking feeling of losing control swept over me, just as it had the day before when I'd gone sliding down the rocks into the cave, almost on top of Shannon—and I fell, once again, without wings.

No sooner had the fear of my tumbling to an untimely death entered my head than I felt my foot jerk beneath me. A rung had given way. As I opened my mouth and screamed, my flashlight slipped away and I felt myself being pulled down by my own weight.

I hit bottom almost as fast as I'd begun my fall. In fact, when I pulled myself out of my puddle of slump, I realized that, had the rung held, I could have stepped down onto the floor with only mild exertion. It's strange how truth can be shadowed by darkness.

Crawling once again on all fours, I explored the space around me. At first I found nothing more than I'd discovered on the floor above, just an empty shell of a room, not even a door. Frustrated, I sat back on my haunches. As I did, I realized there was a wall of sorts behind me, its surface rock hard, certainly harder than the dirt-packed walls I had explored earlier. I reached around to touch stones piled one on the other about waist high. I stood and inched along its side, estimating its length to be about six feet in one direction and three across—about the length of a man, a dead man.

Running my hands over its surface, I searched for an opening, a latch, anything that might provide a look inside. I pushed and pulled on corner stones and shoved my weight against the entire length and width of the structure. If it opened, then maybe I could get a look at the one who had ruined my life. Nothing budged. Exhausted, I sat on its edge. What next? My fingers throbbed and were wet. I put one in my mouth and could taste blood. My head hurt. It felt as though someone had me around the neck, choking me. I wanted to cry, but knew it would be a waste of time and energy. Instead, I started talking to the thing supposedly tucked into the tomb, the thing I hoped was a dead Celtic king.

At first, I whispered. "Okay, here I am. What am I supposed to do? Please, please, please, let me know how to break the curse. Jake didn't mean to take something belonging to you. How did he know?" Tears trickled down my cheeks as my body sagged, my head pressing against the rough stone. I doubled my fist and began pounding the tomb, railing like a mad woman, "He didn't know. He was just a boy. He picked up a stone and put it in his pocket. That's all."

I don't know what I expected, if anything. After all, the man was dead, and unless he came to me as a spirit, as Welzen had done, little was to be accomplished by ranting at a stack of lifeless stone while battering my hands. I pulled my jacket around me, and in spite of the cold and dampness, I stretched out onto the tomb. "How can we make it up to you?" I continued, hoping to stumble on a word, a phrase, an idea that would wake him from the dead—if, indeed, he was lying in the crypt and "all ears." I laughed hysterically. This time, I really wanted him to wake. "Can we bring you diamonds? Pearls?" I named off a list of precious stones, even added in a sizeable amount of money before I realized he certainly wouldn't have any use for any of it.

After what seemed an eternity, my eyes closed. I curled onto my side. The desire for sleep swept over me. I knew I shouldn't, but I couldn't help it.

Gradually, I became aware of movement around me. My eyes flew open. All was darkness—nefarious, heinous darkness. I squeezed my eyes shut, then sat up and stared into the void, turning my head back and forth, trying vainly to make out a form, anything on which to focus. Flailing my arms in all directions, I moved from the tomb and began to inch my way across the dusty earth below me.

"Who's there?" I called out. "Who's there? I know you're there, whatever you are." Strangely, in spite of the fact he gave me the heebie jeebies, I yearned for Welzen to appear in all his phantasmal glory. He could get me out of here, even if he didn't offer an answer to my dilemma.

Within seconds, a faint humming sounded behind my head, and little puffs of light began dancing wildly, careening around the room, whirling round and round until they formed a smoky ring along the ceiling. Suddenly the circle snapped, and one end began backing up into itself until a glob of sorts transformed into a ghostly shape.

At first, I thought my wish had been answered, but it wasn't. Instead of Welzen with his long, white beard and harsh glare, a womanish form swirled around the room once, and then settled softly a few feet in front of me, bobbing slightly as it took shape. I stood silently, anxious, but thrilled it was female. I wouldn't have Welzen to contend with.

I waited for it to speak. If it was anything like Welzen, it would have a mind of its own, and my asking questions or making demands might send it into a rampage. I didn't have to wait long.

Chapter 40

The truck skidded into the drive. Shannon was sitting on the porch and limped out to meet me. I slammed the door of the truck and wrapped my arms around her. "I know how to break the spell. I found out. You'll never believe." I could barely contain myself. I squeezed her. She grimaced in pain. "Oh, sorry," I added, "but you'll never believe what happened."

"Well, come on. You can tell me over lunch, but I think you better go in and clean up. You're a sight."

"Yeah, I suppose I am."

I vaulted up the steps and into our room. Walking across the room, I caught my reflection in the dresser mirror. "Good lord all mighty," I said as I began stripping off my clothes.

After my shower, I found Shannon on the porch examining a table laden with sandwiches, fresh fruit, and lemonade. "Compliments of the house," she said. We filled our plates and walked back out onto the grounds to a weathered picnic table under low-hanging tree branches.

"I found the abbey. Morvreckleven," I said, sitting down on the bench across from her.

"And the king?"

"Well, yes and no. It was just like the poem said it would be. I found the barrel-vaulted door the poem described. And there really was a face of stone on it. And when I opened it, it actually groaned. At least it sounded like a groan." I drank all of my lemonade, and then took a bite of the sandwich.

Shannon sat patiently, her eyes intent on me. I swallowed and continued, "Thank goodness I had my flashlight. It was pitch black. I had to climb down a wooden ladder. Some of the rungs were missing, and one of them broke. I fell, but I didn't hurt myself. And then I found his tomb."

"How do you know it was his?" she said, the ever-present hint of doubt still lingering.

"Let me finish. At the time, I didn't know it was his. I just knew it was something like a coffin, only I don't think anyone could pick it up or move it. It was more of a pile of stones."

"Could you open it?"

"I'm getting to that." I finished off my sandwich and began eating some grapes. "I tried to find a way to open it but couldn't. It was too dark, and I couldn't see, and I didn't have anything to pry it open. And then my flashlight went out—"

"What happened? Just tell me."

"I'm trying to. Just listen without interrupting," I said, realizing we were both a bit edgy. I reached out and laid my hand on her arm as I continued. "I sat on the tomb scared out of my wits. I couldn't open it, but I knew I had to do something. I couldn't leave. And I doubted the ladder would hold me anyway. At that point I didn't know if I'd ever get out." I stood up and climbed over the bench. "Want anything?"

"Please, some more lemonade." Shannon handed me her glass, and I walked back to the porch, wondering if she'd believe the next part of my story. But I guess it wouldn't matter at this point.

As I sat back down across from her, I began again. "I met another spirit." I looked over at her and waited for a response.

"Another? You mean it wasn't Welzen?"

"No, not Welzen. Something quite different. Something female. It was like smoke, all wispy and cloudlike." Neither of us said anything for a few moments. Shannon just smiled and nodded. I continued, "She told me the stone had to be returned and then maybe, just maybe, the King would release Jake from the curse. When I told her I didn't know where the stone was and suggested I bring something in its place instead, she just looked at me and shook her head. Then she walked to the tomb and pointed to a depression in its surface, saying, "Place it there." Then she disappeared."

"A depression? What do you mean?"

I made a circle with my thumb and index finger. "It was about this size. Bigger than a quarter—almost as big as a half dollar.

Shannon closed her eyes and took a deep breath. When she looked over at me, she gave me a look I couldn't read. I didn't know if she was still having a hard time believing me or just sick and tired of the whole thing. When she spoke, I knew I wasn't wrong.

"Now, *all* we have to do is find the stone." Sarcasm punctuated every word.

"Yeah. That's all."

She reached across the table, grabbing my hand. Her expression changed. "Where do we start?"

"At the farm." Truth was, I didn't have any idea where to start, but just maybe Jake had it hidden somewhere around the house. I thought of the wooden box I'd found in his closet. "I have an idea."

Without another word, we made our way into the inn, packed our bags, and headed toward the ferry landing.

We were exhausted when we finally drove onto the road leading to the house. After dumping our belongings on the kitchen table, we began our search. Jake was nowhere in sight. Searching with him around would be impossible. Laura had told me more than once he was not to have a part in breaking the spell. Didn't make sense to me. But neither did anything else.

While Shannon was combing the living room, I ran upstairs to our bedroom. The box Jake had made as a child still set on the nightstand. I picked it up, hoping he had unlocked it. No such luck. The tiny lock still hung on the rusty latch. He probably didn't even have the key anymore. If he did, more than likely he kept it in a logical place, in a dresser drawer or his desk. I replaced the box and then stepped across the narrow space between the bed and his chest of drawers. Pulling open the first drawer, I couldn't help but feel like an intruder. I could only imagine what Jake would think if he walked in on me. Not that I hadn't been in his drawers before. I laughed out loud, and then checked out the remaining three. Nothing.

I searched a few other possible hiding places in the room, and then went back down to see Shannon removing cushions from the couch. "Find anything of interest?" I asked as I sat at the desk.

"You wouldn't believe what I've found. I've uncovered a fine collection of artifacts—a few shillings for your collector's album. But, of more worth, I've collected exactly twenty-three Euros. I think I'll just keep it close to me. Finders keepers, right?" She looked over at me. Her face was flushed, and she was breathing hard from the effort of working with one good arm. "I'll leave no rock unturned... or pillow either," she cracked. I was glad she had regained her sense of humor, but I told her she should rest a while. Her shoulder was obviously bothering her. She kept rubbing it when she wasn't digging for treasure. She argued a few seconds, saying she was fine, but then stretched out on the couch that had just been scavenged of hairballs and pocket change.

I set to work examining each cubbyhole the rolltop offered. There wasn't much of interest, but I did find some old letters his grandmother had received—mainly from relatives. Guiltily, I read each one, scanning for any reference to a stone. Sadly, they dealt mostly with family deaths.

I was ready to move on to the drawers, when the back door slammed and Jake called out, "Anybody home?"

I ran to the kitchen and threw myself into his arms, burying my face into his sweat-stained shirt—strange how comforting his scent was.

"I missed you," he said, leaning down and kissing me on the top of my head.

"I missed you, too."

He started to kiss me for real, but hesitated, asking, "How's Shannon?"

"She's better. She's resting now. We're both kind of worn out from our trip." I walked to the table and picked up both backpacks, setting them on the floor by the stairs. When he asked what time we got back, I lied and told him we'd been home only a few minutes. He gave me a strange look but didn't say anything. Why I lied, I didn't know. There was no reason why I couldn't tell him we'd been home for nearly an hour, except, of course, for the invasion of his privacy.

Later that night, I struggled to sleep, but the bizarre experiences of the last few days had created a blitzkrieg in my head. Sleep tugged at my weary body while my thoughts fired from groaning doors and stone faces to silent crypts and eerie apparitions.

Forcing my eyes open, I turned on my side and peered in the darkness, barely making out Jake's profile. "He's real," I told myself. "I love him, and I'll do whatever it takes to break the curse." Nothing else mattered. I don't know how long I lay there listening to his steady breathing, but when I woke in the morning, he was staring at me, his fingers gently caressing my thigh.

When Jake was home, there was limited opportunity for searching. Of course, it helped that Shannon and I could split up, one occupying Jake and the other sifting through remnants of five hundred years. Who knew? The stone could be buried behind the wall. Maybe there was a secret passage. I'd heard of palaces having passageways for servants. This wasn't any palace, but I'd just have to ask Jake about the history of the house in the morning.

Chapter 41

For the next few days, we spent every spare moment searching for the stone, the key to the box, or anything that would provide a clue. When Jake was away, Shannon and I would work together, methodically covering every nook and cranny possible. We rolled up rugs and examined the floors for loose planking, scrutinizing every board, stone, and corner—even poking at the ceiling. We cleaned out cabinets and closets—or so we told Jake. He thought I was being "wifely." When he wasn't around, I even went through the pockets and seams of every piece of clothing he owned.

I should have just asked him about the house and whether or not it had any hiding places, but I was afraid he'd get too curious. Laura's warning hung ominously around each conversation we had. Even if there were hiding places, he probably wanted to keep it that way—secret.

Then, on a wet and dreary Sunday, the three of us were sprawled in the living room, drinking tea, reading, and dozing. As I lay on the couch, I realized how lifeless I felt, and it dawned on me that since Shannon and I had returned from our trip to the island, my health had begun to wane again. Shannon kept reminding me to avoid Jake—that is, avoid making love to him—but she didn't understand. When I was with him, I couldn't resist his advances, nor could I bottle my own urges. The curse was rearing its ugly head again, and if I didn't get away from him, I'd be in no shape to carry on with my task. I'd have to talk to Laura again. Surely she knew something that might help. In the meantime, I decided to risk questioning Jake—in spite of Laura's warning.

I slid a sliver of torn newspaper between the pages of my book and looked across at him. He sat entrenched in his weathered chair, brow furrowed, lips skewed to one side as if mulling a substantial thought. After a few seconds, I decided the quickest way to get an answer was to ask a question, so I leaned forward. "Jake, does this house have any secret passageways or hiding places?"

Without looking up, he harrumphed, his eyes never leaving the page. I closed my book, hugging it to me. He looked up, his eyes piercing my own. "What?"

I sucked in my breath, my neck muscles tensing. "Well, I was just reading this story and there's a house with a hidden passageway and I wondered—"

"And you wondered if this house has any hiding places," he interrupted, his voice taut. Obviously, he'd heard my question the first time.

I slipped my book under the quilt on my lap so he couldn't see it, an attempt to conceal my lie. Then, in a rush, I said, "Well, you know, it is old, and I just thought there might be a secret passageway or something. It'd be so much fun to explore it and hear the stories behind it… that is, if there is one." My voice trailed off as I fingered the quilt, the book concealed in its faded folds. I moved them both to one side, rose from my place, and fell onto his lap, causing his own book to slip from his hands and close, losing his place. "I guess I'm just getting bored. It's such a dreary day. It's so damp, and I'm tired of reading. Why don't you light a fire and I'll make some hot chocolate."

He forced a smile. "Okay, I'll light a small fire, you make chocolate, and we'll talk about secret hiding places."

After a series of playful kisses, I headed for the kitchen, signaling Shannon to follow me. As I opened the refrigerator door, she pulled up a chair, plopped down, and began drumming her fingers on the age-roughened tabletop. I reached into the refrigerator, grabbed the milk bottle, and placed in on the counter. "Get the cocoa," I ordered, throwing the command over my shoulder. I could hear her clear her throat as she stood, the chair scraping the floor behind her.

"You're really subtle," she said as she reached into the cabinet.

"I only asked for the cocoa," I said, knowing full well what she meant.

She screwed up her mouth at me, set the cocoa on the cabinet, and leaned back against the counter. "How are you feeling?" Her face relaxed and her eyes were soft and wide.

I turned my back to her. I didn't want to talk about how I felt. To acknowledge my sagging energy would somehow make the entire situation even more unsettling than it was—if that were possible.

I began pouring the milk into the pan. "Would you get me a tablespoon? I think we need about three heaping spoonfuls per cup—and some sugar."

"Try heaping *teaspoons* or I think you'll overdo it—just like you're overdoing yourself, Megan." She shoved me gently aside. "Go sit. I'll finish."

Grateful for her help, I slumped onto the chair, wanting desperately to bury my head in my arms, right there at the table, and sleep. Instead, I propped my chin on my hands and watched Shannon as she stirred the simmering liquid, placed three mugs on a tray, and poured the thick mixture. I remember watching the steam as it rose to the ceiling. My head tilted to one side as if to follow its path. Then I slid onto the floor.

When I woke, I was lying on the couch, a pillow tucked under my knees, and Shannon's face next to mine. She was crouched on the floor next to me dabbing my face with a cool cloth. Jake hovered above.

"Are you all right?" she asked.

"I think so. What happened?" My voice was weak and airy, much the way I was feeling.

Jake took my hand. "You fainted. How do you feel?"

Shannon opened her mouth about to say something. I could see from her expression she had more on her mind than this one episode. She bit her lip, looking at me hard. "I think we need to put her in my room. I'll take care of her—just until she's well." She placed a hand on Jake's shoulder and squeezed it lightly. "Sound good?" She didn't wait for his answer, just began giving orders: "Carry her up the stairs and call the doctor while I make something for her to eat." Neither Jake nor I protested.

I don't remember much about the remainder of the evening. I slept, the doctor came with his usual poking, even gagged me with his tongue depressor. He then inquired about my periods. Had I missed any? Of course I hadn't. "I'm perfectly fine," I assured him, though, without a doubt, I was still cursed, both by Mother Nature and a certain Celt.

The curtain billowed gently, its edges lapping against Shannon's shoulders as she sat reading. Faint particles of dust, magnified in the sun's rays, danced somberly about her head. I didn't have to ask her. I knew why she was hovering over me. She wanted to protect me from Jake, from his love, from the malediction that had passed from him to me. She would ward him off for days, weeks, months, or whatever it took. She was in charge now. She knew what was at stake.

I looked past her and out the open window. Last summer I had stood at that window looking out over the sheep-strewn meadows, breathing in my newfound freedom, freedom to explore life—and myself. I had stood there, still wet from the shower, sleek and sweet, a towel wrapped around me. I had spread my arms, the towel loosening from my damp warmth, my skin prickling as the breeze brushed like lover's lips, irresistibly soft and sensual. I had felt so lucky—as if nothing could ever go wrong.

"It's about time you wake up," Shannon said, rising from her chair. "How do you feel?"

"Better. Really rested. What time is it?"

"Three-thirty or thereabout. You slept through the night and most of the day. Are you starving?"

"Hmm, a bit, I think. Really thirsty though."

She handed me a glass of water from the bedside table. "Drink this and I'll go down and bring up something cool. How about some lemonade and a sandwich? Then we'll talk." She reached down to feel my forehead. "No fever. That's good."

"Where's Jake?"

"He's out working. He stayed with you much of the evening, but I made him go to bed. This morning he sat watching you sleep, then eventually went out. Said he'd be back in early. I told him I'd come get him if you woke. But that can wait."

Shannon didn't have much to say until I finished my sandwich; then she took the tray from my lap and sat on the edge of the bed. "After you went to sleep last night, Jake and I sat up and talked a little. He was worried about you and started talking about Laura and how she died. Megan, he said he told you she died of cancer. But that wasn't true."

"Not true? He said that—"

"I know what he told you," she interrupted, shaking her head and placing her hand on mine, "but it wasn't true. The doctors never could figure out why she died."

I closed my eyes and felt my body tumble over itself. I knew what Shannon was saying had to be true. Laura had said I had to break the curse before it happened again. I'd ignored her meaning. The curse wasn't about me. I was just another of its victims. And if I didn't find the stone and return it, someone else could die—not just me.

Shannon continued, "Before we went to bed, he asked me if there was any reason you wanted to know about hiding places in the house. I said I didn't know. Then I asked him if there were any, and he showed me a crawl space next to the fireplace. He said it had been used as a hiding place years ago."

"Hiding place? Why?"

"I don't know. He didn't tell me and I didn't ask. Right now I don't care about anything but finding the stone."

Shannon took the tray from my lap and set it on the nightstand. I sat up, fluffed the pillows behind me, and leaned against the headboard. "Have you looked it over?"

"Yeah, I did this morning after Jake left," she said, looking down at me with a troubled look. "There's nothing there. I also searched the dining room. Megan, we have to do something. Or it's going to be too—" She turned away, picked up the tray, and went down the stairs. I knew she was about to cry. Things couldn't be good if that happened. Crying wasn't her style.

For a moment, it seemed the walls were closing in on me. A strange, dark loneliness seemed to grip my throat. I couldn't breathe. Throwing the covers back, I stumbled from the bed to the open window, draping my sagging body against its frame. The verdant meadows dotted with sheep seemed to spin round me while the breeze bristled my damp, sweating skin. I felt queasy and wanted to vomit. Fortunately, screens were not kept on the windows. I leaned over and retched.

Within moments, I could hear Shannon's steps behind me. She reached around my waist and pulled me to my feet, leading me back to the bed. After tucking me in and wiping my face, she sat by my side.

"We'll figure this out. I know we will," she said. "Are you up to talking to Laura again?"

I nodded.

"Okay. We better do it now before Jake comes back." She placed Laura's self-portrait at the foot of the bed so I could see it. "Okay?" She looked at me, trying to force a smile.

"Yes. It's fine." I stared at the portrait. "She was really beautiful … even with her sagging breasts and hollow cheekbones."

"We both know Jake has a taste for beautiful women," she said as she tugged at my toe through the covers. "Now, make her talk to you," she urged me impatiently.

I reached out and ran my fingers along the curve of Laura's head and down her bony, white shoulders. "Laura," I said, feeling as foolish as if I had rubbed a lantern, expecting a genie to appear. Not unlike childhood fantasy stories, she opened her eyes and gazed at me lazily.

"I thought you'd never get back around to me again. Where have you been?"

I leaned forward, "Well, we've been looking for the king, just like you told us to. And, guess what?" I paused for effect, but she just looked at me. "We found him."

She didn't seem surprised. "What did he say?"

"Well, actually, he didn't say anything. I just found where he was buried, but another one of those ghastly spirits told me to find the stone, then bring it back to his tomb and place it there. She even showed me where."

"Where?" she snapped, hardly giving me time to take a breath.

"On the top of the crypt. There's a hollowed-out place where it's supposed to be."

take it you haven't found the stone yet." She stretched her arms er her head, then nonchalantly placed a hand on each propped

No, we haven't. We've looked everywhere."

Well, obviously not everywhere."

annon spoke up, "Everywhere we can think of in the house— n the secret hiding space in the living room."

aura raised an eyebrow.

annon shifted her weight on the bed. Her eyes met mine for a d, and then looked back at Laura. "We need your help. We've run out of ideas. As I said, we've searched everywhere. Shannon found some old letters written to Jake's grandmother, but there wasn't—"

"Did you find her diary?" Laura interrupted.

Adrenaline buzzed through me. "No, but I found a box... a box Jake said he made for her when he was a little boy. I've been trying to find a key to the lock so I can look inside. I was hoping the stone might be in there."

Laura's hand came to her mouth and she pressed her index finger to her lips. As she nodded her head, she said, "I bet her diary is in there. Where's the box?"

Before I could move, Shannon slipped off the bed and all but sprinted across the hall into Jake's bedroom. Within a few seconds, she placed the box between the three of us and motioned her head toward me, saying, "I told her to just smash it."

"I couldn't bring myself to destroy what he made for his grandmother." I made a face at her. "Just wouldn't be right."

"You won't have to. I know where the key is."

"Where?" we asked in unison.

"In the desk."

"But I've already searched the desk," I said, feeling a wave of disappointed. "It's not in there."

"Oh, but it is, dearie," she stated flatly.

Shannon and I sat staring, waiting for her to continue. Her lips began to form a tight line as she squeezed her eyelids tightly. "Hmm, I'm trying to remember. It's in the second... no, the third drawer inside the rolltop on the right side."

"I looked in all the drawers, Laura. There are no keys that will fit it." I was embarrassed at the sound of my words. They were whiny and childlike.

Her eyes flashed wide, hard, so hard I got the impression she could see clear through me. "But you didn't look in the secret drawer, did you?"

Shannon repeated, "Third drawer on the right side." She stopped at the door, then turned and walked back to the bed. "But if Megan's already looked there—"

"I said it was a secret drawer. Remove it. Then reach inside the space. You'll feel a flat piece at the back with a notch on the upper part.

Just slip your finger into the notch and pull. A tiny drawer will slide out. The key should be there."

Shannon was back on the bed within two minutes, her hand open, her palm proudly displaying the tiny key. "I told you we'd figure it out," she said brightly.

I forced a laugh. "Yeah, well, I'll let *you* take the stone back to the Abbey—that is, if we find it." My voice trailed off as I slipped the key into the lock, attempting to twist it open. "It's not working. It's not the right key."

"Of course it is. Let me try," Shannon said, taking both the box and key from my trembling hands. "It's just rusty, needs some gentle persuasion." She wrestled with it a few seconds before we heard a tiny snap, and the lock popped open. Without another word, she placed the box on my lap, saying, "Open it."

Chapter 42

Minutes later, Shannon and I sat huddled on the bed, peering down at Anna's diary, taking turns reading aloud from the fragile pages. Each entry was headed with a date, beginning with May of 1920. She had been twenty years old at the time and newly married to Jake's grandfather. Her entries were brief and scattered, usually months apart. Occasionally, a year would slip by before she'd pick it up again. Most entries referred to daily life or her babies—her "wee ones." Eventually, we began skimming through the pages, figuring any reference to Jake wouldn't come until a later date.

In an entry dated July 1973, we first spotted a reference to him. Shannon read aloud: *The laddie's come to stay with me. How they do that, I cannae ken. May the good Lord guide them. I can see him now, climbin' up the tree. He's a boy so full of life. So full of joy.*

Pages later, an entry dated October caught our attention. Scrawled in a shakier hand, was the first hint of a possible stone. *I doubt it will bring forth no good.* The word "it" was underlined. Then, *I can't help but think of the story mum told me when I was a child. Of the fairy cave and of the ghosts and the changelings that stole mortal children and left fairy babes in their places. I fear for him, for little Jakey.*

We looked up as we heard the crunch of gravel in the drive. Shannon went to the window. "It's Jake. We'll have to put this away for now." She marked the place with an edge of tissue and slipped the diary under the bed, then fluffed and stacked the pillows behind me. "You lie back and try not to worry. We're going to find the stone, Megan. I know it."

I gratefully eased into the down-filled pillows and shut my eyes, desperately fighting the tears already spilling forth. Her soft-soled shoes squeaked ever so slightly as she walked out the doorway and into the bathroom. Water splashed in the sink for a few moments, then she retraced her steps and sat by my side, wiping my face with a cool cloth.

"Shh, it's okay. I'll tell Jake you're asleep. I'll send him up later with your dinner. Just rest. It's going to be okay. I promise." She leaned down and kissed me on the forehead. "You get some sleep, girlfriend."

I nodded and she left. As I lay there thinking about Anna's words, the door opened. I could hear Jake sigh, then close the door. His heavy boots seemed to drag across the hall. His door shut. It was quiet again.

Eager to continue with the diary, I leaned down and felt around the floor beneath the bed until my fingers found its tattered edge. Opening the book with care, I began reading. Each entry expressed Anna's growing concern about the unnamed "it," and with each entry, I was more certain the stone Jake had taken from the cave had been in her possession. Page after page she fretted: *It might be magic, cursed, could haunt him forever, can't throw it out, they could come for it.* Clearly, she was afraid, afraid to get rid of it or keep it. Finally, after several entries, two words gave me the answer: *the quilt.* Then nothing more. The remaining pages were blank.

I closed the diary and slid it under the cover next to me. *Quilt.* My first thought was of the childhood quilt Jake kept in the living room, the one Anna had made for him when he was living with her, but I knew she had made more—many more. I'd seen a closet stacked with handmade creations of assorted patterns and colors. Besides, how many times had I smoothed his childhood treasure over my lap? More than I could remember. I'd never noticed anything unusual.

A few minutes later I was sitting on the couch, unfolding the finely pieced coverlet. The frayed corners were knobby, hardened by time, grime, and oft-needed washings.

I'd never paid much attention to the pattern: four sets of diamonds in shades of blue and white, each stitched to form a block, then joined by a red cross in the middle, each angle of the cross supporting one of the diamond-formed blocks. Together they formed one twelve-inch block. Four of these had been joined to form the width of the quilt, while five had been pieced to create the length. With the border binding them, it was just the right size for a young boy.

"What are you doing up?" Shannon came out of the kitchen, the apron with cavorting lambs tied around her waist.

"It's in a quilt."

"What? What's in—you mean the stone? It's in a quilt?" She sat next to me and ran her hand over the multicolored coverlet on my lap. "This one?"

"Maybe. I'm almost too afraid to find out."

Shannon picked up the quilt and held it out in front of her. "Well, this shouldn't be too difficult to—"

Jake's footsteps at the doorway sent Shannon's words in another direction.

"Well, you better lie back. You had no business coming down here. We were just about to bring dinner up to you." She placed the quilt over my lap and turned to Jake, saying, "Can you believe this? She came down here by herself. Didn't even tell me."

Jake stood in the doorway staring at both of us. The expression on his face seemed to be a mixture of irritation at Shannon's hovering presence and concern for me. Ignoring Shannon, he walked straight to me and sat by my side.

"You keep her company while I get her soup," Shannon said, scurrying out of the room.

The remainder of the evening, Jake held me close, reading from a book of Renaissance poetry, his voice warm and animated, expressing the passion of love, the pressure of time, the joy, the sorrow, the fear of life—all through the patience and the discipline proclaimed with the poets' words. We marveled at eloquence, sighed in unison at exaggerated expressions of love, and laughed in delight at onomatopoeic cleverness.

He ended our evening of repose with Thomas Nashe's poem, "Spring, the Sweet Spring," his voice full and purposefully singsong. And each time he recited the repetitious lines of the three stanzas, he'd leap from the sofa and stand before me, trying in his own clumsy but sweet way to mimic the twittering sounds of the birds: "Cuckoo, jug-jug, pu-we, to-witta-woo."

By the time we went to bed, I had almost forgotten the quilt—and the stone.

Chapter 43

As soon as Jake left the house, Shannon flopped on the edge of my bed, shaking me gently. "Megan, get up. I've got the stone. It was in the quilt. It has been under our noses the whole time."

I rolled over onto my back and looked up through sleep-clogged eyes. "You really found it? Show it to me." I rose onto an elbow and she stuck her hand under my nose, revealing a brilliant, green gem about the size of a walnut.

Fingering it with her other hand, she turned it over, and then placed it next to me on the bed. "It was in the small quilt. In one of the corners."

"I can't believe we didn't notice it," I said in disbelief. "It's bigger than I thought it would be."

"Well, with all the batting and fabric, it was fairly well concealed." She took it from my hand. "I'll keep it. Otherwise, Jake might see it."

I nodded my consent. "Do you think he knows?" I asked as I pulled myself free from the covers and sat up.

"If it was in the blanket? I don't know. I would think his grandmother would have told him at some point in time."

"What did you do with the blanket? You'll have to put it back. I know he'll miss it."

"Don't worry. It's as good as new—well, not new, but good as it was. I even sewed a small rock up in it so he wouldn't notice. That is, if he knew it was there."

We sat quietly on the bed staring down onto the treasure in Shannon's hand. Exhaustion overwhelmed me. I lay back and curled up on my side. "Shannon, did I ever tell you about the dream I had before we came to Scotland? Before I met Jake?"

She shook her head. "I don't know. Tell me."

"I was riding on the back of a horse, holding on to a man's waist. I was scared and felt I would fly off the horse at any minute and he, the man, turned and looked back at me and it was Jake. He told me to hold on. Shannon, I feel like I'm on that horse again. Things are whirling around me; I can't think, I have no will to save myself."

Shannon leaned down and placed her face in front of mine.

"Megan, I know you love him, but you know what being here is doing to you. Right?"

I nodded and closed my eyes. With the edge of the sheet, she dabbed at the tears forming tiny droplets in the corners of my eyes. She then whispered softly, "I have to get you out of here."

I don't remember much for awhile after that. Just bits and pieces. I remember Shannon and someone else—it wasn't Jake—carrying me outside and putting me in a backseat of a car where I quickly went back to sleep. Then they carried me again and placed me on a bed. I remember getting an injection in my hip. It stung. And from time to time, I saw a figure dressed in white hovering over me. I was too weary to think much about it. Just went back to sleep. Eventually, I woke long enough to notice the ceiling, a stark white, smooth-textured surface with an opaque glass light fixture breaking the center of the space. I struggled to sit up, but couldn't. My arm seemed glued to the bed. That's when I noticed the glass bottle and tubes leading to my arm. By that time, a woman in white was standing at my side.

"Well, hello. It's so good to see you awake. How do you feel?" Her smile beamed down at me, making me instantly self-conscious. Without waiting for an answer, she turned and left the room, leaving me struggling to collect my thoughts.

The first thing I recognized as I looked around the room was my backpack. As I stared at it, thoughts of Jake, the manuscript, my trips to the cairn, Laura, the diary, the stone, and being carried out of the house rushed through my head. I just didn't know where Shannon had taken me.

In answer to my question, the door opened, and she and Colin walked into the room. "Thank goodness you're awake," she said as she leaned over and kissed me on the cheek. "We've been so worried about you. How do you feel?"

This time they all listened intently as I said, "Starved. I want to get out of bed." The woman, who I learned was a nurse, immediately called the doctor. Within minutes, tubes were freed, and Colin lifted me from the bed and carried me to a distinctly modern living room, placing me in a comfortable chair he said was his favorite. With that, I assumed the apartment was his.

After sipping warm broth and tea for a few minutes, I looked up at the two of them. They sat side by side, watching me intently.

"Well," I said, "tell me what's going on."

Shannon cleared her throat and began. "For starters, Jake doesn't know you're here." She paused, waiting for a reaction, but I didn't have one in me to give. "Colin and I brought you here to his place. I didn't think Jake would look here."

I stared at her a few moments, trying desperately to put it all together. I looked over at Colin. "But how did you get to the farm so fast?"

Shannon answered, "I called him the night before, after I found the stone. I knew I had to get you out of there. I was sure Jake wouldn't just let you go. You understand, don't you?"

I nodded, but couldn't say anything. The thought of my leaving without saying good-bye—of his finding me missing—made me ache inside.

Shannon took the empty cup from my hand, went into the kitchen, and came back with fresh juice, and then walked to the window, sipping a glass of wine. "You realize he could show up here? And if he does, you're going to have to tell him something that will keep him from demanding you leave with him."

It took a few minutes for it to sink in. I was afraid to move, even to answer with a flippant comment, the way we often responded, a result of knowing each other so well. I tried thinking of how I'd apologize to Jake, putting the blame on Shannon for whisking me off; but then how would I explain to him I wasn't coming home? Finally, I looked at her and said, "I'd have to lie."

Hesitantly, she said, "Yes, you'd have to lie." Then becoming animated, she said, "But it'd be worth it. You'd get well, return the stone, and then go to him and explain everything once the spell was broken." She walked back to where I was sitting. "Of course, he may not think to come here and you'll get well and be back with him before you know it. Then there'll be no lie."

"I think there already is," I said, setting the orange juice on the table. Anger stirred in me as I thought of how she had taken me from him. "I could have figured something out. Now he'll be worried, calling everyone, maybe even the police."

A look of bewilderment swept across her face, but before she could say anything, I was struggling to heave myself from the chair. "I've got to go back to bed. I have to think." And I wanted to be alone.

I lay thinking for what seemed hours, and when Shannon brought the phone in to me, saying it was Jake, I knew from the look on her face that it was up to me. Cradling the receiver in my hands, I watched Shannon turn and walk away. As she reached the doorway, she looked back and smiled, saying, "Go for it, girlfriend."

I can't remember exactly how I told him, what I said, what I meant to say. All I can remember are his words before he hung up the phone. He said, "You're dancing in the rain again, Megan, dancing naked in the rain. I'll be here waiting."

I didn't try to hold back the sobs that followed—emotion spurred by relief. The memory of the night I'd impulsively stripped and danced and beckoned him to join me in the thunderstorm replayed over and over in my mind. He'd stood at the back door watching, unwilling to disturb my celebration of life. Later he laughed and said, "You're nuts." I didn't take him seriously at the time, but, as I lay gripping the phone, I began to think it was true.

Chapter 44

A slow two weeks followed before my blurry-eyed weakness faded and I was strong enough to consider venturing out on my own. I took long walks in the morning, knotted myself into yoga positions before lunch, napped afterward, and made trips to market with Shannon and Colin in the afternoons, where I weaved in and out of stalls filled with a palette of colors. It was a peaceful time.

Over and over again, I'd retreat into my imagination, stepping across the crumbling façade of the abbey, creeping down the stone steps to the moaning door, shoving it open, crawling on all fours while running my hands over the dusty floor in search of the stone-faced opening, easing down the fragile ladder and into the crypt where I'd finally replace the stone. Then my mind would jerk back to reality and I'd pray to escape from all of the insanity and return safely to Jake. I didn't allow myself to consider the possibility that the curse might still hang over our heads—if there really was one.

As my energy returned, my will managed to take hold, and I sat down with Shannon to tell her of my plans. She argued relentlessly when she learned she hadn't been included in the venture. I knew she'd wear me down if I didn't do something, so I stood up and slammed out of the apartment, an action a bit out of character for me—and a bit dramatic—but it worked. When I returned, she gave me a reluctant smile and said she'd be waiting for me when I got back.

It wasn't that I felt particularly gutsy. I didn't. Since my first contact with Welzen, my every thought had been edged with unsettling stirrings, much like the stirrings of the cairn. I often wondered how much of what was going on inside me was really true. Shakespeare said that thoughts are "dreams till their effects be tried," so it was up to me and only me to conduct my own trial.

The ferry landing was busier than it had been in the spring. Cars and buses loaded with tourists streamed in and out of the parking area, while pedestrians milled in all directions. Clearly, it would do no good to be in a hurry. I eyed the shortest line and eased Colin's Fiat into the queue. In spite of the hubbub around me, I was surprisingly calm.

Once on board, I bought a cola and walked to the top deck, searching the horizon for the island, a tiny speck almost hidden in the glistening water. Gradually, its straggling coast spread before me, revealing sandy windswept beaches giving way to rugged peaks. And on one of its highest points, an ancient abbey lay waiting.

As I drove across the island, the corpse of ancient orders rose slowly out of the earth. Each minute of the drive ticked off a crippled piece of its past until it lay before me, pathetic in its waste. I pulled onto the side of the road and killed the engine. Part of me wanted to rush into its mystery, but another part, my chicken side, urged me to head back to the ferry, to leave the whole situation to chance. Instead, sitting crosswise in the seat, I dangled my feet out the open door, warily eyeing the crumbling mass. I then reached into my backpack and pulled out the ham and cheese Shannon had handed me earlier that morning.

After a few bites, I admitted to myself I was stalling, that the ham and cheese wasn't on my list of priorities. Tossing it out the window, I drained the lukewarm cola, shouldered my backpack, and headed up the path to the waiting doorway, wide in its welcome. Inside, nothing had changed, except a faint outline of footprints, the footprints I'd left behind on the dust-layered floor.

From my backpack, I pulled out a small, cloth bag, loosened the drawstrings, and peered inside. The green of the stone appeared to brighten momentarily. Undisturbed by its chameleon powers, I squeezed it tightly into the palm of my hand, saying, "Please work," then tightened the strings and shoved it into my pocket.

With the light of a new flashlight, the descent into the cloister offered no surprises. As I had so many times in my imagination, I descended the stairs, opened the groaning door, located the stone-faced entry on the floor, and lowered myself into the pit with nothing more than quickened breath.

I splayed the light around the cell until I could make out the shadowy shape of the tomb. Something was wrong. The crypt had changed. It seemed lower to the ground, but I wasn't sure if it was a trick of my memory or the veil of darkness hanging heavily around it. I squinted, straining to make out what I really didn't want to see.

I stepped back a few paces until the earthen clay of the wall jarred me to a halt. I stood motionless, waiting for something to happen, something to appear, some ghost or spirit, even Welzen. I waited. Nothing happened. Nothing moved except for the trickling of sweat down my back and my breath as it passed through my nostrils in short, jagged spurts. As the moments passed, the rampage of adrenaline that had doused me into a state of fright began to ebb. I had to move. With every bit of effort I could muster, I took a few steps forward, then a few more until I was standing over the crypt, looking down into its emptiness. I couldn't believe what I was seeing. It seemed impossible. The entire top surface of the crypt had been removed and lay in pieces, strewn haphazardly on the floor; and there was nowhere to place the stone, and no king to receive it.

I fell to my knees and began to examine each shattered piece on the floor, searching each fragment for a small, scooped out indention, one where I could place the stone. It wasn't long before I realized the piece I needed wasn't there. Something had gone wrong. Laura was wrong. Welzen was wrong. And even that wisp of a spirit, who told me to put the stone there, was wrong. They were all wrong. If there ever had been a king buried there, he was gone, and, with him, my chances for breaking the curse had vanished.

I gathered myself from the floor, thinking maybe I could just place the stone in the empty crypt. I would have upheld my end of the bargain, but then I remembered the warning. The beryl stone had to be left in the very spot that had been hollowed for it on the crypt—an indention a bit larger than a walnut shell, one centered on a crudely etched cross.

Every ounce of strength seemed to drain from me as I slipped to the floor. Nothing stirred within me—no pounding heart, no quickened breath, no tears, no thoughts. No power of my mind could even imagine what to do next.

I lay there for some time, unable to will myself to move. Gradually, a shuffling sound faintly etched its way into my mind, awakening my senses. I sat up and listened. I heard it again. Something was above me. My first instinct was to stay still and hide, but I knew there was no hiding from the forces plaguing me.

In my weakened state, I struggled to climb the ladder, leaving my flashlight behind and me in darkness until I reached the opening above. As I pulled myself up onto the floor, I was relieved to see the reflection of sunlight on the walls of the stairs leading up to the main part of the abbey. I moved silently toward the archway and leaned against the rotting frame, knowing that once I walked up the stairs—

"Hello! Anybody down there?" a voice yelled from above.

I slammed by body against the wall and shut my eyes, thinking, "The king. He's come back." Instantly, it hit me that it wasn't the voice of any king of any kind. And he certainly wouldn't be concerned about my whereabouts. I pulled myself away from the wall and looked up to see a burly and grizzled old man peering down the stairs at me.

"You all right?" he asked, fingering the faded tam in his hand. "I didn't mean to scare you. Sorry if I did that."

I let out the breath I'd been holding since he'd yelled down the stairs. "Oh... I'm... I'm okay," I stammered. "I just didn't expect anyone else to be here." I began walking up the stairs, feeling relief to see another fellow human.

"You aren't alone, are you?" he asked, taking a step back as I reached the ground floor. "This your backpack?" he asked, giving it a nudge with his foot. "I saw it and the car outside and figured someone was in here." When I didn't answer, he quickly added, "There've been some strange happenings around here lately, and I don't think it's safe to be here, especially if you're alone."

"What kind of strange happenings?" I asked.

He was quiet for a few seconds as he looked me over, and then said, "Where are you from? I don't recognize you. You don't live on the island."

I realized my refusal to answer his questions had made him suspicious of me. Deciding I could trust him, I smiled. He certainly wasn't one of my spooks. "No, I'm not from here. My name is Megan McEller, and I live on the mainland. Actually, I'm from the States. I'm a writer. I'm writing about your island. I just happened to see the abbey and decided to stop and explore. I hope it's okay."

He nodded his head at me. "Of course, I'm sorry. It's just that a few nights ago I was taking a walk a bit away down the road and saw some strange lights coming out of this place. And then I heard what sounded like an explosion. I notified the constable. They didn't find anything. Really strange."

I followed him as he walked out of the abbey and onto the rut-filled ground outside the decaying doorway. I could see his truck parked behind Colin's car. He stopped, picked up a small rock on the ground, and turned to face me. "But I found something you might be interested in." He walked to the bed of his truck, reached over, and lifted a large piece of stone. "It's not much, but it has a carving on it." He held it out in front of me.

In disbelief, I reached out and ran my trembling fingers over its surface, tracing the etching of the cross and the hollow of its center. In fear of betraying my interest and enthusiasm of his find, I forced down the elation welling up in me. When I looked up at him, he said, "What do you think?"

"I think it's wonderful. Where did you find it?"

"It was right outside this doorway. I probably wouldn't have seen it, but I'm in a habit of picking up stones and tossing them when I'm out for a walk. And yesterday morning I came over to see what I could find out about the happenings the other night. And I saw it."

"What are you going to do with it?"

"Well, I took it home with me yesterday but decided I'd bring it back. It belongs here." He walked toward the entrance to the abbey, then stopped, bent over, and placed it gently on the ground. "Not going to toss this one." He laughed, wished me luck on my writing, and then slowly ambled to his truck. He looked out at me before he drove away and said, "Now, you do what you need to do, then get on home."

Do what you need to do? I wasn't sure what he meant, but I knew what it meant to me. I picked up the seemingly worthless piece of broken rubble, placed it gently into my backpack, and made my way back into the darkness below.

All the way home, I practiced what I'd say to Jake. In the end, I didn't tell him about the curse. I don't know why. Maybe it was easier that way. I just let him go on thinking what I'd told him on the phone when I was at Colin's, that I wasn't feeling well and just needed some time away, some time to think. He must have wondered why I could be with Shannon and Colin, and not him. But he didn't say anything. Not then or later.

I've tried talking to Laura at times, but she doesn't respond, at least not in the same way. No flickering eyelashes, no questions, no commands. Just a faint smile, nothing you'd really notice if you had the notion to stand in my shoes and look at her—her portrait that is.

I still dance in the rain on occasion and Jake still watches from the door, shaking his head. When he hands me a towel, he still smiles and says I'm nuts. That's something I still haven't figured out.

Just as the sonnet had proffered, the journey into the depths of Morvreckleven Abbey offered solace, solace in a scanty plot of ground beneath its deteriorating walls—relief from my procrastination, from my fear of failure, from the curse tearing me from my love and threatening my very existence.

I worried for months about the manuscript I'd stolen from Jake's desk before I gathered the courage to mention it to him. He acted surprised, as if he didn't know what I was talking about. When I pulled it out from under the bed and handed it to him, he looked at me as if I was crazy.

"Megan, there is no manuscript. The day you saw me writing, I had only written a few pages. And I destroyed those the same day."

"Why did you destroy them?" I asked.

"Because I wanted to put it all behind me," he said quietly.

"Put what behind you?"

"Her death and the fear I had somehow caused it."

"And that's why you wrote—"I couldn't finish.

He nodded and pulled me to him. "Yes. I realized I couldn't allow myself to record every minute of your life, as I had Laura's."

"So there was a manuscript about Laura?"

"Yes. I started writing it when she got sick. I don't want there to be one about you. I just want you right here with me. And I want to live each and every moment."

A few nights after I returned home and Jake was sleeping, I went downstairs and stood at the open window where we had shared so many late night *tête-à-têtes*. As the breeze wafted around me, I smelled the heavy scent of roses, even the Iceberg rose had been urged into full bloom again. The dry-stacked fences stood unburdened of winter's snow, and the sheep, huddling together for their evening slumber, stared in amazement at any movement other than their own. As I stepped back from the window, I glanced at the painting on the wall, the one I noticed the day I met Jake—the day his heavy boots clumped across the room and my heart did that funny, flippy thing. I remember turning away from him to look at the painting, recognizing only the spirited freedom of the youthful dancers. Their nakedness had not registered… nor had the rain, falling in silence around them. I agreed with Jake. I wanted to live each and every moment—come what may.

Made in the USA
San Bernardino, CA
15 July 2020

75484780R00155